IRIS GREEN, UNSEEN

IRIS GREEN, UNSEEN

LOUISE FINCH

SCHOLASTIC

Published in the UK by Scholastic, 2024
1 London Bridge, London, SE1 9BG
Scholastic Ireland, 89E Lagan Road, Dublin Industrial Estate,
Glasnevin, Dublin, D11 HP5F

ISBN 978 0702 33108 4

A CIP catalogue record for this book
is available from the British Library.

Printed and bound in Great Britain by Clays Ltd, Elcograf S.p.A.
Paper made from wood grown in sustainable forests
and other controlled sources.

1 3 5 7 9 10 8 6 4 2

www.scholastic.co.uk

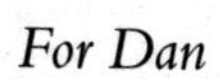

For Dan

1

My underwear is mid-thigh when I notice. There on the toilet cubicle wall. Four little words inked above the sanitary bin:

Iris Green is grey.

I drop back to the seat with a clunk of plastic on ceramic.

Grey?

Obviously it could be worse. Just below, among doodles and epigraphs, I learn "Suzi T's legs don't close". On the back of the door, lingering despite the cleaner's best efforts, is the ghost of an invitation to Jess Arthur's OnlyFans page for buck-teeth fetishists.

It could be so much worse: an unflattering photo turned meme or nasty rumour running wildfire over social media.

It's honestly *been* so much worse.

But "grey"? The casual specificity jabs me like a needle under the nails – sharper and more precise than a thousand empty insults. And it's gutting this is the one immortalized on a toilet wall: Iris Green, notoriously bland.

I dig my camera from my bag and line-up the viewfinder. The graffiti transforms with the snap of a shutter. Now it's mine. Now it's art.

My fingernail rakes the scrawl, but it doesn't shift. Hard to know how long the writing's been there; this isn't my cubicle of choice and I could have easily missed it before. But I have suspicions about what sparked this particular lack-of-character assassination. I'm only surprised I've been allowed to get away with it for so long. Eventually someone was bound to realize I don't belong with someone like Theo Hastings.

The toilet seat complains as I sit back. For a moment, the whole world shifts under me. The edges of my vision sparkle, silver and strange, shimmering fish climbing the cubicle and my chest tightens in what feels like the most debilitating anxiety incident of my life, only different. This time the jittering isn't under my skin; it's over it. Dizzy, I wobble on the seat and brace myself against the wall. My fingers are gone, my edges faded to nothing but pins and needles. I recoil, snatch my hand away from the wall and stare.

I blink and it all stops – no dizziness, no fuzzy vision

or my fingers paling away to nothing – and the skin of my hand tingles like the ringing in your ears after a loud gig. I flex then make a fist. *Get a grip, Iris.*

Pants pulled up, skirt smoothed down, I get out, heading for where I always go.

Whenever sixth form gets too much and I can't breathe, there's a cupboard I hide in. Tucked round the back of C-block, it's what passes for a photography "darkroom" in our school and it's basically abandoned. After one week of intro to photography at the beginning of year twelve art, everyone else ditched it. Either they believe the paintbrush is mightier than the shutter, or they prefer the immediacy and flexibility of digital over film. Fine by me. I've staked my claim. This room's my Narnia, my oasis, my escape.

At least it was. As I swing through the door this Tuesday lunchtime, I'm pulled up short by someone else's work on the drying rack. Someone has been in my room.

I step further inside to see what I'm dealing with and unclip one of the mystery portraits.

The girl in the photos is making *that* face – eyes half closed, lips apart, all sexy-pouty-sultry. It would look ridiculous on me, but it doesn't on this girl with her perfect skin and huge eyes gazing straight into the lens – unembarrassed, confident. And why shouldn't she be? The cut-outs on her dress reveal a belly so flat it looks practically airbrushed, only—

"What do you think?" says a voice behind me.

My elbow smacks the wall and pain streaks through my funny bone.

"I didn't think anyone else used this space," the intruder continues, leaning in the open door. I've seen him before – Baker Something from year thirteen – dark, wavy hair, brown eyes and a smirk that already grates.

"Because the regular users keep it tidy." I rub my bruised elbow, annoyed it's too late to pretend I wasn't looking at his photos. "And they don't leave their dry prints everywhere."

"Hmm, well, the prints were wet when I left them, see? That's pretty much the reason for drying them." His lips twitch. "Reckon I might need a do-over. These look underexposed?" Baker Someone says, reaching for the nearest print.

"She looks pretty exposed to me."

Baker looks at me and I'm very aware I'm uselessly standing here. *Why? What was I meant to be doing?* I push the bottles of developer and stopper back into place on the worktop too forcefully. There. That.

I clear my throat. "Do you think you'll be in here a lot going forward? Because, if so, maybe your things could go—"

"'Going forward?' Do I need permission?" This Baker guy leans against the side, eyebrow raised. He's too close. Less his fault than the minuscule proportions of the room, but it's disconcerting to sniff the minty smell of body wash over boy-skin.

"It's a free school," I say.

"But?"

"This doesn't exactly look like a school project. Thanks to the … uh … naked girls." My cheeks catch fire. *Oh, nice one, Iris.*

"Naked?" He shakes his head, lips twitching again. "There is a singular clothed girl in these pictures."

My eyes slip off his. It's uncomfortable enough to stare people dead in the eye at the best of times, but here? Point-blank range? When I expected to be alone?

He unpegs the photos from the rack but with no real urgency. He stops to examine one and I peer over his elbow. She gleams back – a girl version of Baker – all glossy hair and dark, deep eyes. Even in black and white the girl in the photos isn't grey.

I begin preparing my equipment.

"So I'm Baker."

"Congratulations."

"And you are…? I mean, other than mightily concerned about this young woman's clothing choices."

I shake my head.

"Just saying." Baker holds up his hands. "I see where this is going and it'd be my pleasure."

"Excuse me?"

"I can source a location, but you'll have to style yourself if you want a portrait."

"A … um … I don't think…" I sputter through my fluster. "My boyfriend wouldn't appreciate that."

"Boyfriend?" Baker whistles, his substantial eyebrows shoot up. "And manager or…?"

I ignore the jibe. And I can't help it, not even after four months together, can't help the brag slipping through my teeth. "Theo Hastings."

Seymour from last year's production of *Little Shop of Horrors* and lead singer of Vanishing Fact. People tend to know Theo.

"Oh, that guy."

That guy. Of course. I'm hot and furious with myself for falling into this trap. Of course he doesn't believe someone like Theo would go with me.

Baker tilts his head to the side. "Actually, I'm thinking of the wrong guy. All those high achievers blend into one another. Them and their template faces."

"You know what? I'm going to come back later." I put back the equipment, fast.

Baker says, "Hey, if I offended you… Um, what's your name?"

I squeeze past him to open the door and slip out without another word. Silent, nameless.

Grey.

*

The way my dad tells it, I was born keeping secrets.

"Blind as a bat practically from birth," Dad will say at family parties to an audience who've heard it all before. "Nearly four years old and she never said a word." The story will be accompanied by laughter and wine. The implication is clear. I did that. A deliberate ruse by my small self to make my parents look negligent in front of medical experts.

Of course I wasn't blind – lazy-eyed first, myopic later – but a correction only makes Dad roll his eyes before launching into some embarrassing story from before I was old enough to control my own bowels. It's a wonder he has so many of these anecdotes – small Iris and Dad didn't hang out much.

The thick pink-framed glasses that brought my world into focus were binned a decade ago and replaced with a series of progressively more flattering successors. While I can barely remember the fuzzy time before them, I often think how dazzling it must have been to suddenly see with crisp edges. Maybe it was like being behind my camera lens: shocking and joyful and brilliant. The whole world an endless catalogue of possibilities.

After school, I follow a stranger up the cobbled high street, a guy in a checked suit with a silver-tipped cane, so dapper he belongs in black in white. I imagine tapping him on the shoulder.

Excuse me, can I shoot you?

He'll hesitate – a second of confusion – before noticing the camera clenched between my damp hands.

My bad joke breaks the ice, and he's so charmed he lets me take the photograph.

In the darkroom the portrait will spark to life. It'll speak to love, tragedy, life and spirit. It'll be the ideal start to my exhibition project: a prizewinner, an attention-grabber. Maybe his family come to the preview. Perhaps they'll request a print.

Only they won't.

I stop walking, stop daydreaming. Return to the world. Master of candid photography, Henri Cartier-Bresson, once spoke of the decisive moment, but I watch mine walking away, shining brogues fading in the afternoon sun. A smack of car exhaust finishes off the fantasy.

"Iris, are you *stalking* old men?" Olivia shouts, startling some pigeons.

Bert and Olivia's hands are rammed full of canvas bags stuffed with their post-school shopping haul courtesy of the least weird charity shop in town. Bert's red suede jacket hangs from her arm and her cheeks are flushed with bargain-hunting success.

"You shouldn't harass pensioners," Olivia says.

"Harass?" I blink and Olivia throws an elbow into my side.

"Put an ice-cold frappé in my hand this instant," Bert sings. She wipes imaginary sweat from her forehead and pretends to faint against me. "I must replenish. I swear wrestling my ginormous bum in and out of jeans burns five hundred calories per minute."

"*Gorgeous* bum," Olivia corrects, as I'm distracted by my

phone buzzing in my bag. As I fish for it, I'm dimly aware of Bert agreeing her bum is both glorious and generous and a gift to the world, but she fades out, replaced by him.

Theo: you still in town?

Me: over by boots. be quick?

Theo: incoming

My heart jumps. When I glance back up Olivia's watching me with an odd expression.

"Hmm?" I say.

She says, "You should have come. I scooped a pristine hardback of *Northanger Abbey* and there was a jumper you'd have gone *wild* for."

"Was it grey?" Six hours on, I'm sure the toilet graffiti will haunt me till my final breath.

Olivia's eyebrows crinkle in confusion. I didn't mention the graffiti to my friends. Too embarrassing. A bitter reminder it's only been a handful of years since such commentary was a too frequent occurrence. Olivia's gaze sweeps me, from battered black boots, black tights and uniform right to my mouse hair. She sucks her teeth. It's a source of vast disappointment to Olivia that in all our shopping trips I've only ever made it inside one or two actual shops. But, for me, all the interest is outside.

"I did get you a little something-something," Olivia

says, rifling in her bag, lifting out a hardback. "You don't have it, do you?"

I run my finger up the spine of the white dust jacket with gold lettering, *Rebecca*, and shake my head. "Thanks."

"Did Iris get her thing done?" Bert asks, pointing at my camera.

"Um, so, no," I say, tucking the book in my bag. "Not exactly. The quirky older guy was perfect, but I wussed out."

"Photographing old men is such a normal thing to do with your time," Bert says with an affectionate eye-roll. "At least it's a departure from your recent oeuvre of abandoned trash."

"That was..." I wave my hand limply. "It was my Keith Arnatt phase."

"I know, the rubbish was a beautiful metaphor! You know who else is a beautiful metaphor?" And she nudges Olivia and they lean and put their cheeks side by side and throw their arms high. They look so perfect – Bert and Olivia and their pre-filtered lives.

I take the shot and Olivia asks to see, forgetting that's not how it works. The camera's analogue: no screen – just glass, light and film.

"Take one with my phone?" Olivia says, handing it over so I can create a replica.

"Love the commitment to eccentricity, but it'll be nice when you get your upgrade and join the twenty-first century." Bert waggles a finger as I snap the shot and then fold my hands round my camera protectively, shielding it from her judgement. "We might at least see some of your shots."

"Yeah. Maybe. I mean, don't bank on it." I rub my fingers together with a grimace in the universally understood gesture of skintness and hand Olivia's phone back.

Bert watches the screen as Olivia reviews my efforts. "You're coming into money soon. I can feel it in my bones." And I know what she means: the sixth-form art exhibition.

"I'm fairly sure they only give you money for winning; it's not a participation prize," I say, my words speeding up as I get into the rhythm of Bert's company, brightening, extending my energy to match hers as I hear my voice slip into similar inflections. "Actually, entering would cost a bomb in materials, so it would be the opposite of helpful and quite a massive dent in the new camera fund." I stop, suddenly aware of how long the attention has been on me. I cast around for a distraction and, falling back on my default, nod at Bert's bag. "What else … did you get?"

Bert tuts. "Pretending you're not even entering just to give everyone else a scrap of hope? Crafty."

"So crafty," I echo as I scan the road and check my phone. He said he'd be here.

Bert narrows her eyes. "Waiting for someone? Let me guess."

Right on cue, he comes striding down the hill, his

school bag swinging, hands in pockets, blond hair ruffled by the breeze: Theo. He's a perfume advert, a dream sequence. Somehow he's mine.

He calls a greeting and throws an arm round my shoulder, eyeing the girls as I stretch on to my tippy-toes to plant a kiss on his jaw. He whispers in my ear, "Why're they here?"

"You thought I was shopping alone?" I tease. "Have we met?"

Theo says, "Didn't think, did I?"

"When do you?" Bert snaps. Olivia's absorbed in her phone, not even acknowledging his arrival. It's awkward, as it always is, how openly they wear their dislike. "We were going for coffee."

"Hmm, you sure?" Theo smiles, his perfect lips stretching out over perfect teeth, his eyebrows lifting, yep, perfectly, as I turn to molten caramel. "Because I've got hot choc at my house. Marshmallows. Cream. A bedroom door."

I tuck my lips between my teeth and taste sugar. For a second, I hesitate. Contemplate my best move, the one that doesn't let anyone down. Life would be so much simpler if Theo and my friends could all be kept in separate boxes. Never meeting, so never making for these confused moments where all eyes are on me.

"Don't think I don't see you, Iris Green," Bert says with a dismissive flap of her hand. "Go then, go. Vanish on us, why don't you? Again."

Before I have time to agree, Theo has my hand and is pulling me away down the road.

In the monochrome streets on the way back to Theo's, I keep my eyes peeled, searching for personality in the detail – this girl's neon bra strap matches her lipstick, the red stripe in that woman's hair, a man with a long plaited beard. But there's no one as interesting as the man in the hat.

I glance up at Theo. Painfully handsome. A perfect subject right under my nose.

"Theo!" As he turns from two paces ahead, our hands still joined, I line up his answering frown in my viewfinder.

An unwelcome flash of memory. That boy, Baker, in the darkroom. His face. *Oh, that guy.*

Theo's frown dissolves into an easy smile.

Click. My decisive moment.

2

Only the blue-checked cotton landscape of duvet is in focus. Theo's music's turned up loud and his hand's burrowing under my school shirt. Pink-cheeked and overheated, I imagine how this'd look if a parent or kid brother burst in. If there's one thing I've learned from endless afternoons at Theo's, it's that younger siblings have zero respect for closed doors.

I squirm sideways, reach for my glasses and wipe my wet mouth, all chapped from Theo's sandpaper chin. The bedside table's empty, the promised hot chocolate having never materialized.

"Sorry…" I push my glasses up and flip my phone towards Theo. "The time."

"Your cat again? Why are you solely responsible for his survival?" He peels the edge of my shirt up and I push it down again. "Can't it go kill a mouse?"

"My mum," I murmur. "She's home for once." Tonight, she's promised none of her usual uni work on the sofa, just us, dinner and a film. And that's rare. It's a plan. It's worth showing up for, despite Theo's ideas to the contrary.

"Oh, her."

"Don't—"

"Joking, Ris. Get a sense of humour."

Theo's fingers trail across my knuckles and I shiver. The sensation, the look he's giving me … it's too much. I want to pull my jumper up over my forehead so he won't notice any of my wrong features: small eyes, thin lips, a smattering of pre-period spots.

It's a miracle Theo ever saw me. After a year of unrequited pining, the fates of sixth form – more specifically Mrs Coombes – brought us together in history class. Thanks to our alphabetical compatibility it became impossible to avoid talking and, once we started, impossible to stop.

I liked him. I mean, of course I liked him. And he liked me back, I guess.

The fear won't quiet. Not after four months, not since the start of a new term, not since Mrs Coombes had to separate us again, not even a thousand kisses and Theo seeing every inch of me. One day Theo is bound to wake up and realize he's made a terrible mistake: who he wants is someone bubbly, beautiful and all the bright colours.

"Nobody knows it…" Theo sings and nudges me with

his nose to regain my attention as he hums the rest of the bar against the backdrop of the song on his speakers.

"Sorry," I say.

"Obviously you don't want to leave. So..." Theo's arms snake round my waist and he rolls sideways, dragging me on top of him, giving me whiplash. "Don't go. I have a new song you need to hear all about this girl who's a secret kind of pretty."

"Oh? Who's she?"

"Wouldn't you like to know? In a minute, though. First..." His lips move against my neck, warm breath undoing my willpower. But—

"Nuh-uh." I scramble from his clutches.

Theo groans, arm across his eyes. "Why're you like this, Ris?"

"What?"

"Always rushing off. You never have time for me. You don't even like me now, is that it?" He pouts and I'm not sure whether he's serious.

"Of course I do—"

"Then come back," he says. "And let me kiss you."

I teeter on the edge of surrender. My ribcage stretches taut, as though Theo has all my threads, threatening to unravel me with the slightest additional pressure. But then I think of Mum – her first night off in two weeks – and how she'll come back to a dark, empty house.

Plus, if I let my dutiful daughter mask slip for a second,

there's the slight complication that Mum might discover the existence of Theo. Right now she has precisely zero idea who he is, which is easier than the alternative: questions, interest, attention, worry.

With a wrench, I begin pulling my stuff together: jacket, boots, bag, camera.

Theo huffs. "Guess it's a night of gaming and band chat."

"Ash and the skimpily clad elves?"

Theo smiles down at his phone. "Huh?"

"Ash?"

"Uh, yeah." Theo gives me a squidgy grin, eyes turning to semicircles, and I feel better until, when I lean over to kiss him goodbye, he tilts his phone screen away from me.

*

On the way home I see:

A woman in faux fur and billowing vapour. *Click.*

Two old women in bobble hats waiting for a bus. *Click.*

A battle-scarred tortie cat standing regal on a bin. *Click.*

Nothing spectacular, but I take my time over each shot. I peer down alleys and wander wherever my feet want to go.

Halfway home and the message arrives:

> **Mum:** I said yes to a few extra hours. Sorry! There's £5 on the side for pizza xx

I stop. Mum looked shattered when she woke up for a groggy goodbye as I left for school this morning, but she still took an extra shift at the care home?

Now what? Keep going to an empty house, a pizza for one, TV and homework? As much as I enjoy solitude, the sudden change to my evening plans rattles me. Do I backtrack to a pair of warm boy-arms?

I message Theo.

Me: sorry i had to bail. what you up to? missing me?

Once it's sent, I realize it's the wrong end of the cute–needy scale.

A message pops up in the group chat in time to distract me.

Olivia: what's everyone up to? iris, you still in theo-land?

The profile picture's Bert's fingers – three smiley faces drawn on to represent us. I'm her ring finger, my biro smile all lopsided, Olivia's the elegant index and Bert? The middle finger, of course.

Me: heading home, pizza-bound

I perch on a nearby wall, cold brick sapping my warmth. Olivia's posted the photo of her and Bert swinging their shopping swag and some changing-room pics – Bert sticking out her bum in tight jeans, Olivia, hands to knees, staring over the top of sunglasses.

I snap test shots on my phone: the post office building and my boots dangling against the wall. Boring.

Olivia: shroomy? cheesy? let me live vicariously

Me: ultra-processed margs from the cheap end of the freezer section

Olivia: ah, the iris special. enjoy!

So, no Mum, no friends. What now? Where to?

*

The evening's murky, the street lamps jumping to life as I turn down Theo's road. My camera bounces against my chest. I should stash it in my bag. It's not expensive, but still. A man walking his greyhound looks at me a beat too long. I speed up and clutch my camera tighter.

I imagine how I'll explain my return, making the shape of the words with my mouth. I picture Theo leaning in to kiss my cold forehead. I imagine a scenario in which I ask him for a proper portrait, posing him in front of his laptop, multicoloured lights of his gaming keyboard casting a photogenic glow—

Then I stop.

I'm so immersed in fantasy I almost didn't notice him

turning out of his driveway. Striding, head down and purposeful, Theo walks the way he does everything: full-on.

"Theo?"

He doesn't notice me. His hand fiddles at the side of one ear, adjusting the volume on a tune I can't hear.

On instinct I speed up. I follow him.

He's going to Ash's. Of course he is. I'll catch him up, surprise him by throwing my arms round him, smooch him and send him on his way.

But he doesn't head towards Ash's and he's not heading towards mine. There are only so many places to go in this town at this time of night: friends', shops, takeaways, pub. Railway station if you're looking to skip town, but that's cost-prohibitive for people like me and Theo. Buses barely exist.

He can't be going to Spade's – he lives in one of the villages and Theo couldn't get there on foot. My encyclopaedic knowledge of my classmates' homes surprises even me, but in a small town like this you spend a lot of days on people's doorsteps.

So not Ash, not Spade. Where?

I don't catch up. I don't call out again. Hard to say why exactly. I scurry through the gloom after him, lagging behind on straight roads, jogging to keep him in sight as he turns a corner.

Theo stops in the park, sits on a bench and leans his

head back to look at the sky. Another popular post-school location, but only if you have enough mates to ward off the perverts, drunks and dealers. Theo's alone. He looks pensive, his expression soft. I watch from behind a four-by-four as he rubs his eyes. A lump forms in my throat.

Theo's house is always noisy with three smaller siblings all clamouring for attention plus a rowdy Jack Russell and fighting parents. He's an exhausted overachiever, with a résumé the length of his arm. Of course he needed space. That's all. He needs space and support and what do I do? Stalk him. Excellent girlfriending.

I start to turn to begin the long walk home – during which I plan on giving myself a stern and thorough talking-to – when I see someone round the corner. Someone I know.

Glossy ponytail bouncing, lean legs in brightly patterned leggings. It's the leggings I recognize first. I push my glasses up my nose, but I'd know Olivia anywhere.

Weird coincidence. I should catch her attention and let her laugh at my dubious behaviour.

But I don't. Instead, I watch her. Even after exercise, Olivia's a pristine dream fallen to the pavement, her hair pale gold in the evening sun, her long limbs graceful. She swings an arm across her chest and uses the other to pull it tighter in a stretch as she glances up and down the road. She darts between parked cars and crosses. She stops. And then she flops on the bench beside Theo.

He takes his earbuds out. Olivia's mouth moves. Her hands flap. They wear matching serious expressions.

My brain is too slow to register what I'm seeing. A coincidence, of course. She ran into him and she wants to talk to him about me perhaps, or—

Theo catches Olivia's hands between his and holds them in the space between their bodies. The squeeze he gives them seems to clench my windpipe.

My breathing stops. My eyes tear. Deep down, I already know. And I already can't bear it.

He kisses her. She lets him kiss her.

Olivia. And Theo.

No.

They fall against each other and I see it's not the first time. This has happened over and over.

Again.

And again.

And again.

And neither of them stopped even though it would rip me to shreds.

My thoughts cave in around one single point.

I want to disappear.

His fingers thread through her ponytail.

My hands and arms tremble, all prickly with pins and needles. Dancing, pulsing silver speckles my vision. I want to leave but my feet get confused and I end up across the road instead, standing just a couple of metres from where my best friend is kissing my boyfriend and he is kissing her back.

Look at them. So perfect. So right.

Of course they are. Of course.

My hands move on instinct, pressing the shutter before I know what I've done.

Click.

The sound seems to echo from the trees, as loud as gunshot.

The two of them break apart and lean their foreheads together.

In a rush of breath Theo says, "Jesus, what are we doing?"

Olivia says, "We should stop. We're *going* to stop."

My camera drops from my hands and the strap yanks against my neck. I say, "Olivia?"

They jump apart and stare. Right past me. Olivia swipes at the loose strands of blonde hair on her forehead.

"Oh my god, I thought I heard…"

"Right?" Theo gives a relieved laugh. "Holy shit, O. You're making me crazy." He swings his arms round her and buries his face in her neck as she screams in delight.

They do this right in front of me, as if I'm not even here. Watching.

My hands shake too hard to ever stop. And, although I was sure I'd felt it before, now I really know how it feels to be completely and totally insignificant.

I push my hands into my hair and shrink down, knees buckling on the way to the ground. But as I look down I understand why the others can't see, why they looked right through me.

My trembling stops. A thin wheeze of shock squeezes from my throat.

I look right through me too.

My vision blurs and shimmers. The pavement pricks my knees and hands. I can feel them but there's nothing there. No knees, no hands. No shoes, no tights. No skin.

I'm gone. Worse than grey. Nothing.

I'm not there.

Invisible.

3

I'm home without thinking. Standing in front of my mirror, transfixed by the reflection of my prints, snaps and art postcards on the wall, the black-and-white and multicolour mismatched collection filling the space where my body should be.

My hands should be holding my belly, rubbing my arms, clapped to my silently screaming mouth. I can feel it all, my own cold fingers roaming my skin, but I can't see it. *What have I done? Where have I gone? How the hell do I come back?*

Thank god for the thumping of my blood in my ears. Thank god for the sting of my swollen eyelids and the strands of hair tear-slicked to my itching skin. These are the signs I am still alive. Still me. That I wasn't flattened in traffic staring wide-eyed at—

No.

I shrug off my bag and it appears on the carpet beside where my feet should be: the soft edges sagging open under the weight of the book Olivia gave me. I stare at it accusingly, tempted to throw it at the wall. Rip it. Drop-kick it across the room.

As if I have the coordination for that last one. I pick the book up slowly and it moves through the air, heavy in my hands even though my hands aren't there. I put it flat on my shelf and it sits there looking at me like *what now*? I take off my blazer and it crumples on the floor, suddenly real and solid and there. I hoist it by the back of the neck and let it hang, suspended by seemingly nothing. I pick up my phone from my bed and take it to the mirror where it hovers mid-air. I grope against my invisible trousers to drop the phone in my pocket and the phone disappears, even though I can feel the top of it sticking out of my too-small girl-pockets. I take the phone out and it reappears.

Fun. Sort of. Also horrifying beyond belief.

Does this mean I can call someone? Explain? Ask for help?

Tell them what exactly?

I stare at the black screen until it lights up.

Theo: did i miss you?! i was with ash working on the new tune. you k, babe?

Oh, that.

Am I k? I feel pretty un-fucking-k.

I lie flat on my back on the carpet beside my discarded PJs from this morning, my open sketchbook and a collection of old mugs. I stare at the ceiling, my eyes drying as my thoughts run rings around me.

How could he?

How could she?

How could they?

But I already know. It's me. My fault. If I was a better girlfriend, a better friend, if I was a better, more interesting person.

The worst part is, if they had said they wanted to be together, I would have stood aside. I am the very last person to be somewhere I am not wanted. Surely Olivia knows.

Downstairs there's the muffled thump of the door and Mum's voice. "Iris? You home?"

My heart leaps into action, thudding like I've sprinted across the finish at the end of cross-country. Mum can't see me like this. She can't not-see me like this either.

I yank the covers over my head and force myself still. Clear my throat and exhale slowly. The sound of her footsteps hit the stairs. Coming step by step up the hall. The pause outside my door.

"Iris?" Mum calls from the other side. "Sorry about dinner, love. Thought we could hang out now for a bit?"

I force brightness into my voice and try to keep the wobble out. "Yeah, I'm just getting changed for bed."

A pause and then: "It's nine o'clock?"

"Oh yeah. I'm, um, wrecked."

"Are you OK? Did you get some dinner?"

"Yeah. See you in the morning." *I hope.*

"OK." She sounds uncertain. I hold my breath. But then she says, "Night, night then," and her footsteps begin to retreat.

I exhale. I stuff in my earbuds. Dreamy retro sounds directly into my drums. I hit repeat, grab my camera from my desk and in the mirror watch as I bring it to my eye, at least where my eye should be. I sling the strap round my neck and, like the phone, my camera disappears, as if I have some kind of gravity pulling whatever I'm wearing into nothingness with me. I flip the strap back and the camera reappears. Through the viewfinder, I focus on my missing self. Evidence for later. A camera hanging in empty space is luxury when every shot counts, but these are unprecedented times.

This photo's for you, Theo. Dedicated to the one I—

Click.

I flop back on my bed and type a message.

> **Me:** i'm sorry, i can't do this. it's over – i can't see you any more

I watch the unsent message for a while willing it to self-send. *Can't see you?* A painful laugh shudders out of me. I redraft.

Me: i'm sorry. it's over. we're done. sorry

I add a full stop. I press send.

I curl up on my bed, knees to my chest, and wait to reappear.

4

My brain's a problem. It loves to harp on about stuff I'd rather it wouldn't. Digging up memories like snapshots from a dusty box in the bottom of my wardrobe.

For some reason I can't fathom, today it won't shut up about Dad. Ancient history. Getting left with Gran. Burger King of all places.

We'd had a week together me and Dad. A summer holiday week in which we'd got tickets for *The Lion King* at the very back, behind a pillar, and I'd eaten carbonara almost every night, searching for the best in London, ranking them out of ten for taste, texture and how generous the waiter was with Parmesan, Dad urging me every night to try something different, me clamming up until he finally offered Italian. The two of us started the week strangers, the few months since we'd last had a weekend together stretching out like years. But my shyness wore away as the days ticked by and the treats kept coming, only regressing when he'd get irate over my indecisiveness. Why didn't I have any idea where I wanted to go or what I wanted to do?

Because I was six, I guess. Because I'd already learned whatever I wanted would be the wrong choice, always. Because yelling didn't help, or didn't he notice?

That last night he'd made some tea. A pasta with tomato sauce and tiny bits I had to painstakingly filter out and pile at the side of my plate. I'd tried not to cry when he tucked the duvet round me on the lumpy sofa bed of his flat and said goodnight for the last time.

Mum couldn't pick me up that week. Busy with work. So Gran was waiting at the motorway service station at the halfway drop-off point. The two of them arranging to exchange me like an unwieldy relay baton. She'd bought some fries and looked silly eating them with her swollen fingers with all the gold on them and her pussy-bow blouse. Dad's mum – always impossibly shiny, like antique furniture you have to be extra careful around.

I didn't want to go with her. I didn't want to leave him. I certainly didn't want to stay with him. And the guilt of that last...

I can feel every second. The hot plastic leather under my sticky thighs, salt in my mouth, petrol air and Dad's eyes begging me to stop as strangers at different tables started to look at the girl who was too old to be sobbing.

We'd see each other again soon, Dad said. A lie. It was never soon. We'd be strangers again by half-term.

Gran's mouth got thinner and she fixed Dad with a look like it was all his fault. It was. He could take me back home with him if he wanted. He could come home with me. His face twitched with regret that wasn't real. He had all the choices.

It's a pointless memory to dredge up. Irrelevant.

The important thing is, this morning when I woke up, I was here again. In one piece, my entire body. Maybe I imagined the whole thing. Theo kissing Olivia. Olivia kissing Theo. And then me popping out of existence like the last season of a cancelled show. No one would ever have seen the end of me.

But I'm back.

The relief to look in the mirror this morning and see my normal body was overwhelming. Every inch exactly the same as it left. As three-dimensional and technicolour as it ever was. For one second it was lovely to see, but then I rubbed the sleep from my unfocused eyes, peered into the mirror at my pinched, wonky face and got some perspective. I was convinced I had disappeared. Gone. Invisible Iris. That's worrying even for me.

"Iris Green, get your beautiful bum here!" Bert's yell punctures my reverie from across the quad.

Bert's wearing a hand-embroidered, red-and-yellow hair scarf, appropriate given she's a human fire alarm. Olivia, every blonde hair in place and winged liner on point, is a freshly minted angel. So ends my futile attempt to avoid both my best friends for the rest of my life.

How else was I meant to deal with today?

"Good grief, woman, where were you this morning? We declared you deceased," Bert says when they've caught up. She pulls me into a hug and swings me side to side while I rigidly wait for it to be over. "We've planned your funeral."

"Buried at sea," Olivia chips in.

"Such a moving service."

"Oh, well. Call off the Vikings," I say into a mouthful of Bert's chestnut curls before she finally lets go.

"Are you *sick*?" Olivia peers into my face with concern.

"I'm, uh … tired. Fine."

Liar, liar, life on fire.

"Are you coming down with something?" Olivia's forehead does the hypochondriac crumple as she tries to diagnose whatever I'm dying of. "You're so pale you're basically transparent."

It's not like I'm unaware of how bad I look. My eyes behind my glasses are puffy and sunken. My skin is dry, lips flaky. No wonder Olivia's already planning which symptoms she'll plug into Dr Google on my behalf.

Not that I haven't done a bit of it myself. I have googled almost every word I could think of alongside "invisibility" to try to find answers and have diagnosed hallucinations. Perhaps some temporary psychosis.

It's the only logical conclusion. Stress temporarily twisting my reality. I simply wasn't as close to Theo and Olivia as I thought. I imagined crossing the road. I imagined, well, lots of things.

"Since you're alive, you're coming to common, yes?" Bert says. She threads her arm through mine and all three of us begin walking, Olivia on one side, Bert in the middle and me clunking awkwardly on the end. We meander between clusters of lower years as we make our way towards the brick behemoth of A-block and the common room inside.

As Bert rambles about her adventures in Mr Brandon's German class, Olivia and I trade glances. She searches my face for clues on where I've been all morning (the darkroom, toilets, lessons), I search hers for traces of guilt.

I picture saying it right now. *"I know you kissed Theo."*

I picture the shock on her face. The strenuous denial. The fallout.

The pity would be the worst. Worse than holding it all in. Worse than having to pretend every day that it never happened. Worse than smiling at Olivia while never being able to unknow how fake this all is: her concern, my excuses, both of us playing our parts to a new extreme.

So I'll say nothing. Keeping this secret protects everyone. Friendships are preserved, Bert's not caught in the crossfire and Olivia avoids becoming another bathroom wall victim. Maybe she deserves it, but if I illuminate this situation, it's not just Olivia who'll end up overexposed.

Because if I tell them I know – if *everyone* knew – they'd understand immediately why Theo did it.

Iris Green is grey.

I broke up with Theo; damage contained, disaster averted. No reason to say a word. No need to lose them all.

We swing through the double doors of A-block and amble, me trailing two steps behind my friends, down the corridor towards the sixth-form common room. It runs along the teachers' and admin offices, a narrow stretch of corridor wallpapered with achievements – sports teams, theatre productions, the shining stars of King's school stretching back beyond memory.

I don't appear on the wall.

"What, um … what did you two get up to last night?" I say.

Bert says, "My mother is on a power trip – she's implemented this inhumane practice of confiscating electronic devices until dinner and family time have been achieved and homework completed. Like Dad and I are prisoners getting yard time."

I glance at Olivia, but she's watching Bert.

"Did you and your boy have a nice evening after you left us?" Bert says.

"Huh?"

For some reason, I was sure the news would travel like a winter cold. It's a small school, small sixth form. I figured Theo would tell Ash and Spade and they would tell their mates and by this morning the whole King's crowd would know Iris Green and Theo Hastings broke up.

Maybe not. Maybe I imagined sending that message and the multiple responses from Theo I've been too scared to read too.

I say, "No, I tried to do the mum thing, but … uh, she bailed on me. So I went…"

Olivia's head jerks up. "Back to Theo's?"

Like a bad spirit, as soon as we think of him, he appears.

Theo steps into view between Olivia and Bert's profiles. He's up ahead where the corridor fattens out into the common room space. Theo's head is thrown back, laughing at something out of sight round the corner. His teeth flash.

Nice to see him so clearly devastated.

"Urgh, that boy," Bert says. "Sorry, Iris, I'd rather take a sandpaper cotton bud to my eardrums than listen to his music and he's so not my type of—"

Olivia laughs. "Not your type? The understatement."

"I'm saying! Obviously he's not a lumberjack girl—"

"Or non-threatening androgenous boy," Olivia chips in. "Your other exception."

"Fine. But still, I see it. Why do the good genes always go to—"

"We broke up," I blurt and stop walking.

Their concerned faces swing towards me. And I'm sure I'm giving it all away. Emotions scrawled all over me like graffiti on a bathroom wall.

Olivia grabs my arm. "What? He broke up with you?"

"I broke up with *him*."

I step sideways, but Olivia holds on, the grasp of her hand echoed by the spark of interest in her eyes. A wanting. I taste bile.

"Oh, Chicken, what's he done this time?" says Bert.

Ahead of us, Theo's still smiling. But then he turns. He sees us. Sees me.

"You look *really* sick. D'you want us to go somewhere else?" Olivia says, her hand moving to the top of my arm. The two of them peer at me.

"I'm fine." A lie so deeply learned it's out before I can stop it.

Olivia throws a look Bert catches.

Bert says, "OK, well, we can—"

I wrench free from Olivia's grip and mutter, "He's looking."

Bert and Olivia turn away. I back up. Soon others will pick up on this. Soon everyone will start to stare. I wish, wish, wish I was gone. Wish I could disappear. I take a step back and the corner of a picture frame jabs my shoulder. I push my hands into my hair and my elbows are there for a moment and the next – gone.

No? Way?

I stare at my feet and see nothing. Just the dirty school lino. My heart clatters against my ribs so hard I'm convinced Olivia can hear it. Bert too. The whole corridor.

"Erm, where the hell did she go?" Bert says, turning to stare straight through me.

Olivia rises on tiptoes to look over the top of my invisible head and the students behind.

Bert says, "Seriously? That girl must have legged it at the speed of light. Should I go after her?"

Olivia shakes her head. "She got dumped, Bert. Give her a mo."

"She said she dumped him."

"But the evidence." Olivia shrugs. "Anyway, when Iris needs space, she *needs space*. That's how she keeps her shit together."

I hate her a tiny bit. And then a bit more.

My face twists and my insides follow suit, conjuring new possibilities provided by my lack of visibility: scissors and shining blonde hair.

Snip.

But that ugly idea ricochets back at me.

I turn to go, my bag bouncing on my shoulder.

I'm halfway down the corridor, dodging round Doug New, when his mate shoves him and he steps back into me so hard we both stumble.

"Whoa. What was that?" Doug says, after he's saved himself and turned to look.

"I … I …" I mumble, waving a hand before I remember. *Stop, Iris. Shhh.*

I'm still dithering when Lucy Miller ploughs into me. I lose my balance and tread on her foot.

"Ouch." She jumps back and pulls her knee up, glancing

between the empty space that hurt her and the nearest fall guy. She says, "Watch yourself, Doug! What the hell?"

Her friend says, "What did he do?"

"I didn't do anything." Doug stares. His hand gropes through the air.

I dodge. I run.

My hair gets in my mouth and the world blurs as I fling myself between groups of lower years in the quad. My breath shreds my throat. My limbs burn.

No one follows. No one shouts. No one tries to stop me even when I smack into people and send them reeling. I don't stop or look back and don't try to apologize.

Let them believe in ghosts.

5

In the darkroom with the lights out, everything's invisible. There are no edges to the room, there's no drying rack or worktop, no chemicals or pile of easels in the corner, no cobwebs, no splintered surface of the door. It doesn't matter if I'm here or gone. It doesn't matter if I'm totally losing it. Here I can forget the freaky fact of my non-appearance and pretend it's not happening. Hopefully.

I wander the edges of the tiny room, balling and relaxing my hands again and again. The dark's soothing fingers run up my spine and ease the pressure. Soon there's only the smooth plastic film case in my fingers, the warm vinegar scent and my breathing filling every inch of space. It doesn't matter the mess I'm in or how many people are out there. They're not here. No one staring or asking questions I don't have an answer to like, "What the hell is wrong with you, Iris?"

Wouldn't we all like to know? But this film holds some answers. Once it's developed there's two photos I want to see:

- Number one: Olivia and Theo on the bench.
- Number two: my disappearing body.

It's only this part of the process that demands total darkness. Not even the red of the safelight is safe enough. I bend the cassette until the lid pops off, then work my way along to snip the film and load it on to the reel. Moving from memory, using every sense but sight; this is the exact opposite of a shutter press.

I slide the reel into the tank and twist.

The door opens. A knife of light hits the tank. The tank suspended in mid-air by my *invisible hands*. Holy hell.

"Shut the door! Get out! Shut the door!" I whip round as a boy-shape hurtles inside and slams the door.

"Whoa. Sorry." Baker Whatshisface's voice. Of course.

"Don't you knock?"

"Don't you put on the warning light?"

"Sorry." My heart thumps my ribs. Did he see me? Or, more to the point, not see me?

"*I'm* sorry. Is the film ruined?" In the void I picture him running a hand through his dark curls.

"It's in the tank, so probably fine."

I wait, though, because what happens now? This is the predicament: I am trapped, invisible, in a tiny space with some guy. Not a problem when the room's dark, but I'm about to seal this tank and my film will be safe and the lights will go back on. And when the lights go back on Baker will see I'm… Well, he won't see me.

One of us needs to leave. But I can't boot him out without letting the light in. I can't leave without him seeing.

"Hey, Iris? It's Iris, right?"

"Yeah. How did you … um…?"

"You'd be surprised how few angry girls live in the darkroom," his voice answers. "It was a simple matter of asking any year twelve. Can't reveal my source, though."

Wow. An interesting development: Baker bothered to find out my name.

"Well, Iris, are you going to finish up so we can shed some light on this situation or what?"

I twist the top of the tank and it shushes into place. "There. Listen, if you don't mind—" Baker throws the switch. The light is sharp, sudden, making my eyes water after too long in the black. I shield them with an arm—

A solid arm. Yep, attached to my body and legs. I'm back and Baker's staring at me so intensely I have to double-check my clothes came with me.

"Are you OK?" he says.

"Um … yeah?" My hands run over my hips automatically checking for flaws, but there's no clear reason for the expression Baker's wearing – somewhere between anxiety and awkwardness.

"Your face." He twirls his finger around his own.

Shit. The crying. I turn back to the workbench and surreptitiously lick a finger to wipe over my lids. It comes away black with smudged mascara.

"Do you want to chat about it?" Baker says.

"I'd rather flee the country."

"Sure. Well, if you ever need a shoulder to cry on, I … have shoulders."

"No need to brag." I glance sideways at Baker as he shrugs said shoulders. They are indeed very existent. Very broad.

As calmly as I can, I make a mix of developer and water from the streaky sink and check the temperature before I pour it into the tank. I set my timer for nine minutes. Precisely nine minutes with nothing to do but stand in this confined space with this boy. At least he's started to rifle through supplies instead of staring with that concerned expression on his face.

I take out my phone.

Theo: this is so unfair

Theo: don't I deserve an explanation?

Nope. I pocket my phone.

To my side, the drying rack is pegged full of images and this time there's not a pouty girl in sight. They're street scenes. Long exposures of lights at night.

"Nice to know it's not exclusively pretty girls you're interested in," I say, reaching out for the nearest print.

"Not *exclusively.*" A smile. He's joking.

This new photograph is a view down a dual carriageway. The road snakes out into the distance, lights from cars flowing down in an endless stream, turning the paper white in places where the trails overlap.

It's abstract. Imaginative.

"How long was the exposure?" I say.

"These beauties were a quick pinhole camera experiment. An empty beer can duct taped to hell left overnight."

"Hmm, interesting."

Baker gasps and claps a hand to his chest. "Why thank you. I get the impression that's high praise from Iris Green."

My cheeks heat. Still four endless minutes on the timer. I give the tank another shake.

"Have you got any stuff I can see?" Baker asks.

"Not really."

"You don't have any photos? Do you spend time in here because you enjoy the view?" He gestures at the windowless room. "Or hiding from reality maybe?" My eyes snap up. "Reality is objectively terrible, so no judgement."

"I like the quiet." It echoes in my head, harsher than

intended, so I add, "I've got some stuff in the drawers." I jerk my head in the direction of the tray and the wide peeling label with my name on in block capitals. "It's not ready, though. It's nothing."

"Can I look?"

"If you must?"

He hesitates.

"Sure." My phone timer beeps and I knock it to the floor. *Smooth, Iris.* Silence falls while I drain the tank and add my stop bath and fixer. I rinse and unroll my film.

I could leave. But I can't leave Baker unattended with my art. There's one thing worse than hearing what he thinks of it and that's never hearing what he thinks. If I leave now knowing Baker's seen it, I'll have to live with constant unease. It'll be like Schrödinger's cat: Baker simultaneously convinced that my work is both bin-worthy dross and a masterpiece. No one could live like that.

And there's the small matter of the contents of my film.

I slide the light pad closer to me and put a wet set of negatives on top. I can't resist. I study each of the tiny sepia images over the illuminated panel until I find the last strip of four. There's the cat, the old women, then there it is. My camera hanging in mid-air in front of my mirror.

It happened.

I stare, expecting shock, but there's just the cold flat nothing of knowing.

And there's the other big news of the night. Olivia and Theo embracing on the park bench. They're too small, too far to make out in thumbnail format. But they're there.

That happened too.

Baker leans over and I'm hit by a soft wave of mint. "Who are these two?"

For a moment, I think he means the kissing couple. My breath catches. And then I glance up at the print he's holding. Just another street scene. A couple of interesting strangers.

"It's nothing," I say, on reflex, but Baker doesn't agree. He runs his thumb over the corner of the print. I press my lips together, then blurt, "The girl with the short hair, she caught my eye first."

"Yeah?" His expression opens. An invitation.

"Her and the birds anyway … She had this flaking messy croissant and her girlfriend was picking crumbs from the paper bag to feed the sparrows, this cloud of them at their feet."

"Pretty great capture," Baker says.

I take the print from him. "It was perfect. I mean, they were perfect. This single frame of their whole epic love story just there and then…" I snap my fingers. *Click.*

"It was so lucky. The picture can't even do justice to the moment. The two of them, the birds and the light. Unposed, unfiltered. Nothing performed. That's what I love about street; those moments are always happening. Even in a small town the scene's always changing, so I try to get out there as often as I can, because you just never know…"

I catch myself. Refocus on Baker who probably regrets his polite interest. I realize my hands are out in front of me and wonder if my face has been misbehaving. *Shit, Iris, you big weirdo.*

"Anyway, it turned out OK," I mumble, putting the print face down on the side.

"That's incredible." Baker's two front teeth have a thin gap between them. A tiny imperfection. He moves closer to where my negatives lie on the light pad. "You know, the street stuff is pretty interesting," he says after a while. "As Iris Green might say." I grin; I can't help it. "Someone more effusive with their praise might even say they're amazing. But this one's fascinating too."

I'm still smiling – until I see what he's looking at.

"Ah, that's not even a thing. Don't look."

It's a self-portrait. The ultimate embarrassment. Worse, it's an experimental self-portrait. A double exposure of my face overlaid with a background of my house. I overexposed the print and there's too much background. It is, in short, a mess. Which makes it a fitting self-portrait.

"I like it," Baker says firmly, jerking the print out of reach as I make a move for it.

"It needs work. It was practice, an idea."

"Maybe the execution needs work, but the idea is great. Did you try any more?"

I recoil at "needs work". "Um, no. One spectacular failure was enough, thanks."

"Right, because if at first you don't succeed—"

"Stop. Exactly."

Baker's eyes are on me. I suddenly hate that he saw my photos. This was a mistake. This is why I like to work in secret until things are ready. Until I know they're good enough. From artwork and homework to conversations, everything is finessed before finding an audience.

"Are you pissed?" Baker says. "I genuinely like it. The whole film thing is—"

"A mess."

"Would you take one of me?"

"I'd rather glue my hands together."

There's a pause. Baker gives me a look.

"What?"

"Does being this stubborn work out for you on the whole?"

I tut and ignore the question. Focus on the light pad.

I flip the negatives and take the two I need to the enlarger. The one of me, the one of Olivia and Theo. Evidence the two bombshells of the last twenty-four hours weren't all a figment of my overactive imagination.

And when I see the projection of the image on a plain piece of paper, it's as I remember: the two of them locked as tight as the vice round my chest.

Baker's laying out his own prints. He won't notice these two, I think, as I clip them to the rack. There are so many photos drying and, unless you know what you're looking for, there's nothing to see.

Just a couple on a bench. And an invisible girl.

"See you," I say. "These need to dry."

"Bye, Iris Green," he says, but the door is already closing behind me.

6

The next time I see Theo is third period: history. Appropriate, no?

I pretend not to see him as he mouths a greeting and slips into his chair as Mrs Coombes kicks off a session revisiting the policy of containment. The Cold War is even less fascinating with Theo's eyes burning into me from across the room, making concentrating even more impossible.

At the end of class I pack my bag slowly, waiting for the room to empty. Theo leans on his desk feigning interest in his phone but shooting quick glances my way. I pack slower.

My history desk mate, Neel, touches me lightly on the shoulder. "Do you want me to walk you out?" His warm brown eyes turn cold as they settle on Theo who abandons any pretence of not watching.

I put on a smile to show I'm grateful. "I don't think that would help the situation."

"Yeah, well… If you're sure?"

I nod, knowing all the fake-fine has left my expression.

Neel heads out and Theo trails behind him. I give it another couple of minutes until I'm the last person in the classroom, alone with Mrs Coombes. As the door begins to close behind the final straggler, my history teacher glances up.

"I've been meaning to catch you, Iris," she says.

The door clunks into place. I am caught.

"This year's important, so with everything you're going through at the moment" – I jerk my head up. Does even Coombes know about my tragic love life? – "I wanted to remind you I'm here."

The last time we did this was a couple of months ago. My last little crash. An awkward heart-to-heart when Coombes impressed on me quite firmly that her door was open. Always. The only time it closes is when I'm already inside the room, trapped. Like now. Coombes perches on the near side of her desk, her long flowy skirt hitting the floor. I smile and nod and try to look appreciative. Try to look her in the eye. Wishing I was anywhere else at all.

"Iris," Mrs Coombes says gently, and I realize I've not only not been listening; I've picked off half a thumbnail. I pull my jumper down to cover my hands. "I've had an update on your referral for one-to-one support – the counselling? You can start in the next couple of weeks if you're ready and that's still something you'd like?"

"Oh." My skin prickles. This again. If I could have simply kept everything under wraps none of this would have happened. No singling out. No worry or attention. "Who else … will know?"

"Your classmates won't know if that's what you're wondering?" Mrs Coombes watches me.

I look at the board behind her. At her. Away.

"Have you spoken to your parents about it?"

"No."

"You're sixteen so that's up to you, but it's worth considering whether they might be able to support and understand you better if they're looped in."

"Yeah. Maybe." Maybe on my death bed.

"Someone to talk to can be incredibly helpful," she says. "And we can make sure the pressure doesn't get overwhelming."

I nod. "OK."

"Are you OK?"

I nod again, faintly annoyed by the question. "I do appreciate your concern," I say stiffly, weirdly formal in an attempt to shut this down and get out.

I wonder if I can leave now or if I have to stay. If it would be rude to turn down this "help" after so long waiting. It seemed like a good idea in the abstract – someone to hand all my anxieties over to, for them to hold so I could let go – but now it's here and I'm faced with the prospect of an actual stranger listening to my actual problems with their actual ears? I'm less sure.

Mrs Coombes gestures to the exit. "I'll make sure the details for the session are emailed over to you, but even afterwards I hope you know my door is always open."

*

"Neel didn't take long to move in."

Theo's waiting beyond the classroom, strategically pressed against the wall outside the door so I didn't see him from inside.

"What?" I step back from the slipstream of migrating students and fold my arms round myself to hold back the panic in my chest. How can it be Theo's the one who cheated, but with one sentence he's already made me feel like I'm in the wrong? "You know it's not like that. Neel's a friend. Not even a friend, really."

"Sure. And I'm meant to believe that now?" Theo sighs and wipes a hand over his forehead. "A message, Ris? You didn't even have the courage to tell me to my face?"

"Sorry," I say. "I'm sorry."

"Clearly you're not. No one made you do it, did they?"

I look at him, unable to stop myself. His sad blue eyes.

"After everything we've been through, Ris. Sure we've had our ups and downs. But those ups..." He reaches out, but his hand falls away with touching me. "I deserve some kind of explanation. Don't you think?"

"I just … can't do this any more."

"Since when? Since yesterday?" He eyes me. I wonder if he wonders. Because Theo knows what happened yesterday, I remind myself. He knows what he did. But my knowing is eroded by the sight of this hurt boy right here.

I shake my head.

This is the boy who serenaded me under a duvet tent.

This is the boy who softly traced lyrics on my bare skin.

This is the boy who ran to my house at midnight. He did that. Time has turned the details murky, as though the memory's sat too long in a developing bath. There had been a fight. Some tears. A handful of words Theo promised afterwards he'd never meant. Me in my bed, bunged up with misery when Theo messaged to say, "Outside. Come down." And when I crept out and took his hand and pulled him up the road away from prying eyes, he pressed me against the knotted bark of the tree on the corner. Closed eyes, skin sparking, his whisper against my ear.

"I needed to tell you I love you," he'd said, his breath still ragged from his run. His skin smelled of alcohol and I couldn't breathe as he kissed me.

This is the boy who told me he loved me for the first time under the stars at midnight.

I wish I could reset this year. Go back and keep my Theo as he was before. Not this sullied version with Olivia's fingerprints all over him. I want my Theo. The hurt is doubled, tripled, backdated through all the time I didn't even know I was missing him. I want my imaginary boyfriend, the one who never hurt me. I'm embarrassed for the Iris who let him kiss her eyelids and believed he was real.

"This isn't going to be like every other time, Ris," Theo says. "Still can't wrap my head around why you're throwing this away."

"We can be friends." It comes out strangled and unconvincing.

"Don't want to be your friend. We were never friends, Ris." Theo sighs. He looks over his shoulder then back at me. "Once you've thought about this, you're going to know it was a mistake."

*

I retreat to the darkroom and develop my prints. The two that matter. The one of Olivia and Theo and the one of me. I try not to stare too long at the details. Not yet, not until they're ready. Not until *I'm* ready.

At the end of the day I return, too paranoid to leave the prints overnight, too desperate to rake over the details. The photo is miraculously in focus. Miraculously perfect despite my absent-minded development job. The figures are in profile, crisp and recognizable. But it's not the photo I'm drawn to.

It jumps out immediately, so vivid in the gloom. A neon yellow square. A Post-it note.

ISN'T THIS YOUR BOYFRIEND???

It clings to the bulldog clip holding the print of Olivia and Theo.

There's only one person this note could be from. Somehow the scratchy, slanting capitals are very Baker.

And I see how this is going to go – the way it'll spread all over school. How everyone will know. Because Baker will blab this hilarious heartache and so will the next person and so on and so on.

Bert will know. She'll have to choose between me and Olivia.

I rip down the print, then go to unclip the next one. My empty bedroom, a floating camera, a disappeared girl.

I touch my finger to the paper. It lands in the black-and-white space where my body should be and where, when I push up my glasses and bring my nose close, there's distortion on the image. An out-of-place fuzziness. A change of focus on the wall behind. There's an infinitesimal shift somewhere along the edges of where I'm secretly tucked away, as though existence has split in two and I've slipped through the cracks. A scar where it healed imperfectly.

I trace the edge of myself on the page and feel a shiver up my spine.

Is that where I go when I disappear? Behind. Through.

Would anyone notice if I never came back?

7

"Drama block," Bert says, giving my arm a nudge as she steers me across the quad. "Olivia's having a wobble over *The Importance of Being Earnest* so a little moral support's in order."

A play where everyone's pretending to be someone they're not? "Perfect."

"You absolutely do not have to say a word or acknowledge the existence of any other emerging thespians," Bert adds, jiggling my arm and sneaking me a sideways glance.

Theo, she means. I nod wordlessly, and slap on a weak smile.

It's been a weird day and a half. Only for me though.

Somehow I've kept it inside. Pretended everything's exactly as it seems on the surface – a simple break up, no big deal – as I carry the truth like a deep ache in my centre that makes it hard to talk, to walk, to function.

Bert holds me together. She keeps me on course. "You're doing amazing," she says, as we wait, getting chilly standing outside the drama department.

And I wonder who she's looking at.

But that's unfair. Maybe she knows I'm not coping. Perhaps Bert sees it all on my face, like the dark bloom of blood soaking through a bandage. She's been uncharacteristically restrained over the break-up, not asking too much, not prodding too hard.

Olivia emerges from the auditorium full of the energy of whatever part she's recently been channelling – her spine a little straighter as she bounces past us.

"So?" Bert asks, dropping me and stepping towards Olivia. "Is it carnations or roses I'm meant to throw during your standing ovation?"

I force my tone to be bright as I say, "Who are you again? Ernest?" and don't add:

You kissed my boyfriend.

"Classic," Olivia says with a glance back. "Bert, put a pin in that very thoughtful idea, doubt you'll need it. God, I wish it had been another musical, not a play. Celine Foster's totally tuneless but a phenomenal actress. She makes me feel like a patio slab. Urgh."

Olivia gives herself a small shake before turning a smile on me and Bert.

As we head back towards the school's main building, we're trailed by a familiar bunch of boys travelling in the same direction. Theo's laughter's turned up to ten, just the sound of it spiking my anxiety.

Bert says, "Forget it, O. We all need a break from drama. The Lion? Bad wine? Friday?"

Olivia begs off: her parents are divorced too and this week's a dad weekend. Thank god. One glass of cheap illegal wine in Olivia's presence and who knows what I'd say.

The one positive this week is no one else seems to suspect anything. Not Olivia, not Theo, not Bert. There have been no whispers, no stares. I guess Baker kept quiet.

Baker. There's a roll of film I need to develop that won't see the light of day because I'm too afraid of bumping into him in the darkroom. I hardly ever see him around school – he doesn't frequent the common room – but yesterday I saw him in a corridor. We didn't have a chance to speak, though. Mainly because I fled.

After the Post-it there was follow-up contact. A DM request.

Baker: Here if you ever need…

That's all I know. The preview cuts off.

I didn't accept Baker's request, didn't open the message, but I didn't delete it either. It sits on my phone – a bomb waiting to go off. A proximity bomb, though; if I avoid him, it'll never detonate.

Bert, Olivia and I swing through the doors and make for our usual corner of the common room.

"It's so unfair Celine got Cecily in the first place," Olivia says. "She barely bothered with her lines last year when she understudied Audrey."

"You're still a major role, *Gwendolen*. And you're going to be stunning."

Olivia gives Bert a withering look. "It's always something with Celine. Every year. She was probably the one who gave me gastro in year ten before *Sweeney Todd*."

"All to steal the part of chorus girl number two?" I ask.

Olivia laughs. "It was *extremely* covetable. I was front row, best light … well worth slipping some raw chicken into my smoothie."

"It's probably a bit late for this, but … break her legs?" Bert says as she hits the sofa.

Olivia gracefully drapes her own eminently snappable calves over Bert's lap and I perch on the sofa arm, tempted to say:

Other people deserve good things too, Olivia.

But I don't.

Olivia sniffs. "And Theo's Algy, so—"

"Exactly!" Bert says. "Lucky escape not being his Cecily then. You don't want to act nice with him."

"Is he good?" I say, my stomach twisting.

"About half as good as he *thinks*." Olivia smiles and checks her phone.

I knot my hands in my lap. Even without looking, I know he's here. Over in the opposite corner behind me. We're divided by the crowd and a row of painted brick columns. He and his mates are at the table-tennis table, playing a ridiculous game using textbooks in lieu of the missing paddles.

I hate the common room. Although we're far more involved in the social strata of King's here than we were during last year's lunchtimes in the draughty E-block Portakabins, I hate the exposure of being here. Everyone's eyes. Too many potential opinions. Plus, it's offensively noisy, too bright and full of conflicting smells. Today it's rice crackers versus body odour, but neither Bert nor Olivia seem fussed.

Bert kicks her shoes off. Her gaze flickers over my shoulder and then to Olivia as she says, "Obviously you owe Theo squat, beaut, but don't you want to get it off your chest? You've been unnervingly chill about splattering his heart all over the rug."

My eyes fall to the carpet, scratchy darkest grey with speckles. You'd hardly even notice the blood.

"And you've been very quiet," Olivia adds. "Were you never very keen?"

I wince at the hope in her voice.

"You never liked him anyway," I say. "You were always rooting for us to break up."

"I *never* said that," Olivia says.

"I definitely did," Bert offers. "So what? You came to your senses at last?"

Olivia and Bert shift on the sofa. Clearly the time for silence has passed, and I wonder if this intervention was planned. If so, it's Bert who'll give the game away. Olivia's a seasoned actress with several school plays under her belt, not to mention her long-running performance as loyal friend.

"It was nothing," I say. "Everything. It was hardly going to work out, was it? Olivia had more in common with him than I did."

Olivia's gaze flickers towards Theo's corner. "That … that's irrelevant."

Bert claps her hands and announces, "At least you shed the dead weight in time to make space in your life for your artistic world conquering."

Right. The exhibition.

The other thing I don't want to discuss.

"That's not happening," I say.

"I'll never understand you." Bert flaps her arm against the sofa. "If there was a prize for any of my subjects, do you know how hard I would go for it? You two would never see me again."

"I wouldn't win," I say. It comes out on reflex. Embarrassing to even say it aloud. And it's true. It's definitely true. But there's a nagging sense somewhere pushed down low that I should at least try, because if I tried – if I really tried…

"Um, hey, do you know Baker Davis?" I say, because I

need a distraction and he's been distracting me a lot lately. "Year thirteen? He's kind of … in my darkroom."

"Mm." Bert shifts in her seat. "Chiselled from marble, but with that strange, otherworldly energy? He's odd. Probably glitters in the sun. I heard he once got off with two twins at one party." Bert's eyes go wide with the joy of gossip.

"Two twins? Like … four people?"

"What? No, two. The whole pair." Bert adjusts her ring stack and adds, "Please don't rebound on to another inappropriate love interest, lovely one. What if we make a pact? These next few months, you focus on taking the art world by storm while I wow the academic world by not only *giving* but somehow *getting* a hundred and ten per cent in every exam and one relaxes because she's already La La Landed her starring role."

"There's still a performance to survive," Olivia says.

"OK, but my point stands."

"World domination?" I say and Bert flexes an arm in agreement.

"Don't count on me. It's a miracle I even know my part since *someone* didn't run lines with me as promised." Olivia balls up a piece of notepad paper and throws it at Bert's head.

"That same glorious someone has been very busy working her colour-coded pens to the bone. Iris, why weren't you roped in?"

"Because she was the only one of the Three Kings without a line?" Olivia suggests.

"Um, yeah." I tuck hair behind my ear. "Thanks to my own improvisation."

Olivia laughs. "Freezing is a form of improv?"

"It was a character choice. That king was an introvert." My smile answers Olivia's. Bert fashions a torn piece of paper into a crown for Olivia, who preens and – *click* – I snap it.

I can almost see us: tiny versions of Olivia, Bert and me all on stage in our gold crowns, clutching our foil-covered props. We were friends back then, until suddenly we weren't and I can't explain why, what exactly it was I did or didn't do. For years I pinged back and forth between other groups, being part of something and then dropped without understanding how I had gone wrong. And then in year ten English I ended up beside Bert and we were three again: me and Bert and Olivia, as if it had always been so.

And it can always be that way. So long as I continue to swallow the hurt. These girls are irreplaceable. They witnessed the in-between years when it felt like I couldn't exist without eliciting digs and comments and looks, before I learned to be the right kind of invisible. Bert and Olivia picked me up again. My only ever second chance.

I can't bear to be alone again.

Olivia isn't purely this thing she did to me. Olivia and I have a hundred giggly sleepovers, Sunday breakfasts and sunny days on the grass. The time she capsized our dinghy and I swam for help because she's scared of deep water. The time she took the fall for a botched physics experiment because she knows I can't stand a public bollocking. Cigarettes tried and dismissed, popcorn and secrets shared, sides taken and in-jokes created and never forgotten.

Those were genuine, weren't they? But I can't be sure now I know Olivia has at least two faces. Until last week I only recognized one.

"What's with all the sighing?" Bert says abruptly, eyeballing me. Beside her Olivia is immersed in her phone.

"Um…" I blink, unaware I made a noise. "Just … life. Not Theo. Just…" I gesture at the common room, unable to find a lie.

"This year is such a lot," Bert says with a knowing grimace.

"My dad's on the uni thing still," I blurt. "He floated the idea of me getting a job. Start saving…" I shudder. Finally escaping the polyester prison of my school uniform on a Friday afternoon only to put on a new one and beep groceries within a flickering fluoro hellscape of suspect smells? I'd die.

"After the barista incident?" Bert bobs her head.

Ah. My cursed trial shift at Don't Be Latte, where the pressure of being observed led to spilled coffee beans, an inability to count basic change, crying for two hours after leaving and never daring show my face again.

"There must be something I can do." But what I mean is "probably not".

"Exactly. Play to your vast collection of strengths," Bert says. "This is why you should do the exhibition, though! It'd be amazing for your personal statement – all about demonstrating experience and participation. I need to get a shuffle on if I'm going to make the early deadline..."

I lose Bert's voice as it mixes with the background noise of too many people. Beside her, Olivia looks up from her phone, a quick sideways glance. I twist my head to see Theo answer the look and then swiftly check his hand. I'm too far to see the phone that must be clutched there.

My insides squeeze tighter. I shut my eyes to the feeling of falling. Plummeting.

From way down here I am tuned to his frequency and the sound of his laughter. He's laughing. At me?

My fingers start to tingle. All hot and numb like the feeling's coming back into them after touching snow. The sensation's familiar now. Alarming. I ball my hands into fists and ram them between my thighs and the sofa.

Not here.

As I watch, the toe of my boot disappears.

Not *now.*

The bell goes. My vision dances with silver confetti.

"But the stress is unreal when the margins are so tight," Bert finishes. "Are you still thinking history? Iris?"

I blink and it's back. My foot. My sanity.

My heart's hammering. I might have convinced myself

I imagined it the other night, but if it's a hallucination, it's a recurring one. And frighteningly real.

My eyes fall on the wrinkled, sagging posters stuck to the painted brickwork over Olivia's head. *Exam anxiety? Relationship worries?* it asks. *You're not alone!*

There's a list of helplines underneath, but none for unplanned invisibility or cheating friends.

Where's the helpline for *that*?

8

It's a relief to get home to a dim, quiet house and shut the door on the world outside. The weight of the day is hung up with my blazer and I step into the kitchen, aiming for the kettle. Nothing soothes like a warm milky tea with two sugars and an hour of total silence to offset the stress of my daily post-school ritual: replaying the day, cringing over every word I said or didn't, rescripting conversations I've had and coming up with better responses than I did on the spot.

But when I get in the kitchen, Mum's there. Propped against the counter, head down, damp hair curling against her fuzzy dressing gown collar. So much for my alone time.

"I'm working out what tea fits between now and the pile of receipts waiting for me later." Mum straightens and puts her hands on the small of her back. "Would I be a bad parent if it was beans on toast?"

"Mm, beige," I say.

"Our other options are limited." Mum opens the fridge and peers inside, the cool glow illuminating her lines and the remnants of make-up.

Over in the brightest corner of our small, dark kitchen, the one window is crammed with an assortment of houseplants in mismatched pots. A new addition looks like it's been in a fight: two large torn leaves over a straggly stem.

"Someone dumped it in a skip, can you believe it?" Mum says.

"Completely." I stroke the jagged brown edge of the tattered foliage. "It looks like a foot."

Mum tuts at me then asks, "How's your weather today?"

Our new check-in picked up from one of her books or blogs, a tactic to circumvent the reflex response of "fine". For a while, she had me, but I've adapted. Learned the ambiguously unworrying emotional weather a frazzled parent wants to hear and that's:

"Cloudy with sunshine breaking through." *And puddles underfoot deep enough to drown.*

"Lovely. I had one of those grey, damp, mizzly days."

"Mm, you look tired."

"Charmer. Old more like." Mum nudges me and I brace for a hug that mercifully doesn't come. She smells like moisturizer and honey-scented shampoo, but I swear underneath there's still the faintest hint of antibac and coffee. Her pupils dance back and forth, assessing me, as she says, "Sorry I wasn't around last night for a catch-up."

"It's fine. It's OK." I sigh, feeling the pull of my own silent bedroom but knowing it's rude to leave. So, although it's the last thing I want to do, I reach for another excuse to get a moment to myself. I shake four slices of bread from their bag to avoid having to touch the clammy plastic and tell Mum, "Go. Sit. I'll toast and microwave."

Mum pauses at the kitchen threshold. I stand with bread in my hand, unable to begin until she stops watching.

"You're good for making tea. The best." She hits me with a wan smile and shuffles from the kitchen. I deposit the slices in the toaster; breadcrumbs cling to my fingers like soft grit.

Mum's living proof humans have limited processing capacity. One dependent daughter, one sickly cat, the care home, the freelance bookkeeping plus accountancy studies is a lot for any human. Something had to give and I'm the only one with flexibility. So I flex. I compartmentalize: home problems at home; school problems left at the door.

"Your dad called," Mum shouts from the front room.

Not a question, so I don't respond. Purkoy mewls on the floor and slinks her tail round my leg, begging for love.

"He wants to know if you're going away with him in the summer."

I open the beans.

"He wants to book a holiday."

Beans into bowl.

"He needs to know. Prices will rocket," Mum shouts again and it rattles my skull. I'm bone-tired and busy-brained and the small, awful part of me that craves peace wishes she had been out after all. "What shall I tell him?"

"Nothing."

"Nothing?"

"I'll call him."

Mum goes quiet. I imagine her out there dying to point out my track record on such promises and that irks me too. It's not her responsibility to fight for Dad. He should do his own dirty work.

Sometimes he does. Last week he emailed me a list of the top British unis for history.

I know it's scary to think about your future, he wrote, *but your future's going to happen regardless, Iris. You need to think about a proper career. Teaching is a job for life – you can work your way up.*

He had highlighted the unis that are London-based or London-adjacent, as though increased proximity to him would be an incentive. For a man who prides himself on his smarts, my father has a severe inability to read the room. I deleted the email, but the words were already seared on my brain, veiled critique of Mum and all; "proper career" being, I presume, the antithesis of working two jobs while getting your qualifications at forty-three.

Dad's insistent meddling is just one reason the summer holidays that charmed me as a kid have stopped cutting it recently. That and growing up. Realizing he was the one who left, who moved hours away, who prioritized his career over, well, everything.

I take dinner into the front room. Mum slides her reading glasses up on to her hair and reaches for her plate.

I cross my legs under me in an armchair and pick at my food.

After dinner, I could start highlighting revision notes or sketch out provisional, probably irrelevant exhibition ideas.

Or I could reply to my dad and put an end to my summer holiday dread.

There are many things I could be doing. *Should* be doing.

I glance at Mum, who's wolfing her dinner down with one eye on emails. We could watch a film. Something we've seen a hundred times and know all the words by heart so I don't need subs and can doodle. Burton or Luhrmann – something undemanding and pretty with a decent soundtrack. Hot chocolates, Purkoy curled between us and no chatter. Companionable quiet.

Bean juice has absorbed into my last piece of toast and rendered it inedible. I reach for Mum's empty plate and open my mouth, about to suggest the movie – when she gestures to the textbook by her side and says, "Do you mind if I power through?"

*

Upstairs, in my own room, the walls are humming with the muffled noise of the neighbour's TV. I put my earbuds in and play the song that's been in my head all day. I sit in front of my notes and ignore them. I take out my phone and go to Olivia's profile. There's the picture of her and Bert holding their shopping bags. I study her face, her smile. No one would even know I was there unless they stopped to wonder who took the photo. And then the newest post of her in full theatre make-up:

Painted for the cheap seats. Getting ready for Gwendolen.

So I guess she's already over her nerves.

I finally read Baker's message.

Baker: Here if you ever need a shoulder

Baker: Mine are extremely sturdy

Baker: Not to shoulder brag

Yeah right.

He's so polite. It's so kind. But all I can think is how borderline humiliating it is that Baker felt compelled to message. Being publicly unhinged is clearly good for my inbox.

I need to acknowledge it without guilting Baker into continuing the exchange, so I reply *Thanks* and hope that's the end of it. Baker feels like a complication I don't know how to deal with.

A quick scroll of Baker's profile reveals post after post of abstract photos and short videos. Time lapses of roads and streets, aerial footage of cars and pedestrians. His grid is shot through with casual snaps of him at work, setting up a tripod, ducking behind his camera, pushing his hair back to squint into the sun. I wonder who took them. The girl from his darkroom photos?

His profile shot is a mirror selfie. Black and white, his face half hidden by the flare of a flash. I curse the day I opted to keep my Halloween profile photo. Nothing says well-adjusted human quite like my "vengeful ghost of Anne Boleyn" costume. Except perhaps my date for the evening, the papier mâché severed head of Henry VIII.

At least there's nothing else for Baker to see. No photos of me, no real art. Only sunsets, Purkoy and mangy urban wildlife. A couple of street snaps. There's nothing for anyone to criticize or read into. Nothing to provoke. Not any more.

No one would notice, or care, if I deleted it all. It would be so easy. Erase my pictures one by one. Erase myself.

There's an idea. I eye myself in the mirror. Imagine trying. Squeeze my eyes shut and open them again.

Ridiculous.

Instead, I step up to my wall of photos. In between the art postcards and my own prints there are more everyday snaps: my favourites of all. Bert and Olivia blurry-faced and blotto in front of the bathroom mirror at the White Lion, the three of us in matching Bert-knitted scarves on a rare snow day, Olivia taking a bow holding a bouquet of paper flowers.

I pull those photos down one by one and stash them in the darkest depths of my wardrobe.

There. Olivia's turn to disappear.

9

The sixth-form art exhibition planning meeting has already started when I clatter into the auditorium on Friday lunchtime. I've brought my body with me, all awkward and noisy. No more glitches like in the common room. I cling to excuses. A daydream, surely. Low blood sugar, maybe. There have been so many changes lately, I barely know what's real any more. But I am, regrettably, so I guess I'll have to live life as a fully visible person.

And that means considering entering the exhibition.

Considering. And most likely rejecting. The frames are expensive; the chances are slim.

But then again, every sixth-form art student will be entering. Do I want to be that one person who didn't?

It's a rite of passage, your work out in front of the world for the very first time, a proper group show. An opportunity to be part of the collective. Plus there's the prize fund. I'm skint as shit and could use the boost.

I'd realize that even if I didn't have Bert reminding me at every opportunity. Despite her enthusiasm, I don't bring her with me or tell her I'm here. After all, this is just for information. The thing is, I spent so long nearly talking myself out of it, it made me late. And then the lateness became a reason not to come …

But I do. Trying to sneak in subtly, I lose my grip on the heavy door. As it slams shut, Ms Amin breaks off, eyes on me. Everyone's eyes on me it feels like. And it takes everything in me not to turn and bolt.

I mouth, "Sorry."

A sharp nod and Ms Amin disappears behind a sheet of smooth dark hair as she resumes speaking. "As I was saying, each student will have a one-point-two-metre space to present their work…"

I shuffle round the back of the crowd seeking a hiding spot. These people are my classmates but not friends. Thanks to our forced proximity, through years of schooling, I know an unfortunate amount about these relative strangers. Facts, histories, anecdotes. It's claustrophobic to think they know the same. As I creep round the edge of the group, I try not to look at anyone in particular, but Elina turns and smiles. By the time I've realized it's directed at me, she's already looked away. Great work, Green.

Someone else shifts in the pack. Dark hair, tall, quirky eyebrows, staring right at me? Baker Davis, of course.

I stop moving, lean back against the auditorium window and fix my attention on the front.

Ms Amin continues. "The dimensions of the exhibition space are finite. I can't give you an extra inch, not an extra millimetre. If you want to negotiate additional space with another classmate who's not using theirs, fine. But" – she pauses for emphasis – "do not involve me until you've reached an agreement."

Baker edges up beside me.

"All work will be framed unless it's on canvas, in which case—"

"Hey," Baker whispers.

A series of images flash into my mind, a recap on an episode of my life I didn't catch the first time:

Baker in the darkroom looking at the photograph of Theo and Olivia.

Baker scribbling out a Post-it note.

Baker understanding what a chronic mess my life is.

I stay focused on Amin.

"All work must be submitted with the correct fixings. All work must be clearly labelled..."

"She's going to hand out a list at the end of this," Baker says. "Saying it all again. In case her saying things extra loudly and clearly doesn't permeate our thick teenage skulls."

"Half of us will probably mess up," I say in defence of Ms Amin. And my own brain, which never absorbs verbal instructions.

"Undoubtedly," Baker says. "I fully intend to mess up."

I fix my eyes on the front again. Ms Amin's saying, "This year we have an extra-special addition to the competition—"

Baker starts, "So I—"

"Shh," I hiss gently.

"As you're no doubt aware, the annual Grieg Art Prize is possible thanks to a donation in perpetuity by a local philanthropist, a gallerist and former pupil. And I would remind you all the grant is not available in cash, but for materials, equipment and further learning only, administered by the school, so there are limitations on how it's spent."

Someone to my left coughs, sounding suspiciously like "vodka".

"Quite," Ms Amin says drily. "Anyway, we've recently been approached by King's alumnus Fiona Grieg, owner of boutique gallery chain the Open Fold. This year, in acknowledgement of the tenth anniversary, the grant will be accompanied by an opportunity for the winner to see their exhibition pieces on public display at the gallery and to liaise with Ms Grieg over the hanging and display of the pieces."

"Holy shit," I whisper. A real gallery. How incredible. How terrifying.

"Shh," Baker says with a grin.

"I don't need to tell any of you what a great opportunity this is or how good it will look on your university applications. It's a very generous offer for one of you to benefit not only from exposure and experience, but also advice and mentorship." Ms Amin claps her hands together. "So! Put your name on this sheet or email. If you're not on the list by the end of the day, you're not in." Ms Amin's eyes lock on mine. "No exceptions."

The crowd begins to disperse and chatter.

Baker's hand arcs through the air. "Excuse me, I have a question."

Ms Amin, never a fan of questions, sighs. I shuffle sideways. I'd hate her to assume Baker and I are together. Amin's got this no-nonsense sternness to her that has always left me with the impression she's less than impressed with me. I am, after all, mostly nonsense.

Baker says, "What are the rules on eligibility?"

"Baker," says Amin, "I know you are thoroughly acquainted with the eligibility criteria. One named artist per body of work, the exhibition is open to every King's student with the award going to the most promising *art student* annually. My answer hasn't changed, so I hope that's clear now?"

I cringe soul-deep at the exasperation in Ms Amin's voice. Clearly these two have history and, while I don't understand the root of Baker's question, he's obviously being annoying.

"Crystal," he says. No shame.

As the crowd revives, I stride forward to grab the paperwork, my brain whirring over this latest development. Baker, apparently not one for hints, follows.

"I hope it was OK to message you?" he says. "I didn't want to intrude."

I peel off two copies of each stapled document and thrust my spares at Baker. Of course he immediately wants to delve into the embarrassing, sordid details of my life.

"Thanks, but I don't want to talk about it."

"About what?"

"The boyfriend-shaped hole in my life and how it occurred and how I…" *Cried in the darkroom like the world's greatest loser.* "I'm going to deal with it the old-fashioned way by silently burying my pain, burning photos, taking up day drinking, witchcraft…"

"Making tortured art?"

"Um, I guess." The words on the form I'm holding blur and refuse to go in despite the intensity of my concentration.

"Have you finished your exhibition project yet?"

"Technically I haven't started."

"So you'll need to put in some hours over the next few weeks?"

"Sure. Probably."

"Photography's quite a solo endeavour, but it's kind of nice going out to shoot with someone else, don't you think? Someone to bounce ideas around with. There's this bridge I go to quite often." He waits.

"Oh. Great," I say, and when Baker doesn't fill the pause add, "I tend to shoot alone."

Baker nods slowly and I feel like I've missed something. I awkwardly shuffle my exhibition instructions, and the paper catches the side of my finger. A thin line of bright red wells up and I drag my sleeve down over it.

"But you're going to sign up?" Baker says. "For the exhibition?"

"Um…" There's a crowd of students round the clipboard. A lot of people. A lot of competition. "Maybe. Maybe not. I mean, what's really the point?"

"True. But I also figure art might be the only point?" Baker says. "How else do we create meaning or make sense of our fleeting time in this vast, indifferent universe, right?"

And since I meant *what's the point since I won't win* and not *what's the point of existence*, the pivot throws me. I jam my paper cut in my mouth. The cluster of people putting their names down thins. Baker walks over.

As he signs his name my brain's busy weighing it all up. How much I want it. The effort it'll take. How I'll get my hopes up only to be dashed. The absolute inevitability of defeat. The witnesses.

I suck my finger and taste blood. People waiting for the sheet jostle me.

"I'll see you round, Iris Green," Baker says. Instead of offering me the pen, he hands it to someone behind him, which seems rude until I move closer to see Baker's added my name to the list, right under his.

"Presumptuous," I call after him.

He laughs and shrugs and then he's gone. I'm left behind with the last few students. They empty out with the bell and then it's just me, the sheet, the pen and my name right there in black block capitals.

No one would know if I scratched it out. Only Baker, but he'd quickly forget.

If I enter – if I tell everyone –they'll *know.* They'll know I tried and lost. I wanted to be good enough and wasn't. They'll watch me fail. It's embarrassing to see people miss out on their dreams. The Germans have a word for the feeling, far less well known than its celebrity cousin, *schadenfreude*. *Fremdschämen*: vicarious embarrassment.

I won't inflict that on people.

I pick up the pen and pull the clipboard towards me. Baker had no right to put my name down.

"Iris Green!" Ms Amin's voice cuts across the quiet before I've so much as touched the pen to the "I" of "Iris". I freeze.

She strides over from the storage cupboard, black bob bouncing, and snatches the clipboard from under my pen.

"I'm glad you're going for it." She unclips the list and folds it in half. "It's good to have a focus and put your work out there. Push yourself."

I make a noise somewhere between agony and agreement.

Ms Amin tilts her head to the side. "Here's a secret not many people know, Iris. You don't have to believe in yourself. Not all the time and never absolutely. I know you'll come up with something brilliant."

Something brilliant.

There's something about the words coming from her – stern, unsmiling Ms Amin – that hits differently. Something sparks inside me. And I wish Ms Amin would give me something more. She could tell me what to do, what this brilliance should look like.

"Everyone will see, though. It's the point, but..."

Ms Amin looks at me for a long moment. She opens her mouth and I think this is it – the inspirational, rousing monologue that will inspire my whole project. Instead, she says, "It's good to be seen."

She checks her watch and whirls round, taking the list with her. And now it's just me. No classmates, no list, no teacher, no choice. So no going back, I guess.

I'm in the exhibition.

10

Helen Levitt talked about street photography as following one's eyes. Out here with a camera in my hands it makes sense. The only place I trust myself. The only place I know how to move, where to go, who I am.

The high street is too bright on Saturday. The sun hits the damp cobbles and blows all the highlights. Underfoot is a confetti of last night's kebab meat, chips and vomit. My shoulder slips under a rainbow of mismatched fabric hanging proud of a clothing stall and a waft of incense breaks through the aroma of charred bacon from the butty van. My earbuds are in, the soft croon of Emily Jane White filling my ears, or "bland, depressive lonely-girl music," as Theo called it that time I made the mistake of pointing it out in the background of Coffee Bear, and I let his criticism slide with a nod of my head and an internal apology to Emily.

Theo had a point, though. If the music fits…

I huff the steam from the top of my flask. My gaze wanders the hill. I'm on the hunt: exhibition fodder, inspiration, whatever you want to call it.

Today there's a busker setting up. She's in a floral dress and pink tights, guitar at her feet, getting ready to compete with the fruit man who booms at shoppers to grab a bowl – any bowl – for a pound. I linger at his stall and raise my camera. In the viewfinder a woman with curly hair picks up a mango and inhales. *Click* and away before anyone notices.

I make my way carefully through half a film, picking and choosing, waiting for my decisive moment. It's capturing coincidence. The serendipity of pressing the shutter as something happens that will never reoccur in exactly the same place and time.

In my camera, my own world, I disappear, as though perceiving everything – detail, texture, sound and scent – with almost painful acuity sucks up all the attention on the street, freeing me from anyone else's notice.

I make up stories. Not about people's pasts, but about our future. The way I would strike up conversation with that person using her dog-print umbrella as a sunshade. I'll tell her Purkoy's origin story, she'll ask about the name, I make a joke. In my head I am different. Vibrant. In my imagination I never say a wrong word, at least until my memory barges in with all its receipts.

I silently press the shutter once more.

They're magic these moments. At least, right now they are. But what if when these prints are developed they lose it all? Hours in the dark invested in one image, but at the end it's only a photo of a stranger. Anyone could press the shutter.

I check my phone like a nervous tic.

> **Bert:** This weekend's already too long – anyone want to come save me? O, when are you back from your dad's?

I don't reply for now, awaiting Olivia's response to judge my own, feeling only a tiny bit bad for leaving Bert hanging. She won't miss me.

My phone lights up again; Theo's name this time.

> **Theo:** ignored me all week
>
> **Theo:** thought you wanted to stay friends
>
> **Theo:** are you k?

Friends? I thought it was just something you say.

There's no staying friends here. Once a cheater, always a cheater – it's practically our family motto, drummed into me as soon as I was old enough to understand the word "divorce".

If I had a spine, I'd block him, but the faint sickness from his messages isn't as dreadful as the alternative. He hurt me. I loathe him. I can't be forgotten. So I do things like message him back:

Me: of course i'm not ok

I do things like view our history, scrolling right back to the very first messages he ever sent me. Last year, the start of it all:

Theo: hey, hey, history genius

Me: hey?

Theo: hey

Theo: do you drink coffee?

There's a gap before the next message where Theo waited for a reply that never came because I was busy losing my mind. Screenshotting every moment for prosperity and sending the messages to Olivia and Bert while begging for them to PLEASE TELL ME WHAT I DO WITH THIS.

Their responses immediate, overlapping, frantic.

Olivia: shit! WHAT?!

Bert: AHHH! Finally! Confess your undying love.
THIS IS YOUR MOMENT

Olivia: ok. be normal. play a little hard to get

Bert: Wait. No. What O said

Bert: I defer to O on matters of the heart

Olivia: theo hastings is used to screaming girls throwing knickers at him. be cool

That aged well.

It's weird to see Bert enthusiastic about Theo. Difficult to remember how her opinion turned. And Olivia? I guess I took her advice:

Theo: what are you up to?

Me: inhaling

Me: exhaling

Me: normal stuff

I really did play it cool for a moment there.

"Cheer up, love, it might never happen."

I take a second to recover from the surprise, process the words, locate the speaker. A man poured inside a burger van, glistening forehead obscured by salty smoke from charred meat. He's grinning at me. "I bet you'd brighten up the whole street with your smile," he says encouragingly.

I fold my arms over the body I'm suddenly rooted to, no longer floating in my own daydream but here, fixed to the ground and forced to reckon with my own visibility – my body, my face, my expressions I have to control – wishing I could switch it off. I toss back a weak smile – be polite. The man who shouted nods his approval at my improved appearance. Or my compliance.

I wish I hadn't smiled.

He means well.

Quips I was too slow to throw stick in my gritted teeth.

A compliment, really.

I line him up in my viewfinder and *click*.

As I'm turning away, I spy Lucy Miller and her friends emerging from a side street, all laughing together and it's the final blow. I unwind my camera from my neck and stash it in my bag, turning my back on the familiar crowd.

Theo: i'm in town. let's get coffee?

Theo: please?

And that's all it takes.

*

The bell above the Coffee Bear door rattles and I make straight for the counter. Pastries, stodgy loaf cakes and muffins with swirls of icing in muted rainbows. My fingers tingle in the heat. I used to love this place. The earthy scent of coffee inextricably linked to warmth and sugar, friends and laughter. First it was me and Bert and Olivia, buying every seasonal sugar rush on the menu to instant regret, then me and Theo, curled up in one armchair listening to his songs with an earbud each.

Today the smell of baked goods turns my stomach. I order a latte and espresso and find a bistro two-seater at the back by the toilets, as secluded as it gets and far from the padded chairs big enough for two.

There's a clean napkin in the middle of the table. I snatch it up and twist the corner round my fingers. My gaze pings round the edges of my view. Door, counter, door, floor, door, table, door.

And then the door opens and Theo's here. It's too late to pretend I haven't seen him so I have to watch as he walks over, my face letting out every feeling.

The chair clatters on the floor as he pulls it out and sits.

"Hi," he says.

"Hey."

Our eyes meet and mine slip away first.

"Ris? Jesus, it's you and me here; you don't have to pretend we don't know each other."

"I'm not—"

"Don't have to make this even harder than it already is for me."

"I'm not trying to do that," I mumble and shred my

napkin. Theo's hand creeps over the table and I stuff mine into my lap.

"Can't you even look at me?"

I do. Those eyes fringed with long lashes, freckles dusted over the bridge of his nose and a long neck disappearing into his collar. No. Don't think about that or the spicy warm smell reaching across the table, threatening to reel me back to when Theo was all I could breathe.

And a phantom whiff of Gucci perfume, as though Olivia's still on his skin.

For a moment, I feel it. That pins-and-needles pull towards disintegration. I ball my hands. "Why did you want to meet?" I ask the table.

The barista approaches, all teeth as he balances the tray with my latte and Theo's espresso and I dredge up enough of a smile to make it not awkward.

"You're really pretty today," Theo says when the barista's gone again. "So cute in your baggy jumper. Swear no one but you could make that homeless look adorable."

"What do you want, Theo?"

"I think I've made it obvious enough."

Olivia? I think, as I shake my head.

"I've never known what you wanted from me."

"Then you haven't been paying attention." Theo moves our coffees aside and lays his hands on the table. "You've always made me insecure. Never let me in. And then you ditch me for no reason… I won't ask again, Ris. This is it for us. If you tell me to get lost and it's over, you'll never have to talk to me again. If that's what you want."

His pink palms look all clean and vulnerable laid out like that. His voice sounds so genuine. Maybe I imagined how easily Theo and Olivia slotted together. Perhaps I turned it into something it wasn't. Perhaps it was a one-off. Perhaps I *did* push him away.

So take him back? It would be easy to say what I saw and let him spin me a hundred plausible excuses and beg – imagine – beg me for forgiveness.

He'll be so sweet afterwards. All kisses and held hands. Wrapping me in blankets and taking me out to see the stars. He will press his lips to that spot behind my ear and whisper warmly against my neck. He will be exactly like that again.

It will be so close to perfect.

"Why are you doing this?" Under the table my thumbs circle each other. I focus on the wood grain.

"'Cause we were going to be together till uni, Ris. We had plans, didn't we?"

So many plans.

"Now or never," he says. "Your choice."

My hand stutters as I peel it free from its sleeve and stretch. I give him my fingertips, resting them against his upturned palm.

"God, that's nice," he says. His shoulders lower and a smile fights the pain still written on his face.

I did that.

Theo's fingers tickle against mine. The coffee smell, too strong and bitter, makes me nauseous.

Theo sighs and slips his hand further to hold my wrist and turn my hand over. "You've been making me crazy, Ris."

It echoes. As clear as if he'd said it again here and now.

Holy shit, O. You're making me crazy.

You're making me crazy.

Me and her. The two of us. But the joke is, it's me unravelling, right here, now, holding his hand. As though I didn't see it with my own eyes.

My hands start to tremble. No, not tremble, but tingle as that feeling comes back.

"No." I pull my hands free. The word reflects in Theo's eyes turning them chilly. "No, sorry." I really am. Sorry he ruined everything.

"I *know*," I say, and the tingle turns into a low hum in my chest, like an engine. "I know you and Olivia..."

His expression fixes in place for a moment. Theo pulls back his hands. "Me and Olivia what?"

"You kissed her."

"I what?"

"Don't lie. Please. Just tell me." I can't raise myself above a whisper as I glance at the table beside us to see if they've noticed the scene I'm making. A frazzled dad doing battle with a ham sandwich his toddler won't eat. They take no notice.

"Ris," Theo says very carefully, "where's this coming from? Of course I didn't do that. Who said—"

"I saw it."

"Saw it?" Theo shakes his head and I see how this will never stop. He won't confess. I try to remember a time when Theo has ever been in the wrong, but all my memories are of my apologies. "Have you been going through my messages? Because you've read into something and got it all wrong. You've always been jealous," he says. "But this is—"

"I'm not jealous," I say. Louder now. Blood pounding. I can picture him on that bench and see him now and somehow they're the same person for the first time since he walked in the door.

"You need to calm down." He starts to get up. I stand quicker. I throw the remains of the napkin back on the table.

I walk out first.

It feels good to get outside and take a gulp of fresh cool air. Better when I walk down the street. But when I have to stop at the pedestrian crossing, it's a pause in the momentum that carried me this far. In the pause I have time to think, time to worry. Time to wonder what's going to happen on Monday.

11

When you dread a thing, you can feel it in the air. The changing pressure before a thunderstorm. That's a thing, isn't it? Maybe the whole sixth sense is that: shifting pressure. Maybe it's clues you catch from the corner of your eye – dark clouds gathering. But maybe – just maybe – it's less the weather and more the fact I flipping told Theo I know.

It's probably that.

On Monday morning the air's heavy and my empty stomach's acid, as I walk through the school doors and Bert catches up to me with a "Good lord, if you're still alive who the hell did we cremate?"

I blink at Bert, too tired even for this in-joke then manage, "I do have one of those faces."

Her humour falls away as I turn from the spotlight of her gaze. "Seriously, did you not hear me calling?"

I shake my head. "No, sorry."

"Are you OK?"

"Fine. Yeah, I'm fine."

"You've been more-than-normal AWOL and you kind of bailed on me the other night. I thought we were going to do a..." Bert's chin rumples and her mouth turns down. "Have I pissed you off?"

I shake my head. *No, of course not. Bert can't possibly believe that.*

The concourse smells of Monday morning: weak bleach and artificial lemon. The pale smooth tile floor's blotted with the occasional blackened circle of old gum. My boots add to the scuffs as I reply to Bert in monosyllables.

"Fine." "Yeah." "Good." "Tired."

I can't find any other words. This feels like the last walk we will ever take together and Bert's bright concern is too much.

"Did you see Olivia over the weekend?" I blurt.

We hit the double doors at the bottom of the stairs and turn the corner round the half-dead flower beds into the quad.

"No, she got back late from seeing her dad and, honestly, it was probably for the best. I don't know about you, but I've been marking off the time we have left before exams and..."

I look at Bert. I remind myself to nod, to say "Uh-huh" when the cadence of her words indicates the end of a point. And I am so focused on the performance of listening, the monumental effort of it, nothing goes in. My eyes skid over Bert's ear to the faces of the crowd beyond, to the people moving past whose snippets of conversation intrude.

I settle on Baker Davis. He's propped against the red-brick wall of the library. One foot flat against the wall, knee bent, his head tipped back to concentrate on a girl in his group as she tells a story with her hands, her face, all attention on her.

I swallow and shift my gaze away as Baker's rises, so our eyes meet for a fraction of a second.

And then my focus falls instead on a pair of people sitting on the library steps. He's perched on the top. She's sitting practically on his shoes. They each hold a sheaf of A4 pages and he is mid-flow, one hand gesticulating. My mind picks up the details, slowly puts the pieces together.

Olivia and Theo running lines together for the play.

How wholesome is that?

How sickening. The sight of them is a sweep to the knees, my legs suddenly quaking.

But on closer inspection their faces are serious. Their eyes not dipping to the page. And I wonder…

"…guess I'll just have to suck it up, though," Bert's saying. "Mum obviously needs a project and I guess that's me…"

It's the way they're sitting there. So intense.

"Oh." I can feel Bert's eyes on me. "I don't think it's what it looks like, babe."

I refocus on her. "What does it look like?"

Bert's weirdly blank-faced and I'm struggling to know what to do. Usually I would shrink away, save it up for later. Today I walk over. Somehow I say to Theo, "Didn't you tell her?" My voice less an accusation than a plea. Why? Why hasn't he told her?

Theo puts his elbows to his knees, eyes all puppy. "Ris has this elaborate conspiracy theory," he says, half to me, half to her. "Don't know who's been spreading what, but it's not funny, O. Tell her."

"Oh?" Olivia eyes me worriedly. "It's only a play thing." As she holds up the script as evidence, her eyebrows pucker and her tongue darts out to wet her lips.

The play? An internal stutter. A flutter of uncertainty. Perhaps that was it – a rehearsal, a rehearsed kiss? But something scared lurks behind Olivia's eyes. She leans forward as though she might touch me. I recoil.

"Guess we're too good at acting," Theo says.

"No. No, wait," I say.

And they do. My move.

I swing my bag off my shoulder and tear through my books and papers, my pencil case, my make-up bag, loose pens. It's right at the bottom of my bag. A bit creased now from lying there in the depths like a bad memory ready to surface.

I rip the photograph from my bag and slam it against Olivia's chest, my limbs juddering with adrenaline.

"If it's all in my head, what's this?"

Olivia's fingers close round the print. She turns it over and her pupils flick back and forth over the dusty, crumpled surface. The unmistakable evidence of the very, very bad thing she did. Her and him, the bench, the kiss, all there in black and white.

I feel sped up, aware of everyone around me at normal speed, because only now is everyone else catching up. The attention is beginning to turn on this scene: to me. And I don't care. I don't. I'm trying not to care, because I'm right and they're wrong and they should be ashamed, not me.

So why's it still me?

"Iris," Bert says gently and puts a hand on my arm. I shrug her off.

Olivia touches the faces on the print. She looks at Theo. At me.

"You took a photo of us?"

"I didn't know she had that," Theo says.

"Oh my god," Bert says, but I can't look at her.

My face twists and pressure builds up at the top of my nose and in my eyes, like a dam about to break. *Don't cry, Iris.* Not here where everyone can see. Instead, I lift my camera and point it at them. Theo and Olivia in my viewfinder again. *Click.*

"What are you doing?" Olivia says, rising to her feet and holding out the photo. "This just isn't what it looks like, Iris. Can we go somewhere? Talk?"

I lift the camera again.

"Don't." Olivia steps forward and I step back into Bert. Stop.

Olivia reaches out, her hand zooming up to the lens. "No."

Her hand connects, closes round the lens and wrenches sideways. My fingers bend the wrong way and release. The strap pulls taut against my neck and Olivia holds my camera, triumphant.

"Look," she says. Her face is full of something else now. The pressure in me builds. "You just need to stop. You need to let me explain, OK?"

"Can everyone stop telling me what I need?" Everything is loud. Everything is too much.

Olivia is still holding my camera. I pull away. She holds firm.

I'm trapped. Snagged. All eyes on me and Olivia who is far, far too close. She feels like a threat.

"Iris, stop! Listen—" She reaches for my arm.

My hand shoots out. So quick I don't see it move, as though it turned invisible just long enough to crack against her cheek.

Olivia holds a hand to her face. Bert's eyes widen. My camera swings back against my chest.

I finally slow down.

In the Netflix version of my life, Olivia smacks me back. We pull each other's hair and sling insults until the fight goes out of us and we cry and hug and make up.

Real-world Olivia takes a step back. She lets her hand slip and her cheek isn't even red. It was barely a slap. But still, Olivia's eyes water.

"Iris, oh my god," she says.

"I..." My words crowd in. Too many to get out.

"It was *one* kiss," she says.

I don't know if she's lying, but I don't know why it would matter. One time, three times, ten times – the same betrayal.

Theo clears his throat. "Ris, I know this doesn't mean anything now, but I never meant to hurt you. I never thought you'd find out, you know?"

"Aren't you a hero." Bert snaps.

The bell goes.

People move round us. They cut a wide berth.

Baker Davis walks past and I can feel him trying to meet my eye.

"I'm going to give you some space," Theo says. "Let you work this through."

The rest of us ignore him. When Theo walks away, I realize the quad has almost cleared around us. Even the sky's blank and clean. All the noise is inside now, behind closed doors.

There are rules to school: when the bell goes, you move. Yet I'm still standing here.

"We need to go," I say, taking a step, expecting Bert to follow. But Bert's not following.

"Maybe you two *should* talk," Bert says with a head tilt

and a shifty glance at Olivia. "Take form room. I'll tell Mr Osbourne you're having matching period emergencies or … something."

"OK," Olivia says. "Thanks."

My gaze fixes on the place where Olivia's shoe meets the tarmac as Bert walks away.

Olivia's feet shuffle to the edge of my view.

"Iris," she starts again. "I don't know what to say. It was a mistake."

I fold my arms and they don't fit together. Every movement awkward and manual.

"Iris, can you just say something?"

Her voice is wrung out with pain I don't want to hear, because I can't help but feel it too.

"It doesn't matter. It's OK," I hear myself say. And those aren't the right words. They aren't true. It does matter. It's not OK. My hands begin to quiver deep down in the tissue, all pins and needles. The sensation blocks my ears. All Olivia's weak excuses are far away and I'm underwater. I'm cold.

This is what it feels like to disappear.

It's happening again.

I turn and run. I can feel myself turning to nothing. Dissolving. Fireworks and fragments. I bounce off a wall, grateful the only people out here are the stragglers. Two girls are hurrying across the quad. My vision blurs and sharpens and the ground comes up fast. I fall towards a pair of black shoes, hands outstretched. Eyes open, I watch it happen. No sound, no warning. Air where there was skin. My whole body: gone.

Dazed, I heave myself sideways. The sounds of panic come into focus.

"Oh my god, oh my god. Did you see that? Tell me you saw that?"

I look up at two girls who are looking down at me. At least, me in the abstract.

"Did that girl… Where did that girl go?"

And when I turn, Olivia's staring too, mouth agape. I wonder, when you see something like that, do you believe your eyes or do you believe what you've known your whole life? Do you believe a whole girl went *POOF* into thin air or do you begin to explain it away before you've even finished processing the sight?

I flee the scene to a soundtrack of their confusion. The girls shaking their heads and what-the-hell-ing themselves out of belief. Girls don't disappear, not like this. We disappear in other ways.

Trust me to take things too literally.

12

People give up on you. It's what they do. If they're brave, they'll tell you to your face. If they're scared, they simply fade away and hope you work it out. That's what my dad did to Mum – and me. That's what Theo did, what Olivia did. It's probably what Bert's doing right this moment as she makes the not-so-difficult choice between me and Olivia. I know who she'll choose. I don't blame her.

It's easy to love someone until they're inconvenient. And I am so very inconvenient right now.

Bert: You didn't come to form?

Bert: Where did you go?

Bert: ???

Olivia: are you ok?

Olivia: it was so weird in the quad. you were there and then

Olivia: did you hurt yourself?

Olivia: i'm sorry

Olivia: let's talk later

Olivia: please

Weird in the quad. Weird like I disappeared right before her eyes? Blinked and she missed me?

But it's the last that gets me. "Talk later" like we have plans to make or gossip to dish or notes to exchange. So casual.

Because Iris Green never makes a fuss. Does she?

I stay invisible, sitting in the darkroom. I perch and hunch over my books, but the words won't go in.

My thoughts are full of Theo. Olivia. Bert. My body that won't stay put.

I slam my book shut and check the time on my phone. My body hasn't come back. Two lessons I've missed now.

I take out the negatives from my market haul. My fingers stumble as I load the strips into the enlarger. My hand–eye coordination has never been ten out of ten, but it turns out not being able to see your skin makes everything harder.

I select a few shots, including the final exposure, Theo and Olivia Take Two.

Maybe I won't come back. It wouldn't be so bad to be here without even myself for company, just the chemicals and trays and the negatives and prints. No one pestering me about cheating boyfriends or exams and exhibitions and university.

If this was how it could be from now until next year, that'd be perfect. I wouldn't have to show up or smile or try to learn in a fishbowl with everyone's eyes on me, waiting to see if I live up to their expectations. I could reappear next year and everything would be done: uni chosen, my application accepted or rejected, exams already passed or failed. And I'd leave: a new start in a new place with new people. I could skip this part where I'm frozen, caught between terror at the unknown and a yearning to start again. Because in a place where no one's watching perhaps I could be someone I actually like.

I mix my chemicals. Multigrade developer, stop bath, fixer, all diluted with water as close to twenty degrees as I can get it. I add them to the three different coloured trays.

Negatives set up, focus found and aperture set. I turn off the lights, turn on the safe light and put the photo paper in place for my test print, revealing each few centimetres of the paper at five-second intervals until the full image is exposed.

I agitate the trays, watching the details emerge. Bricks and windows, tarmac and feet, steps, some bodies, faces. I hold my breath.

When it's fixed, I hold it in my hands and swill it in clean water, frowning, but not for the obvious reason of Theo and Olivia. There's a stripe. A pale stripe bisecting the image with fuzzy edges, all out of line with my exposure gauge. When I check the film, my worst fears are confirmed. It's a light leak. Damage to my camera, somewhere, somehow, that's broken the seal and let in light to ruin my shots.

It pops up in my mind like a snapshot. Olivia wrenching my camera from my hands.

She did this. Another thing she's stolen.

The tears spring up again and this time they fall. Big fat tears that get in my mouth and taste salty. Tears that drop on the rough time-worn wood of the workbench and soak in beside the stains. They fall for everything: the discovery, the lie, the fight, the weeks I have been holding everything inside and now this.

How am I supposed to do anything without my camera?

I take a photo of the print with my phone, no longer caring what or who it shows and I send it to the only person who'll understand. Or at least someone who can tell me:

Me: is this beyond repair?

I cradle the phone. No answer from Baker. I put it down on the side and let my face sink into my hands and push my palms against my head and stay like this for a while, feet jittering on the crossbar of my stool, fingers tapping against my skull as something in my head scratches to get out. And it's quiet but still everything needs to shut up. Shut up. Shutupshutupshutup.

I bang the side with a fist I can't see.

The bang of my fist is echoed by the thump of the door. A knock. Another, followed by a shout from outside. A familiar voice shouting, "Yeah, I'll see you there!" Then, more quietly, "Iris?"

I ease from my stool and move to press my back against the door, my feet braced, my whole weight behind it. On the floor there's nothing. Against the door there's nothing. All this pressure I'm exerting against the wood feels unreal when I look down and every scrap of me is gone.

He knocks again and the judder goes through my bones. I hit the light switch and plunge the room into darkness. "Iris?" Baker rattles the door and it shakes my arms in their sockets.

"Sorry. Give me a minute."

The rattling stops.

Think Iris, think.

"You OK in there?" Baker says.

"No."

The door quivers lightly, as though he's put a hand on the other side.

"You think your camera's broken?"

"Yeah."

"Can I come in?"

"No." In my anxious throat there's only space for one word.

"I can't do much out here."

"Um." I wonder if he'll just leave. Eventually he has to. Eventually one of us will crack and I'm the one with the secret to keep.

Or option B.

"You can come in, but only if … if you close your eyes."

"What? Why?"

"It's … complicated."

I imagine the look on his face. Bewilderment changing to laughter. He'll walk away now, relieved to know he dodged the weird girl. He'll see how close he came to forming an alliance or friendship – whatever this was – with the sort of girl who shuts herself in darkrooms and won't come out and won't be seen.

Maybe he'll tell someone else in his class this story. They'll tell him one back. Oh, that girl? I heard about her…

"OK, they're closed," he says.

Still I don't move. *Is he telling the truth?*

My muscles relax as I take my weight off the door. I hesitate, hands on the handle, then open it a crack.

"Promise?" I whisper.

"Promise."

Sure enough, Baker has his eyes closed. His hand comes up, blindfolding him for good measure. I yank him inside and slam the door behind. A knife of light and then gone. Pitch black.

"Can I open them?" he says.

And, god, this is ridiculous. I'm ridiculous.

"Why are you even here?" I say.

"Because your camera – you said it was broken—"

"Yeah, but…" I hear it. "Thanks, I'm a bit—"

"Angry and panicky?"

"My default setting." In the dark I can feel Baker's body heat. Disconcertingly close. He smells of his whole day mingled together. Sweat and sweets and cut grass. Not bad.

"Are you OK?" Baker says. "I saw you this morning, with your guy, Theo. And your friend."

I nod invisibly.

"I didn't tell anyone."

"I know."

"I figured you wouldn't want me to."

"Correct." The dark holds me like a blanket. The silence invites me in. It's easier not to see Baker's face. Easier to hear his breathing and know he's waiting for me. He could be anyone. "I needed time to wrap my head around it. I think the worst is over now. No more crying in darkrooms," I tell him. "You can open your eyes."

A pause and then, "Can I ask why we're standing in the dark? Again?"

"It won't happen again. It's just … thank you … for keeping the secret, I mean. Everyone knows now anyway. You saw."

"Is that a good thing or a bad thing?"

"It's … something." I shrug.

"Is something else going on, Iris Green? Aside from your rather dramatic personal life, I mean?"

I hesitate. A wild thought: *What if I told him?* Out of everyone he might not flip out. Baker knows better than anyone that everything we see is just a trick of the light. Better yet, I could show him.

I move to the door and lean against it, reaching my fingers up the wall, searching for the light switch.

"Want to see something kind of … different?" I say, my throat dry, my heart pulsing in the tips of my fingers as I imagine how this will go. Imagine how freaked out he'll be looking around this tiny empty room to figure out where I've gone. If I stay very still, if he doesn't touch me, how would he know?

So let the fates decide. Let Baker work out what's the easiest explanation: that I've vanished from the room or that I'm still in it.

"Uh, sure," Baker says.

"Ready?" My fingers fumble along the wall. "One … two…" I throw the switch. Bright white light. I freeze, too scared to breathe.

"What am I supposed to be looking at? What's different?" Baker says in a mild tone, eyebrow raised, meeting my stare.

"Me," I say, looking at my body. All of it. Here and back without warning. My fingers on the switch, my shoes and my tights with my feet and legs inside.

Huh.

When did this happen? Why does this happen? And why am I vaguely disappointed?

"Hey, are you OK?" He tilts his head and speaks gently. "Is there something different about you? Did you do something to your hair? It's exceptionally shiny."

"No." I touch it. "Same old follicles."

Baker's eyes stay with me as I turn to the workbench and fiddle with equipment. He says, "Last time I ask, I promise, but why don't you come to the bridge with me? Take some photos? It'll be fun. A once-in-a-lifetime creative collaborative opportunity."

And the funny thing is, I know exactly which bridge he means. The one from his photographs. A distinctive footbridge on the outskirts of town that leads over the dual carriageway. It's weird. Strange how he and I already have shorthand.

I don't remember him asking before, though.

"I don't even have a camera," I say. "What would be the point?"

"Oh yeah, the casualty. Let's see?" Baker holds out his hands and I nudge my camera towards him.

His fingers wrap round it, broad and stubby with nails so short there's no white to them. They turn gentle as he examines my camera.

"No, you're good to go," he says after a while. "There's nothing wrong with this."

"What? No. Look." I pass him the print. The Theo and Olivia one with the white streak.

"Did your camera experience some kind of shock?"

"We both did."

"Did you hit the back release or wrench it somehow? But the camera itself looks solid."

"Oh." Now it's my turn to hold my camera in my hands and check every inch for flaws. Something I should have done before panic-messaging Baker. And I recall my tumble to the ground, my camera hanging from my neck as I fell. "Shit, I think this was my fault. I … dropped it."

"Well, it survived," he says. "So you do have a camera."

"It seems that way."

"So what do you say to a photo walk? The bridge? Today? Tomorrow? I'm at your disposal." Baker claps a hand to his heart.

I fight a smile. My thoughts flicker back to when I last disappeared on school property. I ended up here then, trapped in the dark with Baker. Baker who knew my name. Baker who came running when he thought I was in crisis.

Both these times my body came back and twice isn't enough to establish a reliable pattern, but still.

Still.

Every time he's here I seem to return.

Does Baker…

Can Baker…

Bring me back?

A small smile wrangles its way over my lips and I open my mouth, about to say *OK, why not?* What's the worst that could happen? But another memory: Bert's gossip about Baker, Baker this morning in the quad, the girl in Baker's photos, and how I don't think I've ever seen him anywhere except surrounded by girls who are prettier than me, more confident and sure of themselves. Who hold attention. Girls like Olivia.

And Baker is so very Theo. Pretty, yes, but charismatic too. That's the danger.

I stack up everything I know about Baker and can't get a grip on the kind of person he is or what he wants from me. Going with him means trusting him. It means letting in someone new. I missed the signs with Theo. I missed the signs with Olivia. But I won't do it again.

"No thanks," I say. "I work better alone."

Baker's mouth goes lopsided. "OK." He holds up his hands. "Sorry if I've been bothering you."

"You're…" I turn round. "It's fine. Thanks for coming to check on me."

The sound of the door opening. Closing. And then he's gone. And I'm alone again.

Just how I like it.

13

Barely five seconds into my alone time, there's another knock on the door.

"I thought you might need me, but I guess you've had far more interesting company?" Bert hangs in the doorway. "What's the story with the boy?"

"We're … acquaintances. He's … I don't know. There's no story." I shrug. I stretch up then fall back into my slouch. I'm grateful Bert didn't arrive five minutes earlier. The idea of her and Baker in the same room makes my heart palpitate. Like him meeting her could reveal something about me – a different version of Iris he wouldn't like.

Not that he likes the version he has met.

"How did you know where I'd be?" I say.

"Literally where else?" Bert steps into the room and turns to shut the door quietly behind her. She puts a hand on my shoulder and I let it stay there. "How are you doing, Peach-pip? I came to say, well, sorry. Earlier was a shock and I guess I sucked at handling it."

"It's fine," I say, because I don't know how to tell her it's not.

"What a bastard. Why didn't you tell us?" Bert gives my shoulder a rub.

I shrug. "One of you already knew."

"Yeah." Bert's hand pauses on my shoulder. "I know. I… She messed up. Badly."

"She's meant to be my friend."

"I know." Bert pauses. I wait. And I wonder how this plays out now. How the three of us can ever go forward. How angry Bert will be at Olivia and if I've ruined things, not just between me and Olivia, but the two of them too. It all feels like my fault.

Bert sighs. "All this girl-on-girl emotional violence makes me sad. It's not how it should be." She turns away to the enlarger, fiddling with the focus dial. "Sometimes there's this expectation that girls must be cheerleaders for each other at all costs, you know? Or else we're falling into some toxic girl-fight cliché. But we're all just people who make mistakes. I know it doesn't make it OK—"

An involuntary noise of disbelief escapes me.

"We're all capable of bad things and I know she's so sorry."

I look at Bert and let her words sink in. *Cheerleaders at*

all costs. And I feel like I've been kicked in the ribs. "Did she send you?"

Bert tilts her head, eyebrows furrowed, like *come on.* I sling my camera round my neck and think about standing, but my legs don't move. Something feels off. Although I didn't expect Bert to come here, I expected this response even less. This … diplomacy has me off balance.

"You'd never do something like this." I pick a white cat hair off my trousers. "It goes against your feminist ideals. Ethics. Something."

"Hmm, feminist scheminist. Theo's the bad guy, whatever your ideology, and, frankly, a whomping great twat who I'd gladly throw off a cliff."

"Not very ethical." The smile unfurling across my face takes me by surprise. I sweep my revision notes from the bench into my bag.

"Do you think you could come back to life? I've told Olivia it's going to be just me and you this lunchtime and she's with the drama crew."

I nod. Bert and I is fine. Doable. But before I can get my thoughts in order, Bert's ushering me from the darkroom and across the quad. We swing in through the double doors and round the corner to the common room.

"Canteen?" Bert says. "Or are you packing?" She assumes her best faux swagger and pats the right zip pocket of her backpack. Her dad still provides fancy packed lunches with multiple courses: his magnum opus was a never-repeated day of hand-rolled homemade sushi. Meanwhile I have a withered satsuma and a crumpled fiver.

Bert's giving me a rundown of her lunch, but I don't hear, because I'm distracted by the sight of Theo heading through the same doors we've just come through.

"I'll come with you, though, yeah?" Bert is saying and nodding until she also catches sight of Theo.

"You doing all right?" he says, all concerned, stopping en route to join the rest of his crew in their usual corner. "That was intense this morning. I never wanted that."

"She's fine, no thanks to you," Bert says. "Come on." She gives my sleeve a quick tug.

I don't move, though. My gaze is locked on Theo. He glances at Bert, then touches my arm. "We need to talk properly," he says. "Some other time, yeah? Soon?"

As Theo joins his mates, Spade, the one with a flat face that looks like he's been smacked in the face with a … *yeah, him*, he gestures towards me. Theo tells him something.

The break-up was one thing but being cheated on? And now everyone knows. Everyone saw the drama. There's a burst of laughter.

"Don't give them a second of your attention," Bert says. But it's too late, they have it – all my attention – except it's not on them, it's pressed back on myself. The weight of being perceived, of being unable to escape.

I wish I didn't have to do this. I wish I could wish

myself away and be a jumble of floating thoughts, dust in a sunbeam. I wish—

This. This is it. Moments like this where I'm on the edge of reality, about to slip. But I can't do that. Not here and now.

"Come on, we'll go somewhere else," Bert says as I slump my shoulders down further and force myself forward. "You don't have to put up with this."

And no, I think. No, I don't.

*

At home later, in the quiet, Mum downstairs doing uni work, I go to my bedroom mirror and the feeling returns. A wish to be gone. A wish to no longer be subjected to my classmates' stares, turning me clunky and awkward in my own skin. Even my own reflected gaze is uncomfortable.

Go, Iris. Go away.

I imagine myself invisible, fading round the edges, blurring.

But my body and all its parts remain stubbornly visible.

I close my eyes and imagine the tingle, the fading skin.

What happened each time? Theo and Olivia. And in the common room too – those moments I wanted to escape. I go back to that first memory: the park bench. Focus. But nothing happens. Maybe the moment is losing its sting.

I go back further. Another memory.

Last summer. I didn't get my predicted grade in my French GCSE – a couple of points below. It stung, it was disappointing, but it was a pass and it was over. When Mum made me call Dad with the news, I saved the worst for last and made my little joke, "I guess you can't cram a whole language."

A pause and then:

"I wish you'd take life a bit more seriously," Dad had said. "That's going on your record for ever."

Such a small moment. A throwaway comment, but even now I feel shaken. I'd passed. I'd tried. It was too late to backtrack and tell him that was my best. French never made sense to me. I could never understand the rules.

But the disappointment in his voice. The hot shame in my chest. And, later, the resentment. As if Dad had any claim on my success or failure. As if I should have inherited his work ethic and ambition through blood regardless of his paltry input to my life and learning.

I'd missed my moment to tell him, of course, but I'd have never said it anyway.

My nostrils flare with effort, with the force of imagining. I hold out my hand and focus.

I wish you'd take life a bit more seriously.

My hand glitches.

Flickers.

Does it?

Blink and it's back. A momentary lapse.

I didn't hallucinate this. I disappeared. For real. I have the photo to prove it. I have multiple alarming instances of losing myself. But what does a photo of nothing actually prove – that I'm secretly the world's most mundane superhero?

My hand creeps up to my hair and winds itself up in the limp mousey strands of it, twirling it round my fingers as I let my mind drift.

The exhibition is something I should start taking a little more seriously. Not that Dad would exactly approve. Or he might – after all, his assertion that cash and connections are the key to a successful art career is also his main objection since I don't have the latter and he won't provide the former.

I consider Baker's invitation. The bridge.

I shouldn't go. I'll embarrass myself. It'll be awful.

But then again, it's only a walk. Some photos. A chat. Company. There's nothing else he could possibly want from me.

Photography's a lonely game and advice would be helpful. Someone with a good eye. Someone who takes art seriously. Someone who could tell me if I'm kidding myself.

I gnaw on my lip. I pull out my phone and look at Baker's latest contact.

I imagine messaging him. It'd probably be supremely unwelcome. A total intrusion into the privacy of his evening. Poor Baker. A couple of small acts of kindness and now he's stuck with some needy lower sixth who won't stop hounding him about her broken camera, her broken life…

Me: when are you next heading out to the bridge?

Baker: Whenever. Tomorrow? You in?

I start typing. I pause.

Baker: You're in

Me: friday?

In my bedroom mirror I catch sight of her: a girl wearing a smile far bigger than the situation demands. It's a bad idea. Baker looks like a boy who would devastate me. Theo looked the same. Funny and quirky, musical and dramatic. An artist.

Still … those shoulders.

I put Baker away, clear my mind and focus on the task at hand.

I need to get a grip.

Take life more seriously.

14

I wake up on Friday jittery and full of regret for agreeing to meet Baker. Iris Green's legendary inability to plan logistics strikes again, because what fool plans to go take photographs with someone new after school on the same day they have their very first counselling session?

It's too much for one day. I should cancel Baker.

I think about cancelling before school when I can't eat breakfast.

And at school when I bump into Bert and she doesn't mention that I've been avoiding her and nor do I, so I feel temporarily normal for the first time in weeks.

Yet somehow by lunchtime I still haven't managed it, and now I have more important things to worry about. Spilling your secrets to a stranger in a room one-on-one with nowhere else to look and no distractions and no one to fill the awkward silences? Hell. Literal hell. But here I am, knocking at the papered-over window of a soundproof music rehearsal room with a "do not disturb" sign tacked to it.

The woman who answers my tentative knock has short dark hair and a wide smile.

"I'm Nicole," she says. "You must be Iris."

"Yeah," I say, wrong-footed because the one thing I'd prepared to say was my own name.

Nicole gestures me into the room, before closing the door.

There are two navy tweed armchairs, a small table with tactfully positioned tissues, a fake plant and a glass of water. There's no window. While I'm not averse to unloading my emotional luggage in windowless rooms, the stacked instrument cases at the back of the room conjure painful memories of performance phobia and musical ineptitude.

I take a seat, pulling my arms in so they don't touch the scratchy fabric of the armrests.

"How are you doing, Iris?"

"I'm fine." Pause to appreciate the irony. "How are you?"

"Good. I thought we'd start with any questions you have about the process and also by letting you know how I work, particularly in terms of confidentiality, which I'm sure is on your mind."

I sit very still in my chair, hands pressed together, remembering to nod and smile. Remembering to look Nicole in the eye but not stare.

"Everything you share here is confidential between the two of us, unless you tell me something I need to share for the safety of yourself or others. In that case I'll inform you I'm planning to share that information further and we can discuss the next steps together. OK?"

"Yep." My voice is falsely bright as I try my best to look like no trouble at all. "How many visits…?"

"Typically six sessions unless we agree there's a reason to extend."

"Like I'm especially faulty?"

Nicole smiles and doesn't correct me. She provides some paperwork I can't read while she's watching, so I sign it and hope I haven't agreed for her to harvest my organs. She asks if I'm OK, not too hot or cold, and then we sit back in our chairs and I know it's time, but I don't have a script for this. No one else's cues to follow. Just me and her.

"Why don't we start by reviewing why you're here?" Nicole says.

"Mrs Coombes suggested it."

"Why do you think that was?"

"The woman's a mystery." To occupy my hands, I pick up and cradle the glass. Take a sip. Plain water tastes so dry. I look away to the wall where there's a long grey scuff on the white paint. "It was about two months ago."

Nicole makes a sympathetic sort of movement with her mouth. "I'm afraid the waiting list can fluctuate."

"I guess she knows I've struggled? With, um … anxiety?" I make it a question in case Nicole's heard differently.

"Anxiety about what?"

"I missed school. A couple of days of school. That's why I'm here."

My mind buffers and flashes up memories like unwanted ads in the middle of a YouTube vid. Last term. The time I can't put it into words. The day I got home and couldn't move or think. When it felt like I was wading in deepening water with pockets full of rocks and feeling everything. Sinking with a brain turning on me, full of noise and chaos, and pressure pressing down, down, down at the same time as everything inside me became huge. I couldn't speak. I couldn't stop.

One bad day and an exhaustion hangover that poisoned the next. A sore throat, a banging head, heavy bones and a sluggish brain. The flu, I told Mum. But the following Monday Mrs Coombes held me back after history. I told her I was "fine" while my tears slipped out and the truth did too. Everything I'd kept inside for years suddenly visible.

And there was Theo. Waiting for me afterwards, walking me round school, messaging me every minute and sneaking soft kisses on to my hair as I pressed my forehead into his shoulder and squeezed my eyes shut to stop crying. "I've never felt this way about anyone," he'd said. "You can't be sad or I'll be sad." And there was the weight of that too. The responsibility of finding his heart so suddenly in my hands, having to hold it. Trying, so hard, to be the girlfriend he deserved.

But that was then; this is now. And I am, actually, fine. It's all back inside. Theo's gone.

"I think it was a panic attack," I offer, because I want Nicole to know I've done my research. Gotta get that A* in therapy. "I got overwhelmed."

"How are you feeling now?" Nicole says.

"Still overwhelmed." Nicole doesn't crack. "Not as much. About different things," I add. My fingers dance up and down against the surface of the glass. "I don't know. Sometimes I feel like I'm drowning." I glance at Nicole. "Not drowning," I correct, having heard myself. "That's melodramatic, isn't it? Just … tired from working so hard and … failing and it feels like everyone sees and knows."

Nicole tilts her head to the side. "What do you feel you're failing at? Exams?"

"No. I'm expected to do well. But then there's nowhere to go from there but down. No way to exceed expectations and a hundred ways to disappoint. But no, it's not that." I shake my head.

I am failing now. Failing to speak. Failing to share. Failing to adequately explain.

I'm worried Nicole will give me unhelpful solutions, the way well-meaning people have in the past: change your self-talk, try affirmations, make the cross-stitch kit Bert got me so I can hang "I am capable of epic shit" on my wall in neon embroidery. Solutions that increased my anxiety as I failed at them too. This session is like the helpline posters tacked to the common-room wall: too little, too late, too generic to fix whatever's gone wrong with me.

I could say all that. I could explain the thing I'm working so hard and failing at is life. The unspoken test where everyone else but me understands the questions. How even though I like to be alone, I feel lonely. And how everything is starting to spill out in strange ways, like leaving my body behind.

But once you put something like that out in the world, you can't take it back. I'm not ready. I'm not sure I'll ever be.

"I'm not sure there's much to talk about any more," I say.

15

On the way to meet Baker I see:

One old chair abandoned by a rubbish bin. *Click.*

A woman nose-kissing her nonplussed Westie. *Click.*

A woman feeding the ducks behind the bench where I discovered Olivia and Theo. She looks like a bird herself. Thin wrists and a beaky nose. A brightly patterned scarf round her neck like plumage. *Click.*

I arrive five minutes early, which is bang on in Iris-time thanks to my chronic fear of being late and therefore rude. My thighs are feeling the burn by the time I reach the top of the steps at the footbridge over the dual carriageway, which is, by any measure, a weird place to meet someone. Below my feet rush-hour traffic crawls. If I focus through the fifteen-centimetre gap between the railings and the slabs, it's as though I'm floating above them. It's disorientating. Dizzying.

At the middle of the bridge, Baker's beside a tripod talking to someone. I recognize her, not from Baker's photos, but from school. Her long red hair whips in the wind and swallows up whatever they are saying to each other. I scuff my feet. Slow. I suddenly don't know why I'm here. To hang out? With Baker Davis? Improbable. And he brought a plus-one, which is even odder. But it's too late to run – they've seen me now.

I hold up my hand in an awkward non-wave.

The stranger throws her arms round Baker. My boot toe catches the pavement. By the time I've recovered the girl has said goodbye and is tapping away, making the footbridge shudder.

"Sorry," I say to Baker. "Didn't mean to interrupt."

"Why are you apologizing? I asked you, didn't I?"

He did. "Sorry."

Baker fiddles with his tripod and angles his camera. It's a DSLR and I'm disappointed. This means Baker will be processing today's snaps on a computer screen instead of a chemical bath.

"Another of your long exposures?" I say.

"Nah, I'm finished with those. This is filming." He moves as if to pat the camera but pulls his hand away before it connects.

I glance down at the scene below. Cars travel past in a normal way on a normal, ugly tarmac stretch.

"You're filming traffic?" I say to make sure.

"All will become clear. Please don't question a master at work." My eyebrows shoot up and Baker laughs. "Well, it might. You know, we all need something to strive for in these end times."

"You're big on doom, aren't you?" Baker's mouth twists down in defeatist agreement. "And films apparently?"

"Mainly film." He ruffles his hair. "The stills were a favour for Tash, the pinholes were for fun. So you won't have to worry about me clogging up the darkroom in the future."

"Oh?" My lungs squeeze. "Good."

"But at least you now know about this little-known beauty spot. And you can finally take that portrait of me you've been hankering after."

If I blush right now, I swear I'll need a new identity. "A little presumptuous."

"You know, I get it. You're intimidated by my rakish good looks, cut physique and flawless photography, but you don't need to be. Consider me your dummy run."

It's guttingly true. Deep eyes, poetic cheekbones, thick, unruly hair. Shoulders. He thinks I'm intimidated because I'm so gross, I suppose, and he's masking it with humour. Of course that's how things are and of course he's only asked me here to do me a favour.

Oh god, I'm Baker Davis's charity case.

Baker's smile dims a couple of lumens as he watches my interior tussle. "Shall we?"

I lift my camera. "The photos won't be any good. I hope you know."

"God forbid."

"You'll probably hate them."

"Definitely. On principle." His face goes mock serious. "So you'll try?"

"She who dares..."

"Yes, Angry Darkroom Girl! Dare yourself." His mouth quirks in that way it does and I have to suppress a smile of my own. "Angry Darkroom Girl" is not a nickname I'm keen to cultivate.

It takes a while to warm up to the idea of this portrait even after I've committed. Baker stands by his camera, uninspiring and unhelpful as I try to capture him, until he eventually prompts me to prompt him, which, *Duh, Iris, of course.*

At first, it's difficult to know what I want. I ask him to lean against the bridge railings first on one side, then the other, seeing how the light looks from different angles. Baker adjusts his camera and I snap him again as he concentrates on the road below. The light turns golden, low, and Baker squints and shades his eyes at they catch the evening sun. He says, "Do I look like I'm contemplating the futility of existence?"

Click. The moment's mine.

I take three more: crouched holding the railings, backlit against the setting sun and smiling straight at the camera.

The last one is intense somehow and I reappear from behind my tiny glass window feeling prickly. I push up my glasses.

"So you're Retro Girl?" Baker says, nodding at my camera. "Do you light your house with candles, cycle around on your penny-farthing, watch movies on VHS, that sort of thing?"

"Boil my clothes, dig for victory, sacrifice my neighbours to the old gods?" I resist an eye-roll. Common misconception. "You can't delete anything with film. You have to be careful, think critically about each shot. You have to get it right first time or live with the mistakes."

"Very high stakes. Very all or nothing."

"Trash or treasure," I agree. "But I like the process too. Knowing how the pieces go together and doing it with my own hands."

Baker nods solemnly. "Right. You're practical – good to have on my side after the apocalypse."

"Get in line," I say. As if my short-sighted, cardio-avoidant self would be worth a damn.

The last few shots I try are a bit different. A bit risky. A secret attempt I don't admit to.

Without explanation, I position Baker against the light and ask him to turn to the side, a silhouette against the sky. I adjust the shutter speed to underexpose the shot, holding the camera landscape. And then I walk away from him. I swap my 85mm lens for 50 and take a second shot on the same frame: Baker at his camera on the bridge with the far-off buildings in the background. It could be a mess like the self-portrait Baker picked out. But it's worth a try. Baker thought the double exposure was decent after all.

I try not to think about the angles of Baker's face or the dip at the top of his lip. His dark long eyelashes, unfathomable eyes. Definitely don't look at any of that.

When I'm done, Baker grabs his camera from its pod and threatens to turn the lens on me, but I duck, camera brandished like a shield. Iris Green is no one's subject.

"No way," I say. "I don't need photos of my weird face."

"Why not? You have a good face, Angry Darkroom Girl."

I look at my feet.

A good face? Said so lightly. Throwaway. It's almost cruel to joke about it.

Baker fiddles with the camera, possibly reviewing his footage.

The sun has gone in. Warmth bleeding from the day.

"I ought to go," I say.

"Sure, I'll catch you around?" The lack of fuss throws me. Usually people protest; they try to let me leave on their terms, not mine. It makes me not want to go.

"What … what are you doing with all your footage from today?" I say.

He lights up. He launches into an explanation of his exhibition project, which sounds like street photography on amphetamines. These videos of traffic, pedestrians, cyclists and trains will be set to discordant music – the beats lining up with the entrances of each new player in the video.

"I wanted it to have this Michel Gondry chaotic neatness to it, the repetition, the sense of pattern even though it's random. I'm not sure about the sounds, though. What do you think?" He shows me a snippet of finished work on his phone and it is bonkers and genius and it makes me so happy to listen to him, so of course I say something like, "What exactly are you hoping to demonstrate with that?"

Baker waves a hand around as he says, "With your street stuff, you're trying to find the individual stories amid the noise, right? I'm trying to make all the noise into one story."

"That's…"

"Pretentious?" Baker runs his hand through his hair. "Yeah, but you have to believe your own hype, right? Or who will?"

"Self-deprecation doesn't suit you," I say, but there's a warmth in the centre of my chest and a restlessness in me as I'm tempted to open my phone, to show Baker some of my favourite street shots. But I know if I start, I won't be able to stop.

"Isn't this all some big conflict of interest?" I gesture at the bridge, our cameras, us. "We're both entering the exhibition and we both want the prize. We're direct competition. We shouldn't be helping each other."

Baker begins to dismantle his equipment. "Gotta say, hats off to your ruthlessness, but I'm not in it to win it. I can't."

"Why? Disqualified for submitting nudes last year?" I lift an eyebrow, thinking of his glossy magazine-style photos of the perfect model in the tiny dress.

"Oh, she's a comedian." Baker slicks his tongue over his teeth. "You know, before you embarrass yourself further, I should tell you, the girl? That's my sister Tash. My twin, actually. Please stop suggesting she's a porn star. It's unbelievably gross."

"Shit." I put a hand to my mouth. My mind plays a montage of every unfair comment I made about Baker's sister and I wish the earth beneath me would erupt in lava. "Why didn't you tell me before?"

"I don't care to explain myself to irate strangers." His teeth gleam, very white. "Anyway, would that've been half as funny?"

"It's not funny."

He shrugs, still wearing a huge grin.

I gather myself. "Why can't you win the prize?"

Baker pauses. "I don't take art. Dropped it after year eleven and it's an art student prize, right?"

"I'm surprised they even let you exhibit."

"Well, there's nothing in the rules to say I can't. And who cares about some prize? No one's going to stand between me and my moment of glory on the school canteen wall."

I nod. I feel reprimanded, as though aspiring to the

prize is less pure. Less art somehow. But my eyes fall on his camera gear. I do some sums plucked from my own fantasy equipment wish list. It's probably easier to have artistic integrity when you're not constantly focused on your bottom line.

"I don't care so much about the prize," I say. "Or it's not the money – well, that would be good, but … if I could get some kind of acknowledgement, maybe I could … work things out. What's next. Whether it's worth me even bothering to do this any more." I raise my camera. "I'd know if I'm any good."

"You're good," Baker says.

"No, but…" I sigh. "It's more than that."

Baker stares at me for a long moment. And I wonder if he gets it. It's not about winning or competition. It's about something I made being on the wall in front of everyone – classmates, parents, teachers – anyone who ever wrote me off or put me down. It's about being good enough. For them. For the judges. For me.

"Well, I can't win anyway, so we can hang out again," Baker says. "No conflict. That's my whole ethos for life, actually."

His eyes twinkle. No conflict indeed. And what does he mean "hang out again"? It's a minefield. The magnetic pull of his deep brown eyes, the quirk of his mouth and the tiny gap between his two front teeth – under other circumstances Baker's pretty irresistible. Lucky I have no burning desire to throw myself at anyone new, not while I'm still choking on the ashes of last time. Lucky I'm resistible enough for both of us.

I wrap my arms round my body and look at the darkening sky.

"Are you cold?" Baker grabs the bottom of his jumper and starts to lift. The T-shirt underneath drags with it and reveals a taut stretch of boy-stomach that disappears as Baker wrestles the jumper over his head and offers it to me.

"Um … no." I clamp my arms tighter. An unwanted flash of Theo in my mind feels like guilt. As though I'm cheating on him simply by being here. "Thanks. I'm, uh … already wearing clothes."

"Your lips are blue."

I tuck my offending lips inside my mouth.

"You really hate help, don't you?"

"I tried that double exposure," I blurt, proof that I listen and take advice. "Similar to the self-portrait you liked. A few different ways to see if any pan out."

"Oh yeah? Awesome. See? I inspire you."

"Um. No, thank you."

Baker laughs. "Fine. I get it. Deny my influence as teacher, artist, visionary – whatever you want to call me."

"Arrogant?"

"Whatever, Angry Girl. Admit it – I pushed you." He reaches out and gives me a gentle, friendly shove. My arms fall out of their cross.

"This is why I don't want your input. Anyway, the photo will probably be awful."

"Impossible. It's of my face." He grins.

"I hope your face is a blurry mess."

Baker laughs harder as I turn.

I shake my head. At the edge of the bridge I catch myself smiling.

By the time I've taken the steps down to road level, my smile's drained away.

He's just being nice, Iris. Don't be stupid. Don't even think it.

16

I get home to an empty house. Mum's left a note on the fridge:

Feed Purkoy xox

Purkoy mewls and rubs her body against my shins. I pick her up and inhale her nutty scent, sinking my fingers into her softness as she purrs. Originally I wanted a dog, hence her name, but Mum said dogs were too much work, that cats are more independent. Joke's on her, this fluffbutt's a needy bitch.

"I love you more than dogs," I promise as I put her down to check the cupboard. No fresh cat tins, so I guess Mum forgot. I pour biscuit instead and then fix myself the human equivalent, the speediest dinner possible: porridge with smooth peanut butter stirred through – tea of champions – and take it upstairs. I sink to the carpet in front of the mirror, crooning sweet silly nothings at Purkoy, and throw my phone on the floor.

A series of missed calls. Dad.

I send him a placatory message.

> **Me:** just out tonight working on my photography. speak tomorrow?
>
> **Dad:** Well if you can spare the time for your old man then
>
> **Dad:** Let's make plans for summer

The hard-done-by tone of his message. The fact that ignoring his Mum-transmitted message clearly wasn't enough. The way he doesn't even ask about my art. It gets to me.

The irony is, Dad introduced me to photography. My very first camera, a bright pink digital point-and-shoot. I loved it so much. Treasured it. And I remember at the end of the second day, as I was hunched down in the middle of Trafalgar Square creeping closer to a plump strutting pigeon with a particularly fine iridescent sheen, Dad checked his watch and said, "Don't you think you've got enough photos of those flying rats yet?"

It sounded almost like a joke. Still, I couldn't take another photo on that trip. Not the pigeons, not any of the sights Dad suggested I snap instead. Nothing. Something turns over inside me at the memory. I open my phone to distract myself. Scroll.

Baker's posted a shot of his set-up on the bridge. I imagine responding. I try out several alternatives in my head and imagine the worst possible way Baker will read each. Post none. Scroll on. Olivia's latest video of her fluffing her lines for the play and giggling at herself. Captioned: When you know all your words by heart, but not in the right order.

Bert's liked it.

Yuck. I throw my phone down and it flashes, so I snatch it back up, disappointed when the message turns out to be from Bert.

> **Bert:** What are you up to tonight? Are you OK?

I start typing.

> **Me:** yeah

And then I stop, because I don't know how to finish sentences with Bert any more.

> **Bert:** Are we OK?

Damn, she saw me typing. I abandon my half-finished message still unsent. Maybe I'm being unfair. Bert didn't know she was consorting with the enemy after all. But she does now and taking the middle-ground feels like taking Olivia's side. What else did I expect, really?

Even though she's still talking to me, I don't understand how we are now. How we fit together in this new shape. All I can see is how I will have to try so much harder to hold up my side of the friendship bargain. How much of a downer I will be, unable to stop thinking about everything that's happened. How Bert will eventually, inevitably get tired of me. It's happened before. Part of me wants to fade out of Bert's life now rather than wait for her to give up on me.

I swipe away to another ultra-posed selfie on Olivia's grid. A make-up video. Breakfast with a copy of the script for *The Importance of Being Earnest.* No pictures of her and Theo. Yet.

The thought trickles through me, down to my toes and pools there, keeping me heavy against the floor so I am aware of my ankle bones against the thin carpet and the floorboards underneath.

They probably are together.

Like I never existed.

These thoughts make the dark behind my eyelids spin and crackle. The charge runs through me to the tips of my fingers. And I wish I could run away from my own thoughts, my own body, my own being. But I've still only managed a flicker.

Every time I've gone was a moment I desperately wanted

to escape. So I lean in. Focus. And think about Olivia and Theo on the bench and Theo laughing with his friends.

And Theo…

"You're beautiful," he said, prising my hands from my naked chest. My arms snapped back like living wood as soon as he let go.

"No." The inside of my eyelids pink and red, glowing against the sun through the window. Even though it was slushy outside, it felt like summer with all the bright and the radiators up high. Theo's duvet smelled of sleep and body and I wished it would open up so I could topple into the warmth like a gaping mouth and be swallowed.

Theo planted dry butterfly kisses over my shoulder that made me flinch and pulled me tight against him and I stared at the ceiling.

It wasn't what I imagined. Not the Netflix fade to black. I imagined I'd lose my mind, but there I was, still inside myself, still aware of all my expansive inches and the pieces of me that didn't sit right, exposed for the first time. Wonky and heavy and human. I sucked in my stomach, considered my angles and hoped Theo wouldn't see too much of me.

"Beautiful," Theo said again and I bit back a disagreement. "Come on, Ris. What are we waiting for? I've waited so long."

And he had. I saw it in his eyes when I opened mine to look at him.

"Wonder why I bother when you don't even like me like I like you," he said.

"I do. I'm sorry."

"It's all right. You're worth the wait. You're just killing me here." And he kissed me again and I let him.

Because I knew I wasn't worth the wait. And I knew it was time: the next step, the thing you do. It's in the relationship handbook. Besides, I wanted it too. More than that, I wanted to be wanted.

That first time. It didn't hurt. It was nice. Theo holding me afterwards and gently kissing my forehead. It didn't hurt until after I'd stood alone in Theo's family bathroom staring in the mirror for too long, waiting for some change in me.

It only hurt when I came back into the room and Theo had my phone in his hand and said, "What the fuck, Ris?"

The memory's strange. A mix of the lovely and painful, it's easier than the good ones; the times he was simply sweet, when he would shyly tell me he loved me then smooth my hair back and plant a kiss at the corner of my eyebrow. Those memories are unbearable to touch.

When I open my eyes the room's swimming and I'm no longer here. In the mirror there's an unmade bed, a messy floor, a scatter of prints that need putting back in their box. There's no Iris.

Success.

The world has a sheen on it. A silvery gloss as though I've slipped through the surface of a mirror and the whole world is behind glass, subtly flipped.

I take my glasses off and everything blurs out of existence as they pop back into being inches from my face. I put them on and the frames disappear as everything becomes sharp again. Odd.

Purkoy stares dead at me.

"Can you see me, Fluffles?" I say and give her a slow blink. She slow-blinks back and resumes grooming. "Of course you can see me," I whisper and lean over to run my fingers over her side.

Downstairs the hum of the freezer changes pitch. It's 9.30 p.m. and I could do my homework. I could watch TV. I could start planning my exhibition project. I could go to sleep. But none of those are better when you're invisible.

I'm not a thief or creep, so scratch the obvious.

What actually *is* more fun when you're invisible?

I stare into the mirror at the space where I should be and it feels like a kind of answer.

Nothing.

17

School. A typical day, a typical lunch with Bert and Olivia and it's normal again. The three of us here, hanging out together in the common room, just like it used to be. Sort of. One difference – and I guess it's a biggie.

"It still feels weird without her," says Bert as the two of them flop into position and I perch opposite. Here but not here. Invisible.

"Do you think she'll come back?" Olivia asks and Bert replies with an ominous stare and exactly zero recriminations.

Without a face and body I'm not expected to smile at Olivia or control my expressions as I wonder if every joke is laced with truth. I don't have to pretend it doesn't hurt that she's not sought me out to apologize properly. Or work out how Bert can be so comfortable around Olivia when the metaphorical fence must be poking her right in the tailbone.

I don't know how to be with them. Now I don't have to be.

Bert's feet are in Olivia's lap as she scrolls. Olivia sips at a can of energy drink. The tang of artificial sweetener gets up my nose and makes it twitch. I listen to my friends like the radio. Relaxed now I don't have to worry how to contribute. Tuning in and out, hearing snatches of other conversation around us. After one cursory name-drop, I go unnoticed and unmentioned.

I should feel guilty for eavesdropping, but the place in my stomach where I expect the shame to fit is empty. Or it's invisible for now too. I guess I'd call it all morally grey and everyone knows Iris Green is—

"Urgh," Olivia groans and holds out her drink can to Bert. "Do you want the rest? I'm desperate for the caffeine but any more of this and I'll hurl." She holds a hand to her forehead. "I'm coming down with something."

"A little ailment known as too much wine at the drama party?"

"Rum. And I think I kissed … Ben Jones?"

"Jesus, why?" Bert's eyes get buggy as she asks the question we all need answers to: *Why, Olivia, why?*

I sit up. The clatter of the common room recedes as I shuffle closer.

"Again, rum." Olivia shrugs. She digs a small circular

mirror from her bag and tilts it this way and that, reflecting first one then the other side of her face. She lets her chin dip until it's double, then grimaces at her reflection. And that's it.

That's *it?*

I stare at Bert, willing her to push – what about Theo? What about the boy she risked it all for?

"Look at this," Bert says, flipping her phone round to point to the model in some arty ad. "Where's her head? Imagine getting booked to be a pair of thighs."

"Her choice," says Olivia with a laugh. "She's a free-range model."

"OK, it's not a choice made in a vacuum, though? Who wants to be just body parts?"

"Please, no lectures while I'm dying. How's No Mow March going?" Olivia asks with an eye-roll and a nod towards Bert's pits. "Speaking of questionable personal choices."

Bert lifts an arm and strokes her white cotton armpit. "It's getting satisfyingly silky under there, but the need to wear a school uniform every day is kind of taking the edge off the statement. There's still time to join in—"

"As if. Imagine some guy copping a feel and getting a handful of fur."

"Imagine remodelling your own body for the approval of Ben-freaking-Jones."

"Imagine giving it a rest, Bert."

It's weird this is how people talk. It bounces from topic

to topic, ricochets back and forth. I want it to be scripted. Edited. I want to discard ninety per cent of the words and only see the highlights, like my pick of photographs at the end of a long session. Only the quirkiest moments, the best framing.

I want it to be about me. I want it to be about him.

I'm behind as the conversation moves on.

"Rum makes me boke," Bert says.

"Shouldn't have drunk that much at Spade's house party last year then. I wouldn't have had to lie to your mum and tell her you'd had dodgy prawns," Olivia says.

"Oh my god, shh. That was for science. How was I to know my limits without testing them?"

"I suppose you'd have gotten away with it too if Iris could've stopped laughing for two seconds to sell the food-poisoning deception."

"Mum thinks you're a straight-up bad influence now."

"She thinks I'm a liar. And easy. Her words."

Bert's eyebrows make for her hairline. "Well."

"Hey! My god!"

Bert's mouth pops in faux outrage and then dissolves in a cackle. "Wait, no, stop. Firstly the context you had to remove to accuse my mother … come on. Easy-*going*, she said."

"I heard what I heard—"

"Secondly you could touch up the whole of sixth form – fine by me. As long as it's what you want. Is it?"

"Not the *whole* of sixth form." Olivia smiles at her hands, at Bert, a wonky, unconvincing thing. And I'm queasy watching now, suddenly aware of my intrusion here and how I don't want to hear this. Suddenly aware in the beat of quiet how hard it would be to extract my clumsy, uncoordinated body without notice, even if I am invisible. I don't trust myself to be soundless.

Olivia waves her hand and adds, "Although Ben Jones isn't my finest work, I can't believe he hasn't even messaged me."

Bert gives her a hard stare. A silence to fill.

"I..." Olivia grabs the sofa cushion and bunches it up on her lap. "I'm serious, though. Don't you want to meet Marissa from the library? She's so sososo pretty."

"Does she have a personality too, or is she just some hot, convenient deflection tactic?" Bert says, side-eyeing Olivia at the abrupt change of subject. "Anyway, why would I? Final year incoming! There's no time for that."

"For fun?"

"Fun?" Bert draws the word out. "Is it some newfangled thing the cool kids are all about? I don't *want* anyone else right now. I'm happy solo. Besides, unlike you, my most meaningful and enriching relationships aren't exclusively reserved for whoever wants to bone me."

"Hey!" Olivia smacks Bert's shoulder and chastises her but in a way that makes it clear she's not bothered. Though perhaps, like me, she feels a spark of envy, a wish to be half as self-assured as Bert. Probably not. Olivia probably just enjoys being reminded of all the boys who've fallen at her feet.

Olivia's her usual self today. Her calm, composed ice queen schtick, nicked from every mean girl villain. It was supposed to conceal a soft heart, but now we know the truth I wonder how Bert can bear to sit so close. Bert: the wire that keeps the current running through this friendship group. The one who somehow got me and Olivia on the same level even though we're such different people. The one who makes us best friends. Supposedly.

Across the room, Theo stands and all three of us pivot towards him subtly, like flowers searching for the sun.

"God, I hate that guy," Bert mutters. "You're not still speaking to him, are you?"

Olivia makes a noise of dissent. "Except for essential theatre business. I'm moving onwards and upwards."

"Oldwards more like."

Olivia nudges Bert. They laugh. Some in-joke I'm not in on. It makes my tummy twist. Some casual little joke about Olivia's love life and the way she's throwing Theo away, the same way she threw me aside. Somehow it's worse that he's so unimportant.

As Bert stops cackling and starts chattering on an unrelated tangent, I make the most of my friends' absorption to slip away.

My footsteps are as light as whispers as I jog after Theo. There's no resistance, as though I'm less solid. I'm the air.

I catch him up over by E-block. Good job I know Theo's timetable by heart. He's lagging behind his friends, eyes glued to his phone. Who is he messaging so intently?

I fall into rhythm beside him. Close enough to see the freckles on his nose and the almost translucent curl of stray hair over his forehead.

I open my mouth intending to say … something. Anything. But I can't get it out.

"Hey," he says. His eyes going all in at the edges as his mouth spreads in a smile.

For a second, it's for me. My heart stops. I stop. He holds me there with a hand in his hair and a smile that goes through me.

"Hey, yourself," someone says behind my shoulder.

I step sideways. Pivot.

"We good for tonight?" Theo says.

"Oh, cute," says Sadie Campbell. "You're worried I'll stand you up?"

His head drops to the side with a self-deprecating chuckle. "You should feel the way my heart's thumping. Proper terrified." He puts a hand to it. His liar heart. "You said you'd give me a chance, though."

"Did I say that?" She breaks out in a smile. "So, ice cream?"

"At seven? WTFs?"

"Sure."

"Yeah?" Theo beams.

"It's not a date, you know?" Sadie says.

Under the bright flare of Theo's happiness, she is suddenly less sure, tucking her blue hair behind her ear.

I feel sick.

Sick.

This *is* a date.

How can he be doing this? Brazenly in front of anyone who cares to see. What about me? Olivia? How can he be smiling his squidgy-eyed smile at Sadie instead? My stomach lurches. Theo and Sadie carry on talking, stepping closer, his eyes skimming hers, his fingers lightly running over the badges on her school bag as Sadie leans back into a display on Gothic literature.

"You can't get to know someone in school with everyone watching all the time," Theo says.

"Like your exes?" She tilts her head.

That's me. No longer a named character in Theo's life, just some scratched-out backstory. The mad woman in his attic.

"Exactly." Theo says. "Later I'll have you all to myself."

I shiver lightly.

The bell goes. Sadie lifts her hand in a non-wave and walks off.

I stay. I think about Sadie. I always wanted her hair – long and dark with blue shot through the ends. I could never be a blue-haired girl.

I'm sure I've only spoken to Sadie once in all our years

together. My first day of year eight and I can see it, brighter than Sadie's dye job. Twelve-year-old Iris wearing Mum's scarlet lipstick, convinced after watching *Moulin Rouge!* for the first and fifth time that summer, that a bold new style would be key to her social reinvention: a gateway to being glamourous and admired. But…

"What happened to your lips?" Sadie had said, face furrowed in concern as she clocked me by the school gates, friends smiling behind.

"Allergies," I muttered, as my heart raced with anxiety at the unexpected interaction. The wrong kind of attention. Moments later, as I scrubbed my mouth clean, full of horror at what could have been, I realized I owed Sadie Campbell. I'd been mistaken. Again. Lipstick, like blue hair, like every other style I'd tried and failed to pull off, were only for other people. The right people. Never me.

The memory comes with a realization four years too late: Sadie knew exactly what had happened.

Huh.

And I still can't decide if it was help or ridicule. Compassion or malice. Regardless, Sadie saved me then, so now? I'll repay the favour, because a date with Theo is an even worse decision than taking school-style inspo from a fictional courtesan.

I could fix this with words, with my skin on. I could talk to Sadie and explain, but I can already hear how it would sound, how quickly my intent could be twisted.

So there's always option two: look out for Sadie in another less obvious way. I don't know Sadie, but I know she doesn't deserve to be lied to or hurt or cheated on.

I don't know Sadie, but I know Theo.

18

It's 7.05 p.m. Quiet. Near empty roads, Theo the only pedestrian in sight as he gets to the high-street crossing. He's twitched towards the button when it lights up of its own accord: WAIT.

He does, brow lightly crinkled. The green man appears.

Across the road, past the kebab shop, the bakery, the closed international food store. He passes the dark windows, a silhouette in the reflection. No one behind him. No one at all.

Theo's walking past a pizza place when he hears a voice say, "Hey."

He doesn't stop walking.

"Theo."

Now he stops. Turns. He frowns at his phone, then raises it to his ear. "Hello?"

Nothing.

"Theo." The word is long and drawn out. A whisper. A death rattle.

Another quick glance around reveals no one. Nothing.

As he walks on, Theo looks over his shoulder a couple of times.

*

Here we are at Whats That Flavour, the ice-cream-shop-slash-cafe with an aversion to punctuation. Sadie's waiting. And even though Theo's ten minutes late, she smiles at him, at the ground, back at him as her legs wind together.

He opens the door for her, sweeter than ice cream. It starts to close, the glass panels rattling, and stops as the shadow of a hand print appears in a thin fog against the glass. The door seems to hesitate. And inside, through the window, Theo's pulling Sadie's seat out and she smiles, unaware how quickly this act will melt away.

The sharp inward swing of the door. The whoosh of cold air. The server behind the counter glares suspiciously at a chair that seems to scoot out from a table of its own accord. But she wasn't watching closely – she saw it out of the corner of her eye – and she goes back to wiping the surface with a shake of her head.

Sadie's eyes roam the walls and settle on Theo. "Nice choice. We brought my little brother here for his seventh birthday, I think?"

"Ouch." Theo grins. "OK, but it's got a sort of ironic

old-school charm. And the milkshakes are…" He brings his fingers to his mouth in a chef's kiss, then places a menu in Sadie's hands, launching into an outline of the various options, the merits of milkshakes over sundaes. Sadie glazes over and her attention slips again to the decor. WTFs is as confused about theme as punctuation. A rainforest mural covers the walls: lush green leaves, turquoise parrots and blood-red frogs are splashed behind neon-pink tables, but inside a fishing net stapled to the ceiling there's a scattering of plastic lobsters, lurid red bodies suspended over our heads. Nothing makes sense here.

Theo ends his monologue with: "Mint choc shake can't be beaten, really."

Sadie says, "OK, sold." And no one could judge her for struggling to have an opinion of her own. Not when Theo's so sure and so close, leaning across the tiny table with his freckles and his eyelashes and his necklace, a worn plectrum on a leather lace to prove he's not just a pretty face. He's an artist.

"I'll get them," Theo says, wallet out.

"Are you sure? I don't want you thinking I can't pay my own way." Sadie puts both elbows on the table. "Or that you can buy my affections."

"I'm deeply offended." He clicks his mouth and puts a hand on his chest. "I'm a good guy."

"Hmm, Iris Green would say different, I think." Sadie's tone is playful but with a note of caution.

"You can't believe everything you hear." His voice is troubled. "I did try to let her down gently, you know. Told her it was over way before Olivia." He sighs. "I should have been firmer," he says almost to himself. "That was my fault."

Sadie shifts. "It wasn't your fault if you were honest," she says slowly.

"I tried." He gives a sad smile. "She wouldn't let it go."

Liar. My insides boil and my eyes smart, but I'm frozen here. Trapped in my own invisibility, my inability to intervene.

"Girls! More trouble than they're worth, am I right?" Sadie gives her words a strong sarcastic twang.

"Not at all."

"Maybe you can give me your version of the story? There are always two sides after all."

"Over milkshake, sure."

Silence falls as they study their menus again, but Sadie breaks it. "How's your band doing? I heard you at the Railway last year. You were great."

"Yeah?" Theo's delight is real.

"I'm in orchestra myself, so, not to say I'm any kind of expert, but..." Sadie fans her hands out on the table. "Grade eight cello." She laughs at herself.

"Orchestra sounds kind of fun to be part of too," Theo says. "I'd totally give it a go, but I've never been good at learning other people's music. It's different from lines in a play somehow, because you can put your own interpretation on that character. Bring yourself to it. That's why the band suits me. I write all our original stuff and it's, like, so much of me, my raw emotions in a way only music can express, you know?"

"Right, you do the plays too – busy guy. All those extracurriculars." Sadie sits back in her chair. "I'm not that serious about orchestra. It's mainly about the parties, actually. Brass section are wild … but you? I always knew you were deep." Her slight smile seems to contradict her raised eyebrow, like even she hasn't decided whether it's a joke.

"Can't agree without sounding like the worst kind of guy, can I?" Theo laughs and runs a hand through his hair. "But I was brought up to be a gentleman. And gentlemen always pick up the tab for pretty cellists," Theo adds with a bow as he stands.

Liar.

"Now, now," Sadie says, pretending to fan herself modestly.

"You've got to know how stunning you are."

She tucks a strand of electric hair behind her ear. It falls back. He reaches over and smooths it and if I'd remembered to eat tonight, I'm sure my dinner would be making a reappearance.

This is how it starts with Theo. With sweet things like compliments and chivalry and dessert. Sadie's smiling and

I'm seething. Trembling. The oily shimmer on the surface of the world swirls faster and the memory's so clear I can smell the sugar.

Another date, another girl, another time, same boy.

"Music's life," he'd said. We were at Coffee Bear on a Saturday, the scent of cinnamon filling the air. "You can find basically every human emotion in existence captured in sound. You ever thought about that?"

"Never," I said and licked my lip clean of latte foam.

Theo smiled. Gratified to know he'd had a thought when I hadn't.

And as we'd said goodbye, he'd reached over, tucked my *hair behind* my *ear and he'd told* me, *"You don't even know how beautiful you are, do you?" I'd held my breath, suddenly so full up I was sure to explode or float away.*

"Don't say that," I said.

"I'm going to say it if it's true. You're going to have to get used to it."

He'd messaged me before I was even out of sight.

> **Theo:** i've got to see you again. monday after school?

And I'd laughed because we saw each other all the time. But blink and it was suddenly all *the time and messages between. He sent me songs that reminded him of me. Playlists full of love and longing and belonging together, always. New songs from bands I'd never heard of but quickly memorized. They were my homework. And I loved them, even when I didn't.*

Now it's the same Theo. Same moves, different girl.

He's at the counter. Sadie looks over her shoulder before emitting a high-pitched whistle of a breath into her phone as her fingers sweep the screen sending updates to, I assume, a rapt remote audience of highly invested friends. So Sadie likes him, I guess. I mean, of course she likes him.

Behind the counter, the server sets off the blender, whisking ice cream into milk. Time ticks by.

What now? A warning note poured in sugar on the table or squeaking a path through the condensation on the glass? A whisper in her ear? Every option seems to come with a side effect of snapping Sadie's sanity in half.

So leave?

Maybe I'm wrong. About this. About Theo. Perhaps he will always be this Theo for Sadie. Because she's worth it.

Perhaps.

But the gleam in Sadie's eyes, the smile she's trying to supress, that's what stops me, because what if I'm right?

As Sadie's sucked into her phone, Theo pays at the counter. He leans in to speak to the assistant with the French braid. The words are inaudible, but I can see her fluster. Her subtle glance over here towards Sadie. It's so easy to miss.

Now, Iris, now. A quick root around in my invisible bag with my invisible hand, speed making my fingers blunt and clumsy. A minute later I dump a napkin straight on the table, letting it flutter into Sadie's eyeline.

As Theo returns, the two milkshakes pressed precariously between his hands, he drops a look back over his shoulder at the assistant.

Sadie notices the napkin on the table. Thick black scrawl peeks out as she pulls it over.

Theo places one shake in front of Sadie, then turns towards his side of the table.

"What's that?" he says, jerking his head in the direction of the napkin spread in Sadie's hands.

"Nothing." She balls the tissue, eyes wide and weirded out.

"Some other guy's number?"

Sadie forces a laugh. She stays seated as her eyes dart around the cafe, checking the other diners.

I step forward, my heart racing.

Both milkshakes are mint choc chip. Both are large. As the first whips from Theo's grasp and sloshes into the crotch of his jeans, I can't help but appreciate the contrast of pastel green against dark denim. Chocolate or vanilla wouldn't have been nearly so satisfying.

"What the hell?" Theo jumps back, an accusation on his face.

Sadie stares, open-mouthed, and then covers her mouth to smother a giggle.

"You think it's fucking funny?" Theo says.

"Umm." Her voice quivers with mirth. "A bit, yeah."

He snatches the near empty cup from the floor and motions as if to douse Sadie. One fat viscous droplet hits her lap.

"That's a bit unnecessary," she says.

"I'm covered."

"And that's my fault somehow?"

Theo's eyes pop. "Is it not?"

They stare each other down. Sadie breaks first, dabbing her skirt with the napkin in her hand. Theo rips napkins from the dispenser by the fistful to blot himself, emitting huffs of impotent rage.

Sadie unfolds the napkin, then crumples it again. "It's just a little milkshake," she says, almost to herself, and then to Theo: "Do you want to go home and get cleaned up?"

"What? No. It's already drying."

Urgh.

As the second milkshake jumps from the table in front of Sadie to hit Theo's shins and drop down to his favourite trainers, it's hard not to hope the colour's permeating the white stitching in an irreversible way.

"You clumsy bitch."

As his words hit her, Sadie's expression freezes over. "I didn't do that." She throws the napkin to the table and it slips to the floor. "And I don't think we should do this."

"Shit." Theo drops his wedge of damp tissues and abandons his futile clean-up. "Come on, don't be like this. I was shocked, that's all. That wasn't directed at you."

"It's fine," Sadie says as she stands to gather her things. She'll worry later about exactly how the milkshake came to jump from the table. She'll wonder later about taking dating advice from a ghost.

Because underneath the table, a dropped, crumpled napkin unfurls to reveal the scrawl inside:

Theo Hastings is a liar. Get out. Get out now.

*

I walk. I keep my skin off – invisible, electric, alive and free.

It's late and dark but I'm safe. The sky burns orange. A few brave stars overpower the glow of artificial lights behind black boxy rooftops. A cat dashes from the shadows of parked cars. A man walks right past me, fixated on the glow of his phone.

I dawdle, soaking up the night, not wanting to go home. For once I don't touch my camera. I keep my brain empty so I can relive, again and again, with photo-perfect clarity, the sight of mint chocolate milkshake dripping from Theo Hastings's crotch. Because that? Pure art.

I pass the little corner shop that's never open, the grey shelves inside illuminated by the red glow from a vending machine sign. Opposite, a group of boys huddle around the muffled thump of music from a phone. One of them gives a loud whoop. Another steps from the scrum for a moment, coughing on his laughter.

Fear thrums through me, body reacting before my mind catches up. They can't see me.

Another figure on the pavement. A slight dark shadow. A girl in a thin hoodie. She snatches a glance behind her, picks up her pace.

"Hey, where are you running to?" a boy shouts with a laugh.

She cringes as she hurries past me, round the corner. One of the boys drop-kicks his empty can into the middle of the road and the others cheer as it goes skittering into the gutter near my feet.

Without stopping I pick it up and hurl it at the group. It hits one in the back of the shoulder with a satisfying metallic clunk and he whips round, shock making him stumble.

With my hands stuffed over my mouth to stop the giggles, I leg it up the road.

When I come to a stop, I'm still beaming. I throw my hands wide and spin until the world blurs into nothing.

This. This is what's more fun when you're invisible.

19

I get home at midnight. Creeping in so as not to wake Mum who I know crashed out at 9 p.m., exhausted from an early start and in anticipation of a matching one tomorrow. I'm equally sure she accepted my message telling her I was at Bert's for the evening. Why wouldn't she? I've kept Mum safe from all my drama.

I sit cross-legged on the floor before my mirror and revel in my absence. With my skin off not even the audience inside my head can pick at my flaws. It's perfect. Almost perfect.

If only I had a clue how to reliably return. Other than a good night's sleep or an hour's strenuous meditation in the girls' bathroom.

In the spirit of daring – and testing a theory – I take my phone out and type.

Me: you know, you taking credit for inspiring my work continues a grand tradition of men erasing women from art history

Probably a bad idea. Probably unwelcome. Probably the worst idea I've ever had.

I hit send. Wait. My lip tucked between my teeth, my toes flexing.

Typing…

Baker: Well damn. I'm not trying to erase you

Baker: If anything I'm trying to draw you out

Baker: I acknowledge I failed to consider the historical context I was working within and for that I apologize

It's an effort to keep my mouth controlled.

Me: i forgive you. this time

Baker: Thanks, ADG, so gracious

Me: ADG?

And then I get it and our messages appear at the same time.

Baker: Angry Darkroom Girl

Me: angry darkroom girl

Me: great, i'm glad that's catching on

I cradle my phone in my hands, letting the screen dim. It's interesting how comfortable Baker feels. Interesting and alarming. Alarming, because I have no idea if he genuinely wants to talk to me or whether he's messing with me in the most intricate way. Interesting because if I think about everything rationally, I should probably never trust anyone again.

But here I am. Trusting. Because I believe everyone or I believe no one, and that second one? Too dark to contemplate.

Baker: What are you doing over the break?

Me: exhibition project planning. reading. sleeping. why?

Baker: I'm recruiting for human experiments, you in?

I look into the mirror, startled to see a wide-eyed girl staring out.

Back. Just like that.

Thank you, Baker Davis.

20

"You came back," Nicole says. "I wasn't sure you would."

"Me neither."

We're sitting opposite each other in the music room. My second counselling session and I'm impressed with the logistics. I haven't seen any other classmates coming and going from the space. No one to exchange knowing nods that say, *Yes, we're both troubled.*

"What would you like to talk about today?" She sits back in her chair. "What's on your mind?"

It falls so quiet I can hear the second hand of Nicole's clock moving. And I think there's no harm in telling the truth. I could mention it. The weird thing.

"I guess … I guess I've been feeling pretty invisible."

"Invisible?" Nicole nods, unruffled. There's no reason to take my words literally.

"It's not a problem," I say. "It's a relief when people stop looking. I don't want attention."

Nicole frowns. "I'm not sure I'm following. You don't want people to see you?"

"It, um … hasn't gone so well in the past."

"How so?" Nicole tilts her head. Her speciality, I'm learning.

"I used to struggle with friends a bit. People being critical, friends turning out not to be friends after all." Past. Just in the past obviously.

"Critical of what?"

"Um … me? Being quiet and anxious and trying too hard. Being stuck-up, sitting wrong, having the wrong … face? My clothes? Everything, really. I was an easy target for a while there." The phrase comes so fluently, *easy target*, though I've never said it aloud before. "Don't overreact," my dad told me when Mum let on about my Sunday-night tears circa year seven. "They see you're too sensitive about the teasing and it makes you an easy target."

I heard the implication louder than the advice. Oversensitive – not the first time the accusation has been levelled against me. Easy target. My own fault. Again.

"So now you'd rather no one notices you?" Nicole says.

"I don't know why I brought that up. It hasn't been that way for ages – literally years – I have a good group of friends now. Bert, Olivia, Baker?" The last name comes out with a question mark. Nicole cocks her head. Hilarious that

"Baker" is the name I hesitate on, when I've listed Olivia, the biggest lie of all.

"And I broke up with someone recently."

"Oh?"

"Yeah, he..." *Lied to me. Kissed my best friend.* I shift in my chair and keep control. If I disappear, it'll be Nicole who ends up needing therapy. I rub my thumb in circles over my finger, troubled by phantom pins and needles. "We didn't work out. And it's over now."

"Didn't work out. Hmm." Nicole's voice is flat. Oddly soothing. "And how are you feeling about the break-up?"

"Fine. These things happen."

"Do they?" A tilt.

"I mean, definitely when you find out they've been cheating on you." I laugh and am shocked by the inappropriateness of the sound. Nicole doesn't look horrified and I recompose my face in a more normal expression. "Everyone goes through these things. Everyone has break-ups and relationship issues. Everyone's under pressure to be a certain way. My problems are so ordinary and I don't know why I can't deal with them. It's embarrassing."

"It might be true that a lot of people experience something, Iris. Does it make them any less painful for you or any easier to process?"

I pick up the glass of water and trace my thumb over a tiny air bubble.

Nicole's expression remains the same. Attentive. Empathic. Difficult.

"No," I say because it seems she wants an answer.

"How are you feeling day-to-day at the moment, Iris?"

"I don't know." I sigh and feel my face contort with the effort of that question. "Since the break-up it's hard to feel like everyone knows something about me. There might be gossip. I might be… It's too much."

"So you're not always invisible."

"More's the pity."

"It seems like you're quite a private person. Would you say that's true?"

I nod. "And my ex? Theo? He kind of … won't leave things alone."

"He's bothering you?"

"Not like that. It's not harassing. It's not even pushy…" I consider getting my phone out as evidence, presenting Nicole with the unexpected message that arrived as I lay in bed last night.

> **Theo**: missing you

As if he hadn't already moved on to the next girl.

"It's hard to let go," I tell Nicole now. And I don't know who I mean. Him. But me too and the way my traitor-heart jumped at the sight of his name on my screen. "It's just another thing."

"Do you have people around you to talk to honestly about how you're feeling?"

I bite the inside of my cheek along the ridge I've unconsciously made. I know the "correct" answer to this question.

I also know the true answer.

I give Nicole something in between. "I talk about some things, but I guess you can't go around burdening people with every random thought you have. That's not fair."

"Burdening?"

I look through the water in my glass to the pale squashed undersides of my fingers.

"We all need someone to open up to in our lives, Iris, to say what's on our minds. I do know how difficult it is to start that process and perhaps that's making it difficult to come here and talk to me?"

I study Nicole's shoes. Turquoise pumps over thick black tights.

"I do want to be here."

"OK. So let's start again maybe? What do you want to get from these sessions, do you think?"

"I want to feel better." And that doesn't sum it up and it isn't quite everything. I put my water down and knot my hands together. They're cold and clammy from touching the glass. "I want to understand why things keep going wrong for me and what it is I'm doing wrong."

"With what?"

"Everything."

And this. This is when I start to cry.

21

The high street cobbles are filmy with dust; it's dry and bright – the perfect weather for my last proper time off before revision and exams start to seriously loom. The market's on and the bald guy who mans the fruit and veg stall is already booming. I centre an interesting shopper in my viewfinder: green jeans and high heels she can't quite walk in, bug sunglasses in leopard print.

"Why her?" Baker asks, because, yeah, Baker's here. My patch this time.

"She's interesting?" I shrug. Too vague.

The woman darts behind an artisanal cheese stall and disappears from view.

Baker's not even looking at me; he's watching a busker. She's singing her heart out, eyes closed in the agony of heartbreak. She should've known he would break her heart, should've known he was the wrong path. Amen, Busker Girl.

"She's here every week," I tell Baker. "And she's always got some nice detail to her outfit… I've thought about asking to take her portrait." I twist my hands round my camera.

"So why don't you?"

"I don't know. It's different to street." I shrug. It's true. Street photography has always felt right, being on the edge of life. An observer. Approaching people and asking for portraits is something else. Too involved.

"She's super pretty." I don't know why I add that. So I can feel terrible?

"Yeah," Baker agrees. Mission accomplished.

As we carry on up the high street, I explain my three-point ethical code of street photography:

- Number one: no photographing people when they're vulnerable. No criers, no disasters and absolutely never anyone who looks like they live in public spaces.
- Number two: no getting in people's faces. This one's for my self-preservation as much as theirs.
- Number three: see people the way they'd want to be seen. No unflattering photos, never making the subject the butt of a joke, no reinforcing of stereotypes.

"That last one's hard to nail down," Baker says.

I shrug because I know what he means. "It's open to interpretation, but I know when I see it. Just because someone's in public, it doesn't mean they're fair game."

There's someone coming up on Baker's other side. I lag back and move round, shooting from my waist and waiting until the distance seems right to snap. The low angle seems right for this one. My subject has a loose topknot, a "STOP CHOKING OUR SEAS" T-shirt and a plastic pop bottle tipping directly into his mouth.

Click. The guy meets my eye and I turn away to Baker, telling him in a rush, "My favourite subjects are where there's some incongruous detail or small contradiction. In a fun way, like they're an unreliable narrator telling on themselves. My favourite trope." And as I say it, I appreciate the irony, because my ability to clock the unreliable people closest to me? A solid zero out of ten.

"Eclectic inspiration," Baker nods. "I like it."

"And you're, like, a total film buff or?"

"Mainly music videos, shorts, sure, artists like Sue de Beer. Feature length not so much. Somewhere around two thirds I lose the will to carry on. It'll only end and then what?"

"Everything ends, you know. Books, school, life."

"Look at you getting aboard the nihilism train. Of course, for some of us the next end of an era is coming up sooner rather than later." He blows on his nails and pretends to buff them against his chest.

"Ah, that's right, mister final year."

Baker turns a grin on me. "Think of me next year when you're chained to a desk and I'm hiking Mount Etna."

"You're travelling?"

"And never coming back."

"Oh?" I let my hair fall over my face to disguise any expression. "Are you going by, like … private jet? Or mega yacht? Or—"

"Train. No need to accuse me of hypocrisy at every opportunity."

"So that's it?" I look at my boot. The leather's scuffed. "You'll travel until the world ends?"

"Or the money runs out." He nudges me. "You'll miss me, of course."

"Uh, purely in an artistic support capacity." My traitor-face immediately heats up. Why the hell would I confess to missing Baker in any capacity?

"Well, seems like you don't actually need my help, wunderkind."

"More like beyond help."

Baker sighs. I laugh even though it's far too late to pass off my character evisceration as humour. I take a sip of my chai latte and miss my mouth or forget to swallow, somehow spilling it down my chin.

"Ever think you might be a bad judge of your own work?" Baker says as I blot at my damp skin and hope he doesn't notice.

"Do you know the Dunning–Kruger effect? The less you know, the better you think you are. You more accurately perceive your failures as you improve."

"You must be amazing then."

"Or worse than I could possibly imagine?"

Baker's wearing a sinisterly determined expression. "Today's the day we start."

"Excuse me?"

He gazes off into the distance with overdramatic intensity. "Did you enjoy your time in your comfort zone, Iris Green?"

"Yes?"

"Say goodbye."

I open my mouth to object but don't get a sound out before Baker grabs my hand and marches up the high street. The dregs of chai latte slosh and I don't know whether to concentrate on not spilling or on the clamminess of my hand in Baker's and the way he hasn't let go. Baker Davis is, technically, holding my hand.

He stops on the street opposite the busker. She's packing her stuff away, picking up her well-earned notes and coins.

"Ask her," he says. "Ask to take her photo."

I snatch my hand from his grip and the air feels too cold on my palm. "Absolutely not."

"As your mentor" – I scoff – "and friend I am encouraging you to ask her if you can take her portrait. What's the worst that could happen?"

"She says no."

"Exactly."

"Um, I wasn't finished. She says no and I'm so embarrassed that my skin shrivels too tight, my insides burst out and I die a grisly, greasy death right here on the high street, crackling in the sun like burned meat until I'm flakes of charcoal in the wind."

His mouth twitches. "Well, that would be terrible."

"Clearly."

"But I think you'll survive."

"And if I don't?"

"You can say you told me so."

"Precious." I gnaw on my lip and fidget my boots against the cobbles, the sun bearing down, as intense as a spotlight. "Fine."

Baker waves me off like a proud mother.

The girl sits on the kerb, bare legs stretched in front of her on the pedestrianized high street. Her straw-coloured wavy hair hangs almost to her waist. She's wearing a floral print dress with a white lace trim that'd look good in black and white. On the way over I prepare my words. I clear my throat.

"Um … excuse me?"

Her eyes are so bright and warm. "What's up, did you like the set?"

"No, uh … I mean, yeah! Sorry! Yeah! I like your original songs so much."

"Not a fan of the covers?" She tilts her head.

Shit. "Them too! But, um, I was wondering … I love your whole … energy and, um, can I take your photo?" I wave the camera, wondering how I'm still standing after the bone-weakening cringe of telling a stranger in all sincerity that I love their "energy".

The girl stares for a second, then springs up and dusts her hands on her hips. *Shit, she's going to storm off.*

"Sorry," I say again at the same time as she says, "Sure, where do you want me?"

And that's how easy it is. I stand a few steps down the hill and she poses. The shutter clicks. A couple of straight portraits. On the third I change my settings and stop the film rolling forward. I ask her to hold her guitar and crouch so I can silhouette her against the sky.

"The old-fashioned camera's so cool," she says when I'm done. "It must take some skill?"

"Not really…"

"She's amazing," a voice says. "You can check out her grid, she's going to put more stuff up there soon." I turn to see Baker looking too pleased with himself and my skin prickles at the thought of him watching me all this time. I got so into my project I forgot he was there. And then he's walking past me and introducing us to the girl, Anna, and she's laughing at something he's said and my mood's a dark spot on the sunny day. But he's leaning in to show her my photos on his phone and she says, "These are incredible. I mean, wow – you're so talented."

"You're talented," I mutter, embarrassed Baker has put her in this situation where she has to pretend like this.

"Thanks! You know every time I get started it takes about twenty minutes to stop feeling like I'm going to puke with nerves." She laughs. "It's cool someone enjoyed it today. Some days it's all small change and cigarette ends in my case and people shouting at me to get a real job."

"I would perish."

"No, you get to the end of the song and by then it's not so bad." She turns her phone round. "Will you post the portrait?"

"Um. Sure."

She follows me on the spot. And Baker too as he shows her some of his work.

Their heads bent together, they fit, the two beautiful people, and maybe I should back off and leave them to it. But then the busker is waving and walking away and Baker's nudging me.

"Right, Angry Girl. Who's next?"

"I've gotta go," I say, dragging the sole of my shoe so tiny stones scrape. I don't want to go, but I'm probably outstaying my welcome.

Speaking of, there's a message on my phone:

Bert: I miss you and your fool face. Are you busy this week?

I reply with a photo of my camera.

> **Me:** snap, snap! working hard at the exhibition project – you'd be so proud
>
> **Bert:** ALWAYS!
>
> **Bert:** If you need a break, we could hang? Pub or something?

But I can't. I feel abandoned by Bert. Not because she's left me, but because everything she offers is impossible. Go to the pub, come over, chat – how?

I want someone to walk next to me and point out interesting people. Or maybe sit beside me at home while I force myself to crawl through revision. I want to know I won't have to think about Olivia. Or smile at Bert knowing she chose her.

Baker's different. Baker's only ever known this subdued version of me. He doesn't ask me what's wrong when I walk beside him without speaking for half an hour, or question it when I spew some random fact about feral pigeons, like:

"They're all descendants of escaped and released domestic ancestors, did you know that?"

He didn't know that.

Baker insists on walking me home and my counter-insistence is too weak, so we scuff back through town together. He shows me his latest film on his phone. Behind the floor-to-ceiling windows of a local gym a row of people on elliptical machines loop on and on, set to Baker's soundtrack of train noise, the movement of their legs synced to the rhythmic chugging of the train. It's good.

"Don't you worry people won't get it?" I poke the screen so the video replays.

"Well, thanks."

"No, no, I like it. I meant that entirely literally… I've done stuff before and people think it's just whatever they can see with their eyes when, to me, it's something more. Do you know what I mean?" I think of the trash series: abandoned items – mittens, scarves, shoes – all discovered on the street and taken home for their portraits to be taken. Then there was the attempt to document every interesting door in town, curious about the lives inside. Too many aborted projects I could never quite make work.

"Did you like your stuff?" Baker closes one eye and focuses on me.

"I mean…"

Silly question – a tree-falling-in-the-forest thing. If I personally like something but no one else does, does my own approval count for anything? My whole externalized personality has been constructed according to popular vote and it's probably why I've turned out so nothing. Bland. Grey.

"Do you know Vivian Maier?" I say.

"What year's she in?"

I think he's kidding. "She's this amazing street photographer – so prolific during her life. Years and years of work but she didn't even develop most, so they found reels and reels of film after she died."

"Wait, what? Why not?"

"Um … money?" A ripple of frustration runs up my spine. "There's a documentary. Her life was fascinating but sad. She died without being discovered, probably without even knowing how great she was. But she still did it. She still carried on creating to the end."

Baker muses. "Maybe she didn't need discovering and didn't need external validation to feel good about what she was doing. What if creation was the point?"

"That's such…" I shake my head and stop before the truth can escape. Sometimes this boy is so clueless about other people's limitations: money, confidence, access. "I'm sure she'd have liked to be able to pay her bills," I say. "Rather than, spoiler, a bunch of people profiting from her talent after she died. She was totally invisible in her lifetime."

"Oh," Baker says.

And there. There I go making him uncomfortable. There I go putting him off with opinions and a tone too serious for the subject matter. *Way to go, Iris.*

"Anyway, never mind. Maybe she wanted it that way, maybe she didn't. She's good, that's all." I catch Baker's elbow and bring him to a stop. We're on the corner of my road. "This is me."

"OK," he says.

And I'm stuck. I suck at goodbyes.

I don't want to look at him. I don't want him to see me. I don't want him to come any further and see the chapped, tired outside of this house we inherited from Nan, barely touched since, or my neighbour's garden with the fake plastic flowers bleached by the sun. Baker lives a mile away, past the train station and upward. Meadow Hill. Posh.

"Iris." I'm caught off guard by the sound of my name and the expression in his eyes that I can't look directly at. "You know, if you're going to be so bothered by other people's opinions, you could at least start believing people when they say they like you."

I compose my face in a way I hope is withering or at the very least disguises the swoop of hope at what sounds an awful lot like it is, in fact, Baker who I should start believing likes me.

*

When I get inside, I shut my door, lean against it. I prise my boots off without undoing the laces and sit cross-legged on the floor, reaching for Purkoy with one hand while I take out my phone with the other.

A message from Theo – some music link I didn't ask for and don't want. "*Thought you'd like this*," he says, and even reading it, even swiping away the message, takes more emotional energy than I'd like to expend.

I have a new follower, Anna, the busker from today.

Her most recent post is captioned: A lousy day of mostly getting ignored, saved by one person who stopped to tell me she likes my originals. It's good to know someone notices. The push I need to have more confidence in my own stuff?

A new message arrives:

> **Baker:** Same time, same place tomorrow?

A bubble of something barely contained rises inside me and I swallow it. I take a moment, my phone pressed to my chest. And if there was any doubt Baker Davis was going to be trouble for me, that illusion comes crashing down.

22

Same time, same place. We do it all over again. A long morning lingering with our cameras, walking the back roads of town and searching for new and interesting angles. Side by side and drifting away from each other before looping back. We are quiet except when there's something to say.

"What about her?" Baker says, gesturing to a tiny, neat woman with square glasses and a happy-looking German shepherd threatening to pull her off her feet. "Go fuss the pooch, get a snap."

"You talk to her if it's so easy. You're the one who exists with an entourage of admirers around him at all times, so I assume you're more charming than you've ever let on."

"What an intriguing view of my life," he says wryly. "I think what you're referring to are 'friends'? Mostly close friends of Tash's, actually, who're mine too by default. It's hard to find your people, right?"

"God, yeah, impossible for anyone who's friendly and traditionally attractive." Shit me. Baker definitely hears that last part – his mouth starts to move – so I add in a rush, "Um ... but I guess you're strange in less obvious ways." And he chokes on the sip of coffee he's taking. "In good ways."

But not every interaction is beset by excruciating faux pas that haunt me when I go on my night-time bodyless walks, blasting through film at a rate my bank balance can barely handle.

I'm beyond questioning what Baker's doing hanging out with me. Perhaps his friends have left the country with their families and he's at the loosest end of his whole life.

One, two days together and I don't turn invisible. My body remains all solid and here because Baker anchors me like gravity as I tell him about Gerda Taro and Dora Maar. "You have to remember their names," I tell him. "Dora Maar deserves to be more than a footnote in Picasso's biography, because that guy..." I kick a stone.

"He was kind of a jerk?" Baker supplies.

"The worst! A total prick!" I clap, forgetting myself for a moment in the pure joy of cussing out Pablo. "You know who else is terrible?"

"I think you're going to tell me."

I am. And I do.

And then it's our last day.

Baker meets me holding two coffees, one in each hand, the paper cups stamped with the familiar bear logo. There's a brown paper bag clamped between his fingers. He offers a choice of muffins: chocolate or blueberry. I want chocolate, but surely everyone prefers chocolate, so I take blueberry.

"Not long until the big day." Baker points his muffin in my face. "Think you've got enough material to whittle a decent exhibition sub? Feeling like a winner?"

"It's sad after all the time we've spent together you still don't know me at all."

"That's fair."

"I'm feeling … almost adequate," I say, mentally cataloguing my haul.

"Sounds like you've got it in the bag. What'll you do with the cash? Think they'd let you use it for a research trip? Europe? September onwards?"

I stuff my mouth with the last bite of muffin, poke my thumb through the hole in my sleeve and waggle it. "Priorities, Davis. If I was to win – and I won't win—"

"Of course."

"I'd buy a new camera. A Leica Q maybe."

Baker gives a low whistle. "Digital? You sell-out."

"But to be walking in the footsteps of Taro and Franck?" I shrug. The Leica would be everything, but winning was never about that. It's not even about getting my art on the wall of a gallery, a prospect that fills me with as much horror as yearning. Just entering is enough, but if there could be more—

"It would make all of this real," I say, waving a hand at my camera, the street. "It would prove... I don't know. Something."

I'm still grappling with the inexpressible when Baker says, "OK, idea. Look at this."

He brushes crumbs from his fingers before rummaging for his phone. He shows me a series of pictures. Two perfectly executed street shots and then the camera that produced them: a compact and sleek black body, a fixed lens, a price tag half that of my dream camera but equally unattainable. "People like the Ricoh as a budget version of the Q," Baker says. "You could always get one if you don't take home the big prize. I've got one; it's decent. My dad wasn't using it."

I recoil. An expensive parental hand-me-down. "Where've you been hiding that?"

"I barely use it, but selling it seems unfair, so..." And in one heart-stopping snap of Baker's fingers, I see exactly where this is going. "OK, here we go. If you actually stump up the courage to enter the exhibition, you can have my camera."

I stare at him for a long second. "I don't need charity."

Baker's eyebrows crinkle. "It's a bet."

"How's it a bet? I'm already entering anyway, but if I

didn't, I lose nothing. That's not how bets work – what do you get?"

We stop walking. Our gaze locks. There's a beat of strange silence and I widen my eyes like, *OK?* Because it's definitely his turn to talk. Baker laughs and looks at the ground, swinging his arms out and turning. "Look, shit! I don't want anything, OK? Take the bet!"

I eye the back of his head, trying to work out if he's serious. Trying to work out if I can possibly accept.

"Shake on it?" Baker holds out a hand. I give him mine. "Why do you make everything so difficult, Angry Girl?" he says in an oddly soft voice.

And I could almost swear Baker Davis is blushing.

*

I see them through my camera lens. Of course I do.

I've left Baker and his tripod at the peak of the high street, under the statue of a long-dead bishop and I'm wandering, knowing I'll find him again when I need to be found.

My lens is aimed at a girl whose soft brown hair is blowing over her face, catching between her glossy lips. She's looking up to the sky in a moment of calm and there's a white cloud hanging in the blue above her. Before I press the shutter, a familiar duo enter the background of the scene. Bert's teeth are tearing at a baguette, Olivia's toying with the lid of a takeaway box. Heat swoops through me and I scramble into the nearest alley out of sight.

I peer back and see them collapse on to a bench, Bert's

mouth moving a hundred miles a minute, Olivia's head bobbing along.

I wonder what they're chatting about. Who.

I retreat. Tuck myself further down the alley. Back among the warm stink of restaurant wheelie bins.

I return without my body.

And, when the girls finish their lunch and get up, I follow. Of course I follow.

23

Bert and Olivia end up in the charity shop on Castle Street where the good swag always turns up. Bert once found an ink-stained Mulberry handbag, cleaned it up and flipped it for double.

As Olivia enters after Bert, neither of them notices the door catching on an invisible obstacle before it closes.

"You can't meet men you don't know," Bert says as she makes a beeline for her size rack.

Olivia drags after Bert, trailing her fingers over a scarf. "Isn't that how your parents met?"

"That's different. How do you know they're not full-on perverts?"

"One guy! I've spoken to him and he's normal. He's *sweet.*"

"Did you tell him you're seventeen? Because if he knows, he is, by definition, not normal."

"He's only twenty-four."

"Jesus! Are his knees OK?"

"Can you drop it? I'm not going to meet him. It's harmless. It's just nice to speak to someone who's not some immature sixth-former and also, you know, doesn't think I'm evil incarnate."

Bert softens. "No one thinks that."

Olivia plucks at some vintage jeans. "Do you think these would be cute with a belt?"

"No."

"Shit. Say what you think, Bert."

"I think you should stop caring what random men think of you. You're worth more." Bert sweeps her hand up and down to indicate the whole of Olivia. "And they don't even know how brilliant you are on the inside. The same way that Theo didn't. Or Ben. Or Spade."

"Oh yeah, I'm such a gem. A great friend?" Bert hesitates and, in the hesitation, Olivia hardens. "Exactly."

"I don't have the energy for this, O," Bert says with a noisy breath. "You know what I seriously think about you and her and … this. Who benefits from me telling you again?"

The two of them fall into silence. Bert swipes at a rack.

"It doesn't matter," Olivia says. "No one cares. When it comes to guys, you're either hot or invisible."

"Maybe try option B for a while?"

"Sorry the way I spend my Friday nights doesn't meet

your high intellectual standards." Olivia jams her thumbs in her jean pockets and shoves her chin forward. "What are you even looking for anyway?"

"You're a smart cookie, Olivia Edis. But I see what you're doing with this change of subject," Bert says with a sharp look. "A cute suit for my cousin's wedding." Bert turns back to the rack. "Not polyester and not black, which apparently is too much to ask. My mum wants me in a dress. Imagine. She's far too invested in my life at the moment."

Olivia waves at her with the empty sleeve of a floral dress. "Have you considered that might be too specific for a charity shop haul?"

The two of them comb the rails and Bert pulls out a shirt and some bright trousers to try on. While she's behind the curtain, Olivia stands outside as changing room security, trying on hats from a nearby shelf. With a straw trilby on, she leans close and shouts into the mirror, "Have you seen Iris this week?"

The shock of my name makes me real again. Instead of drifting around the store like a phantom, I'm suddenly aware of my feet on the floor, my hand on my camera. I exist again.

"Nada," comes a shout from behind the curtain. "She's avoiding me. Apparently I'm now the kind of trash she doesn't even want to photograph, so huge thanks."

"You're enormously welcome," Olivia shouts, then

deflates and adds, "Shit. I'm so sorry, Bert. I didn't think I'd take you down with me."

Bert yanks the curtain open to frame her face. Olivia replaces the trilby with a tweed deerstalker. Bert sighs. "I'd understand if she was angry. At least we could have things out and she could give me a well-deserved bollocking. But she's … drifting away."

Olivia says, "Do you think she's OK?"

It's a bit late to be worried about me. The words dance on the tip of my tongue. I bite them back and feel my fingers start to tingle, along with the tears pricking my eyes.

Bert disappears back behind the curtain. "She's had a bit going on, hasn't she? Being betrayed by her best friends and her boyfriend and all?"

Olivia slumps against the wall and says, "I'm sure if we could talk, we could work it out."

"You're giving your powers of persuasion so much credit," Bert replies.

"No, but she has to listen. We're friends."

Olivia invoking our friendship like it's a reason to talk to her has finished me off. I've seen and heard enough. If I stay, I won't be able to be quiet. I turn.

"You should hear Theo talk to me now," Olivia says so quietly I wonder if Bert will even hear through the curtain. "Like he's so disgusted with me for existing and for ruining things between him and Iris. As if I was the one…"

A stray hanger catches and snags on my hip. The rack

jangles and the girl behind the counter startles at the noise. She looks in my direction.

"Iris?" Olivia says.

And she's not wrong.

I hold up my hand. Pink fingers. Jagged nails. I'm back. Right when I don't want to be.

It's too late to run.

Olivia shakes her head and says, "What are you doing here?"

I've never been a good liar. So I say nothing.

"Did you…?" Olivia steps closer. "What are you doing *inside* a shop?"

Bert's head pops round the changing-room curtain. We lock eyes. "Oh my god." A million expressions play out over Bert's face before she decides on careful neutrality. "Well, good, you can tell me if this shirt's any good. I need a little Green honesty in my life."

"Sorry." I step back and the clothes rail gives another ugly clang. "I didn't mean to…"

I back up. Leave. Wrench the door open and speed through. I'm striding away when I hear Olivia's voice behind me. "Wait! Iris!"

I speed up but it's futile. Only one of us trains for this sort of thing. Olivia catches up easily and slows from her jog to match my pace.

"Iris," she says again.

I hitch my bag higher on my shoulders and hunch down,

trying to keep moving, but Olivia jogs alongside then steps in front of me.

Part of me is glad. I'm tired of running from this problem. I want to hear what else Olivia has to say. I want her to undo it all with a simple apology and take us back to how we used to be.

"I want to talk," she says. "We need to talk. We can't avoid each other all year."

"No?" It's hard to look at her. I focus instead on the people walking past. This toddler on her dad's shoulders as Mum hops alongside him, trying to flatten their daughter's ridiculous frilly skirt.

"Please," Olivia says. A word I've never been able to resist.

"Where's Bert?" I ask.

"Probably caught in a static electric forcefield from wrestling all that second-hand polyester." Disgustingly I feel my mouth twitch to match Olivia's.

"Who are you in town with?" she says.

I blink at her.

"Are you doing OK?"

"Except for this."

Her smile dies. Her pupils skitter back and forth, assessing. "I need you to understand I didn't mean for any of this. It just happened."

I fold my arms.

"I don't know why I did it. I got … I got … swept up

in it." Olivia swipes at the stray blonde hairs tickling her nose. "He was Theo – he was charming and funny and at all the drama-crowd parties. He's always there. And we talked and, OK, flirted, but the flirting was nothing. It was harmless." She shrugs. "And then it wasn't and it was too late to stop."

"You could have stopped."

She flinches. "What do you want to know? When it started? Who made the first move?"

"No." I don't want any of that. I want, so badly, to be able to forgive her. I want her to say the right words to make this better. Instead, I can feel the familiar tug towards disintegration. My mind begins to swirl like water disappearing down a hole.

"You must think I'm such a bad person," Olivia says, "but if you knew how sorry I am… I'm so sorry. I'd give anything to take it back."

"Do you still like him? Are you still … with him?" I think of Sadie. Of the messages from Theo on my phone. As though he thinks I want to hear from him. And I don't know why he thinks of me so often now, not when I was so easy to forget when Olivia was in front of him.

"God, no," Olivia says with a curl of her lips. "Look, Iris, that's all over and I'm still your friend and I've been trying to give you space and not pressure you or guilt trip you, but—"

"Do you remember," I say, balling my hand and

running my thumb over my knuckle, running my mind over a memory, "that time you slipped over coming out of Enzo's?"

"I still have the scar." She points to her lip where a faint white line chips her cupid's bow. "Concrete step one, Olivia nil."

"I've never seen someone bleed like that." I worry at the cuticle at the side of my thumb. "We fell asleep on your floor talking about whether there was an afterlife."

She nods solemnly. "Because I'd come very close to death that day."

Last term, last day. It must have been past one o'clock and I almost wept when Olivia drunkenly declared she needed pizza to get her home. I was so ready for sleep.

An hour before Olivia's brush with the greasy-pizza-joint grim reaper, we were wasted on the dancefloor, pasted together, Olivia's arms round me as she slurred into my ear, "You're so pretty tonight. Those guys're looking at you."

"They're definitely looking at you. You're the hot one."

"No, no, no. You, Iris, you." Olivia leaned away and I clocked them through the haze of heat and flashing lights. Older. Good-looking in that ultra-groomed way. Olivia said, "You have that mysterious thing going for you guys love. That dry humour. The sense of challenge."

"None of that's on purpose."

She squinted at me. "No?"

"No one's into it."

"Theo is."

"Is he, though?"

"I just wish anyone liked me like that. No one ever likes me." She swung off my neck. I caught her hand, pulled her back.

"I like you."

Olivia got this sad smashed smile on her face. "That doesn't count," she said, and then she pulled herself taller, smoothed her hair. Her eyes brightened and flicked back and forth between me and them. "Let's go over. They're looking."

I looked. I wondered why we cared. But on any other day perhaps I would have too, my mind in that moment too full of Theo.

And then Bert stumbled back from the bar, shoving wet cups into our sweaty hands as Olivia danced away, transforming as she went, no longer bouncing but swaying. No longer walking but slinking.

I don't know why it sticks in my mind. The sight of Olivia across the dancefloor. The guy's thick hands on her. She was smiling, but she looked so unlike herself.

I wish I could go back, that I could grab Olivia's hand a little firmer and ask her why she needed to leave. Go back further: year eleven, year ten, before then. Year five, back to being those Three Kings proudly cradling foil props. I wish I could hold us together. I wish I'd never known Theo.

"I wish I counted," I say now and Olivia's mouth flatlines. I shake my head. Of course she doesn't remember.

"I want us to be OK," Olivia whispers. "I miss you."

My words disappear. Olivia stares at me with this mix of pity and longing I can't bear.

You did this, I want to say.

"I think … I think this tiny part of me liked that he had a girlfriend. And he still wanted me," she says, voice so low. "Because I must have been *so* irresistible … and that was irresistible. That feeling. Even more than him." Olivia's face crumples. "But it wasn't because it was you. I hate that it was you."

There. The part you don't say aloud. Ugly and true. It's what I wanted to hear and now I wish I hadn't. And perhaps this is why we call it a crush, because of how it pushes everyone else out. Or perhaps because of everything we'll willingly destroy to get what we think we want.

"It was me," I say.

Olivia's shoulders shift. I take a step back. The invisible thread connecting us pulls tight and we pause.

"I'm so sorry," she says for the last time.

And when she's gone, the shaking starts – my hands tingling, my lips turning numb – and I clench and unclench my hands, watching them, waiting for them to go too, waiting for the world to turn silver and carry me away.

I want it. I will it. But the fingers stay. Stupid stubborn body. Stupid hands.

24

My phone lights up as I'm sloping inside. Dad. There's no sound, but the flashing red and green is urgent and harassing. I pin my tongue between my teeth and consider swiping it away. A phone call and Dad is a fatally stressful combination and the last thing I need.

"Good to know you still exist," Dad says when I pick up, his mock-jovial tone making me grit my teeth.

I'm halfway through the door. Inside the kitchen, Mum's head dips into view. Eavesdropping.

"How's life?" he says, and, without waiting to hear, adds, "Imogen sends her love."

"How's Imogen?" No further encouragement needed, he rattles on. As I prise off my boots, I clock Mum again and kick myself for mentioning Dad's girlfriend by name.

"What's new with you?" Dad says.

"I'm, um, busy." I wedge my phone in place, freeing a hand to stroke Purks. The time period between now and last speaking to Dad blurs into oblivion. Not a single shareable detail remains. "School starts again tomorrow. It's going to be … busy."

There's a subtle smacking on the line. A tiny wet tut. "That's everything in your exciting teenage world? School's busy?"

My hand freezes on Purkoy's back. "I have … an exhibition coming up?"

"Your photography?"

"Yep."

"Sounds major. I hope your other subjects are getting a look in? Exams must start soon?"

"They're fine. Still a while off." Typical Dad. What he does for a living, I'm not sure. Something with businesses, being paid a lot of money for his opinion, so naturally he thinks his opinion is valuable. Must be nice. I consider mentioning the prize: maybe it would appeal to Dad's competitive side? But I let the idea pass.

"You'll need a break in the summer?" Dad says. "If you're too busy for a holiday, you can at least visit. Get yourself to London and it's all on me. If you want to do anything, that is."

It's never a question, always a demand.

"I can't afford the train. Maybe autumn?"

"I pay your allowance."

A pause. All my money's going into the exhibition. The frames I picked out with their matt black woodgrain and deep off-white mounts. They were perfect but pricey. My entire-zilchy-life-savings kind of pricey.

"I'll pay for your ticket too," he says, another excuse crumbling before he issues the ominous command that I "make a decision on dates" and hangs up with a curt goodbye.

"How's your dad?" Mum shouts. She bangs a saucepan against the edge of the drawer and the sound clangs in my skull as I hang round the kitchen door.

"I don't know."

"You've just been speaking to him." She laughs and looks at her hands, awkward. Reluctant to look at me as though I'm an extension of him. Tainted by association.

"You can ask him yourself. Next time you talk about me."

"We don't talk about you. I only give him the headlines because you won't."

"So you do?"

"I'd rather not." Mum's back flexes as she pummels the saucepans into submission. "As you're aware."

On the window sill Mum's phone is plugged into a speaker. I lean over and hit play. The Goo Goo Dolls start up mid-song. I take a stack of plates from the drying rack as Mum sings a line, checking her own phone and interrupting herself to say, "He's messaged me now. Your dad, I mean."

"What did he say?"

She taps at her screen, typing a reply. "Requesting mediation."

There are things you understand without being told. It's like I was born knowing how my dad makes Mum feel. It's in her guarded expression and the way she won't say exactly what's in his message. She translates. Obfuscates.

"It's not up to you," I say.

"Of course—"

"Did you tell him?"

Her body slumps. "You weren't exactly clear with him yourself, love."

That's different, I want to say. He'll kick off. He'll twist my words. He'll make it even more difficult next time. It's different because I have to see him sometime. He's my dad. Half of me. I can't say no, can I? And the worst part is wishing I didn't want to. Wishing, every time, that the next visit might be different.

"He won't care. I'll be letting him off the hook."

"That's not true," Mum says, her voice going low. "He doesn't always show it, but he values his dad–daughter time; I know he does."

That makes one of us.

"How was work?"

She gives me a hard stare. Then relents, filling me in on the care home, her favourite residents: Meggy the former romance novelist with a passion for cryptic crosswords,

Geoff with his stock market insights and conspiracy theories.

My phone lights up. No doubt Dad's looking for round two. But when I check, it's not him.

Bert: I hope you're OK after today. Olivia wouldn't tell me what happened

Bert: We'll speak tomorrow?

Unsure what to say, I like the message, then hold my phone till it goes dark.

As I exit the kitchen Mum says, "Pick a date. He's your dad."

And I grab my camera from the sofa where I left it and open the front door.

"I'm off to Bert's," I shout and let the door slam.

That's not where I go. My body falls away and the world turns silver and I walk and walk and walk, until my mind quiets and my feet ache. I pass Victorian bay windows lit like lanterns, discover a pedestrian underpass collaged with graffiti; I go to the fringes of town, past the station and the park, away from the sprawl of new houses, their light scarring the dark. Across the rugby field, the concrete bridge over the stream, I sit and watch traffic streak across the horizon.

I always liked motorways. Being a passenger on a long

trip, looking into passing cars and seeing clues about the families inside. Bikes or canoes strapped to the racks, boots full to overflowing with bedding and stuffed animals. Families together, kids in the back on their Nintendos, a couple bickering, a lone driver singing along in their bubble. My favourites were the families, always. The complete ones. Two parents, two kids. That looked like perfection to me.

I watch the faraway traffic and think about everything ahead of me: facing Theo, Olivia and Bert again at school, the countdown to the exhibition, exams, the end of education. The rest of my life.

It all feels impossible. Every bit. But especially tomorrow.

25

Here's how I deal with Monday: I walk in without my body and sit at the back of class without remembering to switch myself on again. Easily done. In first period, attendance is called and, for once, there's no rising anxiety in anticipation of my name.

"Iris Green?"

"Here."

No one notices – not the sound of my voice emanating from nothing, not my absence.

I love it, though. Sitting in class and not needing to remember to sit a certain way or maintain a certain expression. Not dreading a teacher shooting me a sudden question. Information goes in more easily.

My visibility is like training muscles. Probably. The

more I use it, the more intuitive it becomes. No more involuntary reappearances.

*

At break I wander between classmates catching snippets of conversation amid the usual white noise. In my daydreams I uncover confessions or stumble over someone joking that "Iris Green is grey" and revealing themselves as my bathroom wall assassin. In reality there's no trace of me. Not a mention. So much of everything else.

I catch sight of Baker with his friends and veer away knowing I would never. Could never. And not just because of my history of pinging back into existence whenever he's around.

I go to the darkroom and bring myself back – relaxing my brain and focusing on good things – before disappearing in a different way, into my own head and making other things visible instead. My print blooms in the bath, a whirl of detail on a formerly blank page. As the busker emerges, so too do the high-street shops stretching the length of the paper.

Magic. Sort of.

I flick on the light. The busker's sketched in black and white, a cobbled road tracks through her hair and I'm unsure about the alignment. The drying rack's filled with attempts at recapturing my first double-exposed portraits of Baker. I keep that one at my fingertips, here on the side like a talisman, but it hasn't helped. Its successors feel too self-conscious, too try-hard.

I need a second opinion, so I take a snap of the shots with my phone: the one of the busker and the one of Baker and send them to someone I trust.

Baker: Look at him! A good-looking guy for sure

Baker: I guess I'd better start planning a farewell party for my camera

He likes it. Possibly. Or perhaps he's simply being generous because he knows I'm out of ideas. I squint at the print, try to imagine it framed.

Baker: Where's the rest of your haul?

Baker: Updates when you're done?

I roll my eyes for the benefit of the empty room.

Baker: I'm imagining you making the face. Like you want to smile but you also want to disapprove of my demand

Me: i'm not making that face

Baker: You are, though

Baker: The Iris face

He's right. I was making the face. But not any more. Now my smile strains at my cheeks.

Bloody Baker.

> **Me:** you can stop now. i've signed up, i'm developing work, i'm committed. your work is done
>
> **Baker:** I'm just trying to feel needed
>
> **Baker:** And it's dull being back here – I'm missing your impassioned monologues about why each and every shot you've taken was bad and terrible and the worst photo ever

I read the message. I put my phone down and pick it up. Read it again.

Missing my impassioned monologues is very different from missing me.

I let my fingers circle the glossy surface of a portrait, its white edges, and try to see it as the judges would. All these years of being too scared to show my work press down on me as the countdown begins. Not long to go. Just a few short days to show the best I can do. And hope it's enough.

An impulse shudders up my spine. To reach out, take the work in my hands and rip it into pieces so small that no one will ever see.

Instead, I occupy my hands with my phone. I can't keep distracting Baker, but I have no problem distracting myself, falling into everyone else's lives. It's all there, curated online, a more reliable source of updates than eavesdropping invisibly in the common room. I check on Theo and Olivia. I can't not. Theo's updates are dominated by band rehearsals, his guitar, notebook pages full of scribbled genius. Everything's in black and white recently and I hate him a little, as though he stole my aesthetic. There are snippets of a music video in progress, Theo's hands moodily strumming intro chords.

Olivia's whole grid is a blur of cute trips and outings with her mum, Bert, her drama friends. I scroll back to highlights from the play that give me a brief, inexplicable pang of guilt – as though missing it meant it's *me* who let *her* down. A photo of her all made up and lightly drunk, her tongue sticking out sideways is captioned This mess, and the comments gush that she's adorable and stunning.

If I was to post the same photo, the same caption, it wouldn't elicit the same result. It wouldn't be received in the same spirit. I would simply be a mess.

The lunch bell takes me by surprise. Somehow hours have disappeared this way – sitting and thinking without thinking. I haven't finished developing my haul or begun to filter what I have into some semblance of coherence. I've missed a lesson. Panic knifes my ribs, but I breathe it away. Think about that later. Maybe.

My phone lights up. A new message from Dad:

Dad: Iris, DATES?

He's such a caps lock kind of guy. I sweep him away.

Another:

Bert: You in your cupboard?

Bert: You can't hide from me for ever

I poke at my phone screen. The group chat has been dead since that one fateful Monday. Every time I open my messages, I see it there, the last insignificant message still unread.

Olivia: hmmm, yeah, they both did. did...

I'd have to open the thread to read the rest. I should leave the chat, but I left it too late and now I'm trapped. Story of my life.

The door swings open in a rush of cold, fresh outside air and noise and it's Bert, pompom earrings and patterned tights breaking up the regulation dress code. And she's here and I'm here and she looks so relieved and disappointed.

"Well, thank god, you and your debilitating self-esteem issues are still with us. Where have you been? I haven't seen you ... well, let's say all day for a start. Have you been here all alone?"

"Yeah. Hey. It's been… Yeah." And my heart gives a lacklustre kick of anger at Bert for coming here and acting the wronged party when *she* hasn't been alone. *She* has been with Olivia. *She* has been fine.

"I've been working." I pick up the double exposure of Baker and wave it at Bert. "Look at what I did."

"Words I never thought I'd hear from Iris Green." Bert takes it with an arched eyebrow. "Oh damn." Bert holds the print up to the light. "The effect on this is so good. Is this Baker?" Bert studies my face and tuts. "Ah. That's where you disappeared to all break? You were hanging with manic pixie dream boy?"

"We're not calling him that." My cheeks give Bert her answer. "We were working on our exhibition projects."

"Weird euphemism…" Bert lingers over the Baker portrait. She moves closer to the worktop and glances over the portraits and street work. "These are kind of amazing, Iris. You're going to smash this exhibition."

I shake my head, my skin prickling all over like the praise is bringing me out in a rash.

"What else have you got here?" Bert says. "Where are the trash photos? I suddenly realize I may have been unfairly disparaging about the concept."

"No, you were right. They were nothing."

"You can't accept the word of a woman who didn't even see the damn things, Green. Gimme."

I hesitate. It's so ingrained in me that this idea was a joke.

Is it true that Bert never even saw them? She opens and closes her hands in a grabby motion and stares me down. "You can't be so secretive all your life."

"You're going to be so sorry you asked." I slip from my stool to rummage in my tray, under layers of street to where my failed projects are hiding.

I pull out the top three trash photos and fan them out on the worktop, my heart beating faster as Bert looks at them and then me.

"These are not quite what you described."

One print shows a pair of mittens on a string, the first clean and laundered, the second exactly as discovered – filthy with mud and damp. They're both spread out over the paving slabs of my garden at home. Another shows a hat perched on a mannequin's head, adorned with a dried-leaf corsage. The last is a children's shoe lying at the bottom of a slide. They're all simple still lifes. Nothing special.

Bert looks up, serious. "I'm sorry if I made you think I was taking the piss out of these."

"It's OK." She definitely was. I carefully sweep my prints back into a stack together, leaving just the shoe showing.

"We should hang out," Bert says, eyes still on me. "Properly. I need someone to save me from Mum's attempts to make me endure every nineties romcom ever committed to celluloid."

"They stopped using celluloid in the fifties," I correct before I can stop myself. "Too flammable."

"Not entirely my point."

My phone lights up. I see Baker's name and make a dive for it.

Baker: Want to do something later?

Bert's attention drops to the screen before I can whip it away. "Or we could do now? Lunch? I feel like..." Bert's mouth twists sideways. It's not like Bert to self-censor. What does she feel like?

I hesitate, then realize there's no question. I have another engagement. One I'm on the brink of being late for. Shit. Nothing says "mess of a human" quite like being late for counselling.

"I actually have to be somewhere," I say as I start to shove things in my bag. "Soon, OK?"

"Ah, yay. I can't wait till it's my turn for friendship rations."

"I really do have to go," I say, freezing as I realize how this sounds.

There's a pause.

Everything in me screams to relent – to offer tomorrow lunch or night or the following day – but Bert cracks first, flicking at the edge of one of my prints and saying, "I don't understand why you've been avoiding me. Don't you want to hang out?"

My body tenses. I can't tell her I do. I sort of do, but it's complicated now in a way it didn't used to be. I do, but not now because I have somewhere to be.

"Wow. OK," she says. "Message received."

"I do," I say, and I think if I could make her understand… "Everything's too hard at the moment."

"Hanging out with me is too hard?"

"No."

Yes.

"No," I say again. "Everything … else. I'm…" I put a hand beside my head and make it explode. "Shit, Bert, I'm a mess. I'm sorry."

"Oh my god! What? Come here!" Bert makes grabby hands and I give her mine so she can shake them, saying, "You've been going through a lot, but you're not a mess – you're fine."

She smiles in a way I know is meant to be reassuring, laced with concern that may or may not be real. Either way, I don't feel reassured. I press my lips together in a poor imitation of reciprocity, extricate myself and move closer to the door. "I have to go."

"Where?"

"Just…" I imagine how long it'll take if I start to explain. "Somewhere."

Bert looks me up and down and sighs. She opens her mouth again. And then shuts it without saying whatever else's on her mind.

26

"The worst thing now is it feels like the Olivia and Theo from before didn't exist," I say. "Because I thought I knew them. I trusted them both and I was wrong, so how do I trust myself now?"

In her armchair across the room, Nicole nods. Despite my small breakdown last session, she welcomed me with the same friendly neutrality today. Perhaps that's why, despite the scratchy armchair, airless room, long silences and constant attention, I feel almost comfortable. Perhaps that's why I opened with Theo and Olivia, the easiest place to start. A clearly delineated problem with a beginning and an end.

"They did this knowing it would hurt me and I can't even wrap my head around why. Even if I was the worst person in the world. It would have been so easy to break up with me first."

Nicole considers me. "You feel like they deliberately set out to hurt you?"

"Surely they knew I'd find out. And they didn't care."

"That's a very understandable way to view things. But it's also worth remembering a lot of people aren't very considerate of others for all sorts of different reasons. You think about things very deeply and thoroughly while they might not. They might prioritize their own feelings in any given moment and live to regret it when they see the consequences of those actions."

My mind whirrs. "Like what?"

"Getting dumped by their girlfriend? That's a big consequence Theo might have hoped to avoid. After all, by choosing your friend, the other party in the betrayal was also incentivized to keep quiet and prevent you finding out. Maybe he thought he had the situation under control?"

Control? I sit back and fold my leg up so it's lying across my opposite knee. I rest my elbow on it and cradle my chin. "Theo told me once…" I start and then stop, because it feels so pathetic to say aloud. But Nicole waits. She makes space and it feels genuinely safe. "He was always trying to get me alone; said he didn't like my friends. I guess that was half true."

"That does sound like someone who likes control. And maybe not a great way to treat someone you're supposed to like – you're allowed to have other relationships."

I run my thumb under my chin and feel the skin stretch

against the bone. "I suppose I made him feel insecure sometimes too, though. I do think that was real."

"And how did he make you feel?"

"Replaceable."

"What was it he did to make you feel that way?"

"He … he literally said he could replace me." I almost laugh. I drop my foot back to the floor and bunch my hands up in my lap so I can run my thumb over my finger in small circles. Round and round like the inside of my mind. "He's here all the time. I still have to see him in history and sometimes he'll message me and I have to be polite. It's exhausting."

Nicole nods. "Have you considered not talking to him any more?"

I blink at her because no.

"Obviously it's entirely up to you, but it's not unreasonable to set a boundary with people who've hurt you. You don't have to see or speak to people to make them comfortable at your own expense. You are allowed to prioritize your own feelings. Do you ever do that?"

I purse my lips. I have the awful sense I might cry if I speak.

Nicole uncrosses and recrosses her legs. "Were you angry about the way Theo treated you?"

"No." I watch my thumb tracing circles. "The funny thing is … he did replace me, didn't he, in the end?"

Nicole doesn't so much as twitch. I guess it's not funny ha ha.

"It must be me. There must be something so wrong with me." I catch the inside of my cheek with my teeth and look sideways at the blank space of the wall.

"Iris, his behaviour is a reflection of his own character, not yours. The things he said to you, the way he made you feel, would you tell someone that or make them feel that? Your friend? Your ex-boyfriend, even – anyone?"

"No."

"And why not?"

She's not smiling, but I wonder if she feels it, deep down. The triumph of this gotcha moment. The corner of my own mind she's backed me into. I know what she wants me to say: I wouldn't tell them that because it's cruel. I wouldn't tell them because it's not true about anyone.

The only person it's ever been true about is me.

"No one deserves that," I say quietly.

"No," Nicole agrees.

*

I can't go from Nicole straight back to class, not when she's had her hand in my mind, stirring it all up. I'm too dizzy, too muddled to sit in a silent room. Instead, I switch my body off and go back, not to my darkroom, but the scene of the original crime.

Third cubicle on the left.

Iris Green is grey.

There's been an addition.

LOL so dull theo hastings falls asleep in her

Ouch. Someone didn't get our break-up bulletin. The words – old and new – have been scrubbed over by a sympathetic cleaner, but they are still legible. Clearly a bit of permanent marker on chipboard is harder to eradicate than my whole body.

I dig for a pen. A biro isn't ideal, but I go to work, the pen seemingly working away in mid-air in my invisible hand, cross-hatching, scrubbing away the letters one by one. *Green is grey.* Grey. Gone. But never erased. The words are seared across my memory like they've been branded there.

The thing about toilet graffiti is it tells accepted truths. Everyone knows Suzi T likes the lads and Jess Arthur's got enormous teeth. So, I guess, everyone knows Iris Green is a personality-free space. Not for nothing did Joss Steadman nickname me Resting Blank Face.

I slip my camera from my bag and take a photo of the blanked-out graffiti. A twin of the first, only now the message in the frame is obliterated.

The main door of the toilets bangs open so hard the cubicle walls quiver. I yank my underwear down and crash to the cold seat, determined not to be accused of the criminal act of standing in a locked toilet without intent to pee. Only belatedly remembering a person without a body doesn't need excuses, followed by the swift realization that noisily smashing around inside my cubicle was the worst possible choice.

Shit. Now the other person knows I'm here. The someone yanks open the door to the next cubicle and slams the door with excessive force.

I wait, willing myself back, but seized by a strange performance anxiety, despite the wall between us.

The someone exhales, breath wobbling. There's no telltale toilet sound, just uneven breathing and the unravelling of toilet roll.

A crier. I tense up. *Come back.* But panic steals my focus so I'm stuck, invisible, hoping someone else's bladder needs emptying or the person beside me will cry herself out and leave. I could go. Sneak out and even if this person leaves right after, no matter how quickly, she'll think I disappeared by completely legitimate means. But I am defeated by the thought of them sad and alone in a cubicle like … well, me.

My neighbour blows her nose. Only a monster would keep quiet at this point, invisible or not. And although history teaches us that in any given situation, Iris Green will say entirely the wrong thing, saying something imperfectly is better than keeping perfectly quiet. Anything.

I lean forward for a view under the cubicle wall, my mouth cracked, willing myself to simply say it: are you OK?

The toilet seat clunks as my weight shifts.

All sounds cease. I picture her frozen to the seat, listening.

Then I see them: the shoes. Black (obviously), suede (posh). They're these flat almond-toed things with decorative lacing. Affected and retro in this vaguely Mary Poppins way. They're drama-girl shoes.

They're Olivia's shoes.

My words of sympathy die in my mouth.

What the hell is Olivia doing crying in the school toilets?

The bell clatters overhead and I use the sound to hop on to the toilet rim and peer over the top of the divide, hoping she's using the space purely for privacy.

Luckily I'm right. My bird's-eye view shows Olivia sitting on top of the cistern, feet on the closed seat, chin in her hands.

I shuffle awkwardly on the seat, struggling to maintain balance now I'm using my feet and not the considerably greater surface area of my bum. The clunk of plastic against ceramic makes Olivia's head come up.

"Hello?" she calls. "Are you OK in there?"

I freeze. She hops off her toilet and crouches down, peering under the divide. No feet. Nothing to see there.

She stands back up.

I should run. Leave. Lurking in the toilets is a bad look even for an invisible girl.

Olivia steps up on to her toilet rim and her face comes hurtling up towards mine. I shift my grip wider as Olivia's hands land between them on the flimsy cubicle divider.

We are face to face. Only she has no idea.

She's red. Puffy. Strands of white-blonde hair clinging wetly to her cheeks. I study her and, no matter how I stretch my brain, I cannot fathom what Olivia Edis would be doing crying her face off in the girls' bathroom at this particular moment in time.

She peers down into my seemingly empty cubicle and I follow her gaze, skipping over her white fingers smudged with black ink on the dividing wall, right down into my own empty space. The strangest fear bubbles up: I'll return. Now. Here. While we are eyeball to eyeball.

And then she's gone. Out into the toilet block. The squeak of an ancient tap, the splash of running water and the rustle of paper towels. The slamming of the door. The heave of relief from my own sore throat.

I step down shakily from the toilet and leave my cubicle. Outside there's the sound of students beginning their next period migration.

On instinct I open the door of Olivia's recently abandoned cubicle and peer in. Nothing. *Duh, Iris.* What else did I expect? But then I turn back on myself and, as I let go of the door, thick black lines of ink catch my eye. Fresh and bold and not unlike the ink on Olivia's fingers as she looked into the hollow of me. Capital letters on the reverse of the door:

YOU ARE UGLY UNDERNEATH

I stare at the words for a moment and then slam the cubicle.

As I'm making my way out, I stand in front of the empty mirror, breathe the damp, ammonia-scented air of the girls' bathroom and try to bring myself back. I shake my head to clear it of Olivia. The words. The mess of it all.

One of the last things Nicole said to me was this: "We can't control what people have said; past criticism has already happened and so has the hurt, the same way Theo and Olivia will always have cheated. But we can try to let go. Of the words, the self-blame. We can be kinder to ourselves."

As easy as that? Let go of the voices in my head. The ones from way before, buried deep, pointing out I'm wrong, wrong, wrong. The voices of my classmates, my old teachers, my dad, Theo, all the people who've told me I needed to be different. The ones that have become so much a part of me, they use my own voice now. Not so much words as sinew – threading me together in this shape I've been holding for so long.

If I let go of all that, what would be left behind?

Later – much later – when I'm lying in bed and the day is playing over in my head, the question comes back to me again and gets tangled up in those black words inked on the cubicle door and I wonder whose words are haunting Olivia Edis?

27

It's a mistake to meet Baker after school. The day weighs down on me: exhibition stress, Bert, counselling, Olivia. I shift my tie, uncomfortable in my uniform, aware all over again of the differences between us. Baker's leaving soon – study leave, exams and then he'll be done. And after that?

"Venice in January will be cold, but at least I'll avoid the crowds," Baker says, midway through a breakdown of his travel itinerary. He leans over and gives me a nudge. "I'll be sending you personalized updates on my artistic progression, naturally, and trying to get you out for a visit."

"Right," I say.

"Or … not?"

"Just how *do* you pay for all your stuff?" I blurt. "The cameras, editing software, your trip? Where does that … come from?"

"Films mostly. Little social media trailers for businesses. My dad recommended me to one of his mates who has a carpentry business and needed a video."

"Oh. Nepotism?"

"If you want to call it that." Baker's mouth quirks. "That's how I'll keep travelling. Make videos, take pictures."

"How..." *Incredible. Enviable. Impossible.* "... great. For you. You're serious about the never-coming-back thing?"

"Yeah, I guess. Not for a good long while."

A group of students overtakes us as I pause to take a photo: a toddler lunging for a passing tabby cat. "What if the grand plan fails?" *Click.* "You end up broke and unemployed with only a bunch of photos and memories?"

"Doesn't sound like failure to me." Baker cocks an eyebrow. "If I don't get to stay out there, at least I tried. I took a running jump into the void while others chose to drop straight into the safety net. Maybe I'll get bruised and battered, but failure would be being too scared to try." He has a hand clasped to his chest by the end of this little speech. A self-aware grin on his face. It's meant to be charming.

I shake my head.

"What?" he says, teeth flashing as his hand drops.

"Of course. Your whole life plan is a back-up plan." It comes out a little harsher than intended, but Baker chuckles all the same. "And your parents are fine with this?"

He shrugs. "They're coming round. It's my life. I don't owe anyone else anything."

"They've kind of fed you, raised you…"

"OK, but they're the ones who brought me into this world. A broken economic system? War? Environmental collapse? Thanks, great party. They can't blame me for wanting to make my own existence more tolerable."

"I guess…" I focus on the houses, the pavement, the cracks made by tree roots. I pick at the edge of my thumbnail until it starts to peel.

"What else am I meant to do, Angry Girl? Sit at a desk and fill up my piggy bank hoping to get a life later down the line?"

I shake my head. *Stay*, I think. And that's not OK. A selfish thought.

"I reckon they owe it to me to get behind what makes me happy and if they don't? I'm done making concessions for other people." Baker's grin is gone now. His face gets that closed, determined look. "So no. I'm not coming back if I can help it."

"Huh," I say, the edges of my mouth turning down. "Sounds kind of selfish."

"I don't know." Baker sighs. "I gave them two years – finished sixth form. If it was up to me? I'd already be gone."

And never met me.

Over a low wall, I spot a pale brown pigeon lying, whole and perfect and dead underneath someone's window.

Baker's too busy watching me to notice, the weight of his eyes too heavy, and I wish he'd stop.

"Do you even know how lucky you are?"

"How?"

"Are you serious? No one hands me anything. Not free camera gear, not opportunities and travel and who knows what else. I..." My words are too fast and I stumble. "I couldn't even imagine—"

"OK, sorry." He holds his hand up.

"Don't be sorry." The fight goes out of me and my last few words trail off. "Be aware."

We walk on. I feel guilty about leaving the bird all alone, like I should go back. Give it a decent burial. They mate for life, pigeons.

"Are you OK?" Baker says and I realize my hands are knotting of their own accord.

The red-brick terraces turn to a busy arterial road, a crossroads, the barber's with the quirky window displays. Outside a guy with waist-length ginger hair drinks a can of supermarket-brand lager. A car honks and it shakes my bones.

Baker says, "We could do something else tonight, you know? Give your shutter finger a break?"

I stop walking. "Like what?"

Baker laughs. "Whoa. Like nothing, I guess."

"No. I don't want to do this if you don't want to." The whole evening I've constructed in my mind comes crashing down. The crackly atmosphere between me and Baker and the disjoint in the conversation seem to rub uncomfortably against my skin. Clearly Baker's had enough of this. Of me. God, I need to learn to take a hint.

"Do you want to go home?" I say.

"What? No. I was thinking a picnic? Feeding the ducks and rats, all your favourite urban pests." Baker waves his hand in circles. "A photographic scavenger hunt? A drink? Pool? I was trying to seize the day."

"With pool?"

"No worries. Another time."

"I haven't finished my exhibition project and we'd already talked about—"

"Got it. Loud and clear. I guess you'll need coffee at least?" Baker says, pointing across the road.

He won't look at me. I want to ask why, but I don't. I want to ask what's wrong, but I don't, because I'm sure it's me. I know how this goes. The familiar sinking feeling. This is the start of the end.

The thick glass door of the coffee shop cracks open as we approach and Baker rushes in to help a woman with a pram as I stand uselessly, feeling faintly nauseous.

Of course Baker doesn't know the places Theo and I used to come. How I'll never go up to the old war memorial in the park, because it's where Theo and I shared our first kiss. Or that there's a bench I'll never pass without thinking of him and Olivia. Baker doesn't know Theo's favourite drink is an espresso with a whole sachet of sugar emptied into it so it leaves a sweet grainy slurry at the bottom of his cup or how we used to pile in the same armchair, even though there were two.

"I'll wait outside," I say, digging in my wallet and shoving a crumpled fiver at Baker. I lift my camera and gesture down the street.

It's pathetic. Just a coffee shop with too many memories, but I can't go in. And I need a moment on my own, to gather myself, to get a grip and work out how to fix things between me and Baker. I drift to the side of the windows and aim my lens pointlessly at a bollard. My own senseless words echo in my mind.

Selfish. That's what I called him.

Selfish. What's wrong with me?

And karma hits like a bus as a group of three boys emerge from an alley: the blond at the front's easy smile faltering at the sight of me.

He's a perfume advert, a dream sequence. Like I've summoned him here with pure anxiety. Theo Hastings.

Bloody small towns.

"Always roaming the streets, Ris," Theo says, waving a hand full of colourful paper. He jerks his head and Spade opens the coffee-shop door, waving Ash through before disappearing after him. I peer through the glass after them, but the reflection's too severe.

Theo runs a hand through his hair. "This's awkward

now you don't even reply to my messages. I feel like some sad groupie who won't leave you alone."

He gestures at the camera. "I guess you're part of that big exhibition thing Spade's all hyped for? He's had multicoloured nails for two weeks now working on some massive abstract finger painting, bless him."

"Yeah. Maybe. Lots of us are in it. I don't know." I look down the road past Theo. He watches me. I tangle my hands together and consider leaving. I could message Baker and tell him where to find me, but how to explain? *My ex made small talk so I bolted. Be normal, Iris.*

"Got a gig next Saturday and we're sounding epic. Giving more time to rehearsals has finally got the guys understanding the material." Theo peels off and holds up a single sheet from his stack. The wind folds it and gives me a flash of Spade's bright artwork. "Be great to see you there. We've got Plastic Highways on support – some kids from year eleven, but they were keen and I've heard worse. We've got a load of new songs. We miss you at rehearsals. Spade was saying it's not the same with no audience."

One time Spade asked Theo if I even knew how to speak. I was right there.

"You should invite Olivia." I watch it land. "Or Sadie."

Theo's eyes narrow. "I tried to tell you, you know? About O. I wanted to confess, but you were always so fragile. I thought I was doing the right thing not telling you."

My boot flexes as my toes clench. There's a crack in the cobbles underneath.

"When did you try?" I say.

"I never wanted Olivia. She's very … surface, you know? You're the one who got me – my music and poetry, your arty stuff. All that."

I force my eyes up. The constellation of freckles over Theo's nose has darkened in the sun. I try to feel nothing. Just the knot in my stomach. The faint disgust that Theo thinks I want this – him to put her down – as though making her less could somehow make me more.

"You don't give second chances, do you?" Theo smiles sadly as he adds, "I used to think you held a lot back, but maybe I got that wrong. You're just cold."

Cold. Fragile. Which is it to be? Both.

Frozen and brittle, unable to speak or defend myself.

"I can't…" I say.

And I think about that time. Our first time. Me, emerging from the landing with a blanket round me and a dopey smile on my face. Theo, there on his bed with my phone in his hand.

"What the fuck, Ris? he said. "Why's Neel messaging you?"

And I took a long minute to understand. My phone in his hand. The expression he wore. The tone of his voice. All wrong.

"Neel? He's asking about history homework."

"Why's he asking you? Is he into you?"

"Don't think so." The wrong response. Theo looked apoplectic.

"Theo, it's nothing." I gestured back at the rumpled bedsheets. I gripped the blanket closer.

"Let me see the rest of the messages then." He held out my phone in his palm.

"I love you."

He ignored that, only looking at me to hold up the phone to my face and unlock it.

"What are you looking for?" I said as he swiped. "There's nothing."

Eyes on me at last as he held my phone to his ear and the two of us listened to it ring and then—

"Iris?" A deep, kind voice on the end of the line.

Theo turned away and cupped his hand over the phone. "No, not her. Guess again?" A pause while Neel spoke. "Who do you think this is then? Yeah? Too right it's her boyfriend."

"Theo?" I whispered.

"You shouldn't be messaging other people's girlfriends."

I shrank. Too embarrassed to talk. To watch. To exist.

"Yeah… Yeah, you have made a mistake, mate."

Theo threw my phone back at me.

Afterwards he wouldn't speak. Not when I apologized or pleaded or cried. And when I'd stopped, when I couldn't speak, after I'd sat quietly at the end of his bed and listened to the noise of his family arriving home – the lively, upbeat backdrop of sound making my wait even more painful – after waiting for one word from him, I said, "Should I go?"

"Why? You have someone else to see?" he said, then sighed. "Just, shit. Just let me calm down."

So I stayed.

After a long time spent listening to the tapping of keyboard keys and the faint music from the game, Theo relented. He curled up sideways on his bed and patted the space beside him. When I lay down, he pulled me right against his chest.

I fit there so perfectly. I felt so safe. Mostly. And in the time after a fight, there was always the euphoria of being welcomed back. Forgiven.

"I just love you so much," he said. "It hurts that you talk to other guys."

The irony.

"You can't expect me not to see anyone else, Ris," Theo says now. "Can't wait for you for ever."

"I don't want you to wait."

Behind me there's the sound of the coffee-shop door. I turn round and Baker's standing there, coffees in hand, waiting.

"You good?" Baker asks me. Only me. "Ready to move on?"

*

"Do you want to talk about it?" Baker says when we're back on the high street. I'm glad he's finally said something instead of watching me like I'm a cracked pane of glass waiting to shatter.

I push up my glasses. "There's nothing to say."

Baker looks at me. My eyes find the ground.

"What about him?" Baker says, pointing.

I follow his finger. Some guy with a leather jacket and a mohawk. "He's got 'portrait material' written all over him."

"Under all his ink," I say, admiring the guy's neck tattoo. A skull threaded with flowers. Baker's right: he'd be perfect in black and white.

"The busker's here again," I say, stretching my arm back towards the top of the high street. "Anna. Do you want to go see her?"

"Do you?"

"You two got on so well." I kick the floor and kick myself too. There's no need to be this way just because Theo got under my skin.

"Go shoot the mohawk guy."

"Believe it or not, even I eventually tire of humiliating myself."

"Your humiliation tolerance is upsettingly low."

"I hang out with you, don't I?"

But Baker laughs, his self-esteem bullet-proof. Perhaps because he doesn't care for my opinion, or perhaps he's never experienced genuine dislike, so my semi-real grumpiness doesn't bother him. Potentially everyone worries they're unliked and it's only me that lets it drag her down, holding my wrongness like a weighted blanket – a comfort, a suit of armour, a way of preparing for next time.

"Don't regress, ADG. You know you want him. And you have to—"

"Push myself? Do one thing a day that scares me?

Getting out of bed should count." *Shit, Iris, shut up.* "I… Fine. I'll do it."

I adjust my settings with clumsy fingers. This is what I deserve for staying after the Theo incident. I should've anticipated Baker pushing and prodding at all my bruised places. I'm his project after all.

"Attagirl." Baker grins and I give him the closest thing to a withering glare I can muster.

As I'm walking towards the guy with the mohawk, I keep my camera held to my chest. The familiar sense of shrinking hits, even as my body is suddenly huge and awkward, my feet ready to trip, as all the distractions of the high street pile in: the sun itching my skin, the rot of the bins, a yapping white terrier tethered to a bollard and some kid shrieking over spilled sweets.

When I reach him, I forget what I'm meant to say. All my words vanish. His eyes are frosty blue, his lashes pale, too much like Theo's. There are studs on his jacket, gothic lettering spidering his knuckles. I smell tobacco as he asks, "Are you lost?"

"Can I … um … take your picture?"

"Me?" One eyebrow shoots up, the inky star above it emphasizing the movement. "What's so interesting about little old me?"

"I'm a photographer and—"

"Oh, really? Where do you show your work?"

"I'm a student."

His gaze sweeps me from boots to eyebrows, taking in my uniform.

"I leave you for five seconds and you're getting hit on?" someone says. A bushy beard, crooked teeth, a checked shirt. Now it's both of them looking at me and I can't tell if I'm welcome and he's about to say yes, or if I'm a freak standing here ignoring their signals.

"She likes my face." The first guy chuckles. "A woman of taste."

"What's the going rate for modelling these days?"

"I'm sorry," I croak out.

I retreat, their laughter clinging to me like cigarette smoke.

"What happened?" Baker holds out his hands and I stride past without answering. He shouts my name and more, his words drowned by the noisy shame of being me.

He puts a hand on my shoulder.

I wrench free. "Are you happy?"

"Hey, no, are you OK? Did they say something?"

"Why did you make me do that? What is this for you? Some messed-up way to pass the time until you leave? See how far you can push pathetic Iris before she snaps?"

Baker stares.

"And I'm embarrassing myself for what exactly?" I brandish my camera, the strap chafing my neck. "Another piece-of-shit portrait in my nothing portfolio? It's not worth it. It'll never be worth it."

"Iris," Baker says softly.

I turn my face away. "I'm tired of pretending I even have a chance." The words blur and merge and so does their meaning. The exhibition. Baker. Ever, ever feeling right.

A tiny part of me knows this is unreasonable. Even as I unhook my camera from my neck and pack it in my bag calmly, as though my hands aren't shaking, my muscles sparking. Everything inside me is urgent and heavy, too big to be contained in my skin.

I'll regret this later but I don't stop.

"Are you leaving?" The surprise on Baker's face brings some cheap satisfaction. "Whoa, Iris, I didn't mean—"

"Did it ever occur to you that I don't need this? I don't need you coming into my life, pushing and pressuring me and trying to make me someone I'm not."

"I didn't mean to … do that. You seemed like you needed—"

"Needed what?" My hands flap. My vision tunnels. Baker's far away, face unreadable. "You think you can, what? Fix me? There's no fixing me. I'm fucking broken. And I hate…"

Myself. I hate myself.

But I stop. That's too much.

"I know you're upset about Theo…" Baker says and he leaves it hanging there like that. An unfinished accusation. I hate that he says it, that he sees straight through me. I hate giving him even more of me to pity.

I hate it, but I let him have the last word, because this is when I walk away.

*

I'm home. Curled up in a tight ball on my bed in the gloom. The rumble of Purkoy's snores and her rising, falling ribcage close to my nose. An unyielding object pokes sharply into my hip. I draw out my phone and it lights up, illuminating new messages.

> **Theo:** so you're with baker davis now?
>
> **Theo:** what's that about?

I block him. But the damage is done. A sleepless night. Lilac bruises under red eyes.

Theo Hastings doesn't let things go.

28

The final exhibition planning meeting. I stand at the back of the room. Alone. No Baker.

He's not the only one missing, enthusiasm for standing listening to Ms Amin obviously waning as the date creeps closer – there'll be an email with these final details, so why attend? I should have given it a pass too.

This morning I woke up shattered, dragged myself out of bed and into an endless loop of regret. Over and over again, wincing through the fragmented memory of the incident. Yelling at Baker. In the street. Over nothing.

Strange that even as I lost control, I stayed visible. Proof, I guess, that there will be no more involuntary invisibility. But now I'm worried I made Baker disappear instead.

Of course he didn't show today.

At the front of the crowd Ms Amin's saying, "All artwork

will be delivered to my desk Friday by end of first period or your space will be gone. No exceptions."

A faint thrum of terror runs across my skin. It's soon, but I can get it together. I can get something together. I have enough.

Ms Amin's chin raises to address the back of the room. "Obviously the prize will be on your mind. But this isn't about a prize, really. This is a practice for the real deal." She turns her stern stare on the front row. "I don't want your most technically accomplished pieces – give me a body of work that's important to you and represents the type of art you want to make. Does it respond to current affairs? The human condition? Is your work confessional or pure fiction? What do you want to say and how do you want to be seen? These are the questions to ask yourself."

No pressure then.

"Layout plans and a list of allocated tasks and timings for Saturday's preview night are on the board."

The crowd starts to disperse. Immediately the plans are three deep with classmates checking they bagged a prime spot beside their bestie. I check the rota. Canapé duty.

"Iris Green, a word." Ms Amin beckons. My classmate, Chloe, meets my eye with a grimace of sympathy.

"I didn't expect to see you here this morning," Ms Amin says, as I shuffle guiltily after her. "We missed you in class yesterday."

"I'm doing the work and I'll be ready," I say. "And I'm sorry—"

Amin holds up a hand. "Art is art. I'm not asking for your excuses."

I hold my hands together in front of my chest, confused now.

"You know what you'll submit?" she says.

"Maybe some new portraits I've been working on? Maybe some street?" Hearing it aloud it sounds weak that I haven't yet decided. If either will do, perhaps neither will.

"Mmm-hmm. You're a perfectionist, Iris. That's commendable, but don't let it become a hindrance."

"I don't think..." I try, because "perfectionist" sounds too much like a compliment and I can't allow it to stand. "I'll get something together."

Ms Amin smooths her hair. "Next year your world will expand hugely. But, for now, this is where you are and I'm aware it's not always where you want to be. Perhaps there's something in that?" She breaks into a rare smile. My cheeks warm.

"Perhaps that's what your street work is pointing to? The sense of place and people and your relationship to them?"

The door of the canteen opens and I'm distracted by the sight of Baker at the threshold. I refocus on Amin, trying to process her suggestion.

"Something to think about," Ms Amin says with a final enigmatic smile.

I trail after her, back to the exhibition planning boards to pick up a timetable. Baker makes a beeline for me, but I can only look at the paper.

"What were you and Amin talking about?" he says. "Looked like preferential treatment to me. Unfair advantage."

"She definitely picked the pretty people for door duty." I shove the exhibition timetable print-out towards Baker and it crumples against his chest. "She was giving me a last-minute pep talk and, reading between the lines, I think the gist was that my current ideas aren't quite … it," I finish incoherently. "I need something more basically."

I let my hand drop to my side. I had to stop talking some time, but now I'm hyper aware of both the unsent apology in my drafts and Baker who's here. Not avoiding me after all.

He has this expression sometimes. Serious and focused, like I'm a scene he's trying to find an angle on. It's disconcerting. He wears it now and I'm sure he's about to mention it: the freak-out.

"I might have something for you," he says instead.

"Oh? Another bet? Another camera? The rest of your gear?"

"I watched your documentary."

"Wait, what? What happened to everything ends, a waste of precious life hours – the whole existential yikes?"

"Artificial happy endings are a strict no," Baker says, waving his hand dismissively with a rustle of recycled paper. "But something true and bittersweet that makes me re-examine all my life choices?"

"OK, I can see that," I say. "What documentary?"

"I'm in love with Vivian Maier. She's a genius."

I blink. "You remembered?"

"Believe it or not, I listen when you speak. I take it in. Sometimes I digest the information and turn it into long-term memories. This was one such occasion."

"I'm…" I drift away from the board, trying to think about the exhibition, but all I can think is, Baker paid attention. He listened and he liked Maier. He came back. "Happy you liked it," I finish flatly.

"I did like it." He has a twinkle. A dangerous half-smile. "And I was thinking about her work and her way of working: alone, secretive, all those years and never stopping … everything you said about her."

There's a tug of war inside me, a nervousness. "What did I say?"

Baker grins and roots around in his bag. He offers me the camera. This sleek black compact thing. I turn it over, surprised by its light weight.

"This is mine now? Premature."

"It's a loan."

"For what? Until when?" My patience starts to unravel as Baker smirks. I hate surprises and secrets and this is starting to feel like both.

"How do you fancy a little outing, Angry Girl?"

29

I stand at the train station ticket machine, ignoring creeping terror at my own disobedience. It's not like this is the first time. Besides, Baker made a good case for the educational merit of the day and my brain makes a good case for spending a whole day with Baker.

Next to me, my own personal bad influence, is outlining his grand plan. "We'll get our Vivian Maier on, take photos like no one's watching and at the end of it we'll pick five shots each." He glances sideways at me. "No promises, no judgement, no expectations."

"Does it have to be London?" I say.

"Other major cities are available, but a change of scene, a bit of inspiration, a chance to get away from this place and all its baggage?"

My eyes flick up, but Baker's watching the empty tracks.

The stranger behind me tuts, clearly frustrated that I've exceeded my allotted ten seconds at the front of the queue. I shoot him a deadly look as I jab the screen, my mind elsewhere. The day return is expensive. If I didn't have a body, I wouldn't need a ticket. It would, technically, be theft, but the train will depart regardless of whether or not I'm on board, and whether or not I buy a ticket. Still, I shake away the thought and reluctantly pay.

"And once I've taken these five perfect shots?" I say as the tickets fall into the trough.

"Did I say 'perfect'? Forget about quality control. Take something: a record of the day, an experiment, whatever – no one will ever see."

"We're not swapping?"

"Imagine these photos locked up in storage until your untimely demise. Completely undiscovered. For your eyes only."

"Unfair to give me a project to do on day one of new gear, don't you think?"

Baker leans over to pluck his camera from my unsuspecting hands, before turning the lens on me. There's no time to hide. No time to object. No time to compose my expression as the shutter clicks.

"Easy. Give or take a few settings. I'll show you the zone focusing later." Baker holds out the camera. Our fingers brush as I take it back.

The air begins to crack and rush. The steady build of

an incoming train. Passengers surge forward to the yellow line as it whips in.

I glance at that Iris on the screen. Half in, half out of sunlight under the station canopy. The lighting gives my face a drama it lacks in reality. Interesting. Intense.

"How'd it turn out?" Baker says as the train doors chime.

I flip the camera away and say, "Terrible."

*

In the train bathroom I loosen my school tie, pull it over my head and meet my juddering eyes in the clouded, scratched mirror. I remove my blazer and try to rearrange my shirt to resemble anything close to casual clothing, but it's futile.

Back at the main carriage door, I seek Baker's distinctive unruly hair over the headrests. Tempted, again, to tuck my body away – no face, no uniform, no judgement from strangers wondering why I'm out of place in the middle of the school day.

And I imagine returning to Baker that way. Slipping invisibly into the seat beside him. I have the fleeting impulse to do it, heart speeding at the wild thought that, somehow, Baker would recognize me anyway. He would, I'm sure. He'd see me for the same reason I can't seem to disappear around him: Baker's the boy who brings me back.

And he came back too.

"What are you smiling about?" Baker asks, when I slide into my seat again, fully, solidly visible.

I shake my head and look out the window at an industrial park whipping by. "This train always takes for ever."

"Your company's enthralling too." Baker waves away my apology, adding, "You know, all you reclusive, genius street photographer types are the same? So focused on the work."

I laugh. "You're the one who hates being still for five seconds."

"True. OK. In the spirit of the day..." He disappears into his bag and pulls out a fine marker.

"OK, here we go. Hold out your arm like this," he says, laying his arm out flat exposing the smooth underside of his forearm, palm upturned. "I know you think I'm just a one-trick pony, but..." He waves the pen. "I have other talents."

"Draw on me?" He nods. "You draw? You're good?"

"I dabble. I'm working on it."

"What if I don't like it?"

"Then I guess you won't have to permanently tattoo it on your skin."

I fold my arms. Baker squeezes his eyes closed in a brief, silent plea, but then caps his pen and sits back against the train seat. He lets it go.

In the quiet, I wait for him to say more, my eyes flicking to him again and again, seeing him in tiny snapshots. I like all the detail of Baker Davis, from his practical double-knotted laces to the gap in his teeth. I like the brush of stubble over his jaw and his endless patience. The way he has encouraged me, bit by bit, towards what I want. But now?

Something's changed. I've broken something between us. Baker will never be able to unknow how I'm only ever a few inconveniences away from disaster. Fragile, like Theo said. And I want to get the old Baker back, the one who could talk to me without being careful. Who could laugh with me without knowing how easily I break.

"I'm sorry…" I start, but then lay my arm flat and beckon my upturned fingers. "Do your worst, I guess. But this better not be anything weird."

"Close your eyes?" His grin is the last thing I see before I comply.

Baker's fingers encircle my wrist. The pen hits my delicate skin and begins to trace, the unpredictability unsettling. It gets easier. I relax. Baker keeps the pen strokes light. Swirls, dots, dashes and long trails that tickle.

"A bird?" I say.

"Shh, accept your fate."

I swallow my smile and the rest of my guesses. With my eyes shut, there's only me and Baker. His warm hand, his fingers flexing against the beat of my pulse. It goes on and on and I don't mind at all.

And then he stops. He lets go.

"We done?" I crack my eyelids and raise my arm.

It's more impressionistic than I imagined. The black ink has bled, blurring into my pale skin, distorting the lines.

"Overambitious maybe," Baker says, tutting and capping his pen. "It's an iris."

"I can see that." And I can. Upside-down and spikier than its real-life counterpart. I lean my head for a better view. "It would be a classier origin story, but I'm not Iris like the flower."

"Ah." He clicks his teeth. "Goddess of rainbows?" Baker says and then, "What's so funny?"

"Nothing. No. Not her either." I sit back. "The drawing, the line work, it reminds me of your handwriting. It's bold. Distinctive."

"Well." He shrugs. A rare moment of Baker modesty. Or uncertainty.

"I love it." I twist my arm and study the drawing. And I do. Because it's a gift and because it's Baker and it would be impossible not to. I push my hair back. Baker watches his handiwork and I have the disconcerting thought he might reach out again. Touch me again.

"Thank you," I say, dropping my hand to my lap. "And thank you … for still talking to me after … everything. I'd have understood if you didn't want to. I'd get it."

His deep brown eyes flicker over my features.

"Why on earth would I ever stop talking to you, Iris Green?"

Baker holds up his hand, little finger crooked towards me in an offer, an old-fashioned promise. I wind my own little finger round it. That's how we stay, all the way to London.

*

The city's an assault on the senses. People everywhere, cars, buses, bikes. Everyone rushing. As we emerge from tube to street level I pause, suddenly unable to find Baker in the crowd, and I am buffeted by bodies too busy to avoid me, until a hand slips into mine and guides me away.

We head for the South Bank, stopping and starting as scenes take our interest along the way. At first, Baker's camera is exactly as I feared, the instant preview providing an opportunity to doubt myself after every shot. But then I force myself to stop looking; I just work. I'm so absorbed it's a surprise when Baker catches up with me and I realize I've lost several hours. My feet hurt, and I'm suddenly ravenous.

We take street food down to the river and sit cross-legged on a curvy metal bench eating buttery arancini, watching tourists pose in front of the Thames.

"Can we stay?" I say. "There's somewhere else I want to go."

*

An imposing brick box topped with a glass lantern. The chimney stretching up to the sky. A stream of tourists to be carried along with as they flow into the cavernous entrance to the gallery. There's no entry fee. No one stops us. No one questions us, despite our school uniforms. No one looks at us, because there's so much else here to focus on. And although I've been here before on my visits to Dad, too many times to count, I've never been allowed to wander the way I wanted to – the way I do now.

I soak them up. Mari Katayama's vibrant, sculptural

self-portraits and Jenny Holzer's wall of flashing furious words. Goldin, Sherman, Rist.

Baker's there and not, lured away by what interests him, returning to check in. Allowing me time.

I sit on the floor in front of Barbara Kruger. Black-and-white photographs juxtaposed with text in bold red frames. A room to herself.

Kruger didn't even take the photos the words are splashed across. Found images. Found art. A collision of ideas. Deceptively simple. But I feel it deep down in my bones in the place only art can touch you. A hit of recognition. I wonder what it's like to make something like this. Something a stranger can stare into, connect with and understand. Here, it hits me that this is what I want to do. Days like this, hours whisked away by pure focus. And it's such an obvious realization, but I know why it took me a while to get here.

All my life I've been waiting for permission, even for this: for someone to tell me what I want to do and who I get to be. Sitting alone on this gallery floor, I realize I could just decide. The exhibition would help. Maybe. My work on the wall, proof that I'm capable of putting it there. And if I could actually win…

So try. Stop holding back and doubting myself. Be brave.

I hold up Baker's camera so I'm staring down the lens and *click*. It's not a perfect photo. The words in the background are small and out of focus but they're there.

We will no longer be seen and not heard.

I just need to figure out what I want to say.

*

On the train home Baker and I are quiet. I have my phone in my hand and the beginning of an idea taking shape in my mind. I google fine art and photography courses and read the details with more interest than I've ever summoned for history BAs. I flick through brochures for degree shows and think of Ms Amin's advice about our sixth-form version. I think I know what's missing now.

"Feeling inspired?" Baker asks, and I nod without taking my eyes off the screen.

My pits begin to prickle overdramatically as I type:

> **Me:** hey, we left things weirdly, so sorry if this isn't an ok question, and no pressure at all, but
>
> **Me:** would you ever let me take your portrait?

There. That's a start.

30

The front room behind the curtains is dark – not so much as even the telltale flicker of light from the TV. I unlock the door and slip inside. I creep upstairs, avoiding the creaky floorboard at the top and pause.

Mum's door is ajar, a thin wedge of weak light thrown across the landing. The faint murmur of her voice. "Hmm, maybe," she's saying.

I squeeze into the gap. Mum sits slumped forward on her bed with her head in one hand and a phone clamped to her ear. She makes another sound of disagreement.

"Mark, I don't know what else to tell you. She's genuinely not in. This isn't some big conspiracy between the two of us. I'm not lying if that's what you're accusing me of?"

Dad. I move silently away, tucking myself round the corner and leaning my head against the wall.

"She doesn't talk to me either honestly. She's sixteen, so it's hardly surprising neither of us are flavour of the month, but try giving her some space maybe?"

A pause. Mum sighs. And I know what comes next, because I've heard it before, the way she placates him, gives way as he bulldozes through our lives demanding we meet him more than halfway – literally, figuratively – always.

"Mark," Mum says after a while, "if she doesn't want to see you, I can't make her. I don't want to make her. So … I'm going to hang up now."

A couple of seconds. The most enormous sigh.

I count to ten. To fifteen. Twenty. Thirty. And then I peer round the corner. Mum's flung back on her bed, starfished and staring at the ceiling.

"Hi," I say and she startles, groggily clawing her way back to a sitting position.

"I didn't hear you come in, love."

"I'm stealthy like that." And then I go in and kneel on the side of the bed to fling my arms round her.

*

I hit my bed. My laptop's open on the pillow and the dark screen reflects me through a fine layer of dust until I snap it shut. As I play the day over, it registers that I survived a trip to London without incident. I could do it again. Another day, another gallery or a few hours on the South Bank snapping tourists. I could visit Dad. Just a few hours of my life on trains. It would be easy. If I wanted.

And I think about that time, at the hotel in Portugal with all the feral cats when I got so sunburned on the back of my legs I could barely tie my own shoelaces. At dinner I didn't want anything on the menu and Dad wouldn't let it go. And the waiter waited while Dad berated me for what felt like hours, because I wouldn't choose. And I couldn't speak and I couldn't say it was him who was being unreasonable, not me.

When I finally opened my mouth, it was to be sick on the floor. The shouting stopped, the fussing started and that seemed better until we walked back to our room.

"Why can't you just talk to me, Iris?" he said as the door beeped green. "Being around you is such hard work sometimes."

I believed that. I believe it. But being around him is hard work too.

I take out my phone and I type a short message:

Me: i won't visit in summer. i'm busy and i just can't make it this year. sorry

Before I send it, I delete that last word.

31

Someone belonging to another era in their white stetson and matching jacket. A man facing off against a giant ice cream. A woman absorbed in *Girl, Woman, Other* on a crowded tube. A white-haired man in a hat reading a newspaper against the backdrop of the city. My own face against the white gallery wall.

I turn them over and send a snap of their blank backs to Baker.

Me: step one: complete

Me: what now?

*

"Like this?" Bert throws her arms over her head and stands back against the wall, leaning into the ivy.

"Yep. Perfect." I nod encouragingly, more for myself than her. "Rotate this way to face the light?"

This lunchtime we've swapped the gawkers and gossipers of the common room for the park and Bert's swapped her school uniform for a brightly patterned sleeveless boilersuit and trainers, a combination I argued her down to last night as she spammed me with wildly ambitious and impractical inspiration shots, making my flimsy confidence waver.

But now all that recedes as I peer through the viewfinder. Bert stretches to the sky, showing off the soft dark hair under her arms, her lips curl, and that's the moment.

Click.

Her eyes pop open and chin tilts. A smidge more. A touch less. A twist. Shoulders back.

"Next?"

Bert picks her way through the shrapnel of broken glass littering the bottom of the wall. Although the brick is crumbling and there are cobwebs in the ivy, all I see is the contrast of texture and tone, brick red against lush deep green. Perfect light. Perfect model.

She hunkers down behind some low railings and throws her arms wide, gripping the iron bars.

I get close, my own camera back in my hands, my 50mm lens.

Click.

"In the middle of everything else going on this year," Bert says, "it's wild that these wispy little armpit goatees might be bringing me the most satisfaction."

"It's surprisingly cute."

"Isn't it?" She moves her arm to stroke the hair. "I love it." My grin answers hers, I hit the shutter and it's so easy, all this, that I can't remember why I ever thought it wouldn't be. It's just Bert. Just me.

"That's the concept." I wiggle my camera. "A mix of street and portraits, people who seem comfortable in their own skin."

"For the exhibition?" Bert's mouth pops open. "Am I going to be art?"

"You're already art. But if you're happy to be included...?"

"Always." Bert layers her hands under her chin and bats her eyelashes. "Sounds like you have a plan and who am I to stand in the way of greatness?"

"In theory I have a plan." I swap my camera for Baker's loan – it needs returning, really – and retake the shot in 28mm. "At least five previous plans all went in the bin, but the deadline is ... soon. So this one has to stick."

"Whatever you end up with will be brilliant," Bert says firmly, throwing a shape.

I shrug. "Or a huge mess. I guess we'll find out."

Bert narrows her eyes. "Please. I've seen some of your other work now—"

"The literal rubbish?"

"Chicken, let's not. Have you met you? Your entire history of academic success rests on your ability to pull something spectacular out of the bag last minute."

"Academic mediocrity." Bert glares, but it's true. "Anyway, maybe this time I don't. It's only some photos of people, you know? Even if they're OK, maybe everyone will think it's nothing. Maybe it'll just be … bad."

There. That. It feels good to say it aloud and let Bert hear it.

"Maybe what I want to say isn't important."

"Your self-perception is so out of whack," Bert says. "All will be perfect, crowds will cheer, victory will be yours." She extends a hand out implying, *Come on*, her face bright and determined, and I smile back trying not to care that these are empty words without evidence. Or that I don't want to hear I'm great, golden, incapable of failure – all those impossible assurances. I push my sleeves up and touch my fingers to the faded remains of Baker's iris.

"You're probably right," I say. "Nerves."

Bert comes to my side of the railings and leans across them, arms at shoulder height.

Click.

"Last year," she says, switching poses, "Last exam season, I was thinking about my anxiety as this nervous friend constantly there, trying to be helpful, but always making it worse. Like, *Hey, thanks for your concern and all the adrenaline, but stop.*"

"OK?" I say, unsure if this is an anecdote or advice.

"It sounds ridiculous, I know, but it helped."

"I didn't know you were that stressed last year."

Bert shrugs. "I held it together. It passed. Everything is temporary and, besides, falling apart wasn't an option."

"Falling apart is always an option," I say solemnly.

We walk. Bert chatters between shots as we explore all the dazzling backdrops the park has to offer: some grass, a tree, a different brick wall. Spoiled for choice.

Bert perches, hand to her knee, on the concrete stairs of the bandstand with its flaking turquoise paint. Her eyelashes kiss her round cheeks, pink from sun and the pose, and it feels wild to me that Olivia is considered the only pretty one of our group when Bert exists like this. Her expressiveness, her honest brown eyes, even the way she asks, "How's this?" And trusts me to tell her the truth.

I move back, crouch. I swap to Baker's camera and hold it low.

Click.

There's laughter nearby. The sort that yanks me abruptly from my mind and back into my body. Over my shoulder I clock some skeevy girl in ripped jeans mimicking Bert, grotesquely contorting her features and angles as her mate looks on and cackles.

I straighten up and my head spins.

"What?" Bert says, dropping her pose. "Don't let them get to you. They're laughing at me, not you."

"Pretty sure they're laughing at both of us."

"I mean, one of them just said 'Chewbacca', so..."

"That's..." I feel the start of a smile. "They could have been talking about anyone."

"I wish. You know I'm trying to start a movement here. I was saying to..." Bert shakes her head. "Everyone. Everyone, honestly, should try some fuzz once."

I focus on the screen, deleting shots where Bert's mid-blink or strange-looking. *Olivia*, I think, plucking the end of Bert's half-sentence from her hesitation. This pause.

"Let's see?" Bert says, gently lifting my camera from my hands.

"Those aren't the final images," I say quickly. "They'll look different – better – after processing."

Bert rolls her eyes without comment as she scrolls. She stops and turns the camera round to show a mini Bert frozen in place, arms and expression open, joy exploding from the frame.

"Who were they laughing at, anyway? Not her, or they must be as short-sighted as you." She looks over to where our unwanted audience have finally lost interest, then jiggles the camera. "Your turn?"

"No way." I push up my glasses and Bert pouts. "I'm in my uniform. And ... no. Iris Green is never the subject. I don't fit the theme."

"Shame." Bert hands back my camera and I slip it into my bag. "You're a subject worthy of study."

"You and Baker would get along so well," I say, giving in to my compulsion to drop him into every conversation. Purkoy's definitely sick of hearing his name.

"Ah. The boy. Maybe I should meet him? Vet him?"

Bert winds her arm through mine and we fall into step. And it feels like old times. Familiar hope sneaks back into my heart: Bert and I will be OK after all. I don't have to think about everything that's happened. We don't have to mention it. We can be exactly as we were.

"Come to mine tomorrow night?" Bert says, as though she's reading my mind. "Eat enough sweets to make my skin riot, stress over the next few months? You can help me with a little craft project of my own if you want to repay the favour," she says, reaching out to lightly tap my camera. "We can even dissect the boy, since you're *clearly* desperate for my opinion."

I laugh and watch my feet step in and out of view, regretting my impulsive name-drop and all the unanswerable questions it raises, wishing I could retreat to safer territory like art, bodies, my impending public failure.

I say, "All of that please. But not the boy."

"Oh." Bert grins. "Definitely the boy."

*

"How's your weather today?" Mum calls.

I'm struggling through the front door, awkward thanks to the tray of prints I'm carrying, and she's tucked inside the kitchen by the washing machine. She's wearing her baggy dungarees and an expectant expression and I don't like either.

"Uh ... breezy?" I say, as I deposit my armful of artwork on the sofa.

"Good. I'm glad." She drags laundry from the machine and stands, blowing a strand of hair off her face, not taking her eyes off me. "I have about a million things to do before my shift to stop the house from falling down."

"OK?" I walk into the kitchen past Mum. On the window sill behind the sink her ragged houseplant has regained some of its enthusiasm for life. I touch its leaves in silent solidarity.

"And a somewhat ominous grey cloud hanging over all that was an email from King's," Mum says.

Oh.

"You're missing school?"

"Uh ... yeah." There's a stack of dirty dishes in the sink and I'd rather climb into the cold, stale water alongside our breakfast bowls than have this conversation. "You could say that."

It's frustrating because I've been attending. Mostly. I've been there, taking in the information and doing the work. Following the rules in my own way. Mostly. Just a few missed lessons stressing in the darkroom and one unauthorized school outing.

"Is there some particular reason why?" Mum says.

I touch my fingers to the side of the kettle. Warm.

I grab a mug from the cupboard, throw in a teabag and the dregs of the kettle. As I watch the water darken, I wonder how I can minimize this. Explain it away without concerning Mum with petty school squabbles, my tragic love life and chaotic mind. I say, "It's nothing. I'm sorry, I'll go."

"How did I not know about this?" Mum says.

"You're not at school, how would you? And I … didn't want to involve you, because there's no need. Everything's under control, so you don't need to worry about me." I put on a smile. For a second, Mum looks like I've punched her in the stomach. She moves closer and leans against the draining board.

"I'm here for worry, love. That's what I'm meant to do."

"Sorry." I drop my spoon in the sink.

Where's Purkoy when you need her to break the tension?

"Do you want to talk about it? Or anything else?" Mum's face stays bunched with disappointment as her eyes flick over mine.

"Not really. I didn't expect them to email you."

"Where were you?"

"Does it matter?"

"Iris…"

I shake my head and put my hand against the side of my mug and say, "It's all fine. Honestly."

"OK." Mum shifts her weight. "OK." My inside-out pillowcase dangles from her hand. She watches me, her head inclined in a Nicole-esque tilt. "If you're sure there's not … more?"

I fold my lips together, wondering what that would sound like. More. All of it. Theo, Olivia, Bert, school, counselling, future fears and the general anxiety of simply existing, of not sleeping, of turning invisible in my skin, all these things I wish Mum knew that I've deliberately kept hidden. Where would I even start?

"Well," Mum says, "I'm glad you're OK."

I nod, hearing the truth of that. "You never missed school, back in the day?" I say as I turn away. "I know it's not ideal, but it's not like I was out selling crack."

"Ah, my faith in my parenting is restored," Mum deadpans. "OK," she says again. She lays the crumpled pillowcase on the worktop and it sags half off. "If there was anything though – even confessions of criminality – I'm here. I hope you know that?"

When? I almost ask, but that wouldn't be fair, so I roll my eyes at her weak joke. Mum reaches out a worn hand and smooths my hair. I flinch, feeling a pang of guilt as her fingers curl and retract. We exchange looks. Another apology sits uncomfortably in my stomach.

I lift my camera and centre Mum in the viewfinder. With her glasses on her head, hair all mussed up and the light from the window, she's beautiful. I can see the echo of my nan's features, the blueprints of my own.

"Don't do that," Mum says. "My face is awful."

"Your face is lovely."

"I raised a liar, did I?" Her forehead wrinkles, but she stays still and waits for me to emerge from behind my camera before she adds, "Your dad called the other night. I told him you won't make the summer. But he could come here instead? He's your dad after all."

I nod.

"But it's OK if you'd rather not. I know it's hard, love. I think sometimes you think I'm on his side over—"

"I don't think that." I grab my tea, prickly from being confronted and scrutinized and the knowledge of all these conversations happening out of sight.

As I'm leaving the room I pause in the doorway. "He could come here," I say. "If he wants to see me. He could do that. And … thanks for … sorting it with him."

*

Bert's portraits from lunchtime are splayed out on my carpet, my legs tucked under me as I go through the rest. I dig back through my older work. I find forgotten prints like old friends and I catch myself by surprise. It's me in black and white and shades of grey. A self-portrait. Straight on, staring down the barrel of the lens. There are others. I find myself in corners of street shots: a shadow here, a reflection there, a ghost at the edge of the frame.

I pull out the one Baker took at the station and the one I took at the Tate and then I sweep myself aside – there's no point in dwelling on those. My exhibition piece will be Bert, Baker, the busker – a chequerboard arrangement of portraits alternating with street, the candid juxtaposed with the posed. There's a coherence to the idea. It works. It's fine. Yet somehow I'm still rifling through old work when Baker messages:

> **Baker:** We need a suitably dignified burial site for our shots. Thoughts? Ideas? Questions?

As weird as that request is, I have an answer immediately. I find a space on my noticeboard and pin up Baker's portrait of me.

> **Me:** i have a place

32

The night's so cold I can't work out where my nervousness ends and my shivers begin. The sky's blotted with inky clouds that obscure the moon and make the night even darker as I lead Baker to the spot. Beyond the rugby field, a line of trees, a trickle of a stream with a concrete slab over it giving way to a long scrubby bit of land where people dump rubbish and ride dirt bikes over the humps. At one end there's a steep-sided man-made mound with an unimpeded view of a motorway services: a petrol station, drive-through Starbucks and the road beyond.

I spread my arms wide and let them flop to my sides with a weak "Ta-da" as my last vestige of confidence deserts me. This place is a mess. What the hell was I thinking?

"Wow." Baker blinks at the horizon and then at me.

"You like?" I lace my hands together and hold them in front of me like a shield.

"I'm a big fan," he says. "How did you find somewhere like this? Do you regularly make a habit of wandering in wilderness-adjacent spaces at night?"

I snort and wrap my arms round myself. Because yes. Yes, I've wandered a lot lately. It's what I do when sleep won't come and my mind is too loud.

"It's such a Baker spot," I say, and he laughs.

"What's that supposed to mean?"

"You like these weird places where worlds collide. You're out for a nice Sunday stroll in the woods trying to pretend wilderness still exists, but then, bam, suddenly there's a Starbucks and a massive road. You're not alone in the universe after all."

"That's very me," he agrees. "Would you want to be?"

"Totally alone?" I think of the respite of turning my body off. The tranquillity of no longer being observed in my girl-skin. The peace of my night-time walks. "Yeah. For a while."

He nods. "If it could be me and you and the Starbucks lights for company, that'd be a good world, I think."

I stub the toe of my shoe against the ground. I didn't realize Baker meant alone together.

He dumps his kit bag, unzips it and pulls out a tripod, camera. I sink to the ground. The grass is sharp and dry, rocky soil needling my palms. I cross my legs and watch the headlights of cars speed by like shooting stars. It's beautiful. If I narrow my eyes the background blurs and the lights are starbursts. Bokeh. The rush of traffic could be the rolling of waves. The gritty air, sea salt.

Immersed in his equipment, Baker doesn't say anything, but it's not uncomfortable. There's no grinding desperation to fill the gaps. I pick a strand of grass and wind it tightly round my fingers.

"Long exposure?" I ask, nodding to Baker's set-up.

"Maybe later. A little filming."

"For your exhibition project? A bit last minute… Hand-in's in two days. Are you nervous?"

"Never. Are you done?"

"Nearly." It's mostly true. I blow out a breath and it flows out in a cloud, hanging in the air then dispersing. I pull my arms round myself tighter. I push my feet out so my legs flatten against the ground and close my eyes.

"So what did you bring?" Baker says, raising his voice to puncture my reverie. "Your five shots."

"You said I don't have to show you."

"I wasn't asking." Baker sets his camera rolling and hits the ground beside me. "But did you get something you liked?"

The temptation is to shrug, to shake my head or play it down. Make my efforts sound smaller, don't brag. But the one of the older guy on the bench – I liked that. The selfie in the gallery was a good memory.

"Maybe," I say.

"What did you like about them? Don't describe the shots; what was good."

"I… You're so bossy." Baker winds his hand in mid-air, encouraging me to go on. "They captured … character. Quirky little moments where people wouldn't think there was anything important happening … and there wasn't, but it was still … kind of lovely."

Baker grins like I've given him the moon. "That's the thing about you, Green. Everyone else is walking around in their own little world with no awareness of anyone else half the time, but you? You see people."

I shake my head.

"I'm serious. No, it's not even seeing; it's" – he tilts his head to one side – "acceptance. You're not trying to transform them. You see all this incredible detail and you believe people are interesting in moments where no one else is paying attention. It's kind of a nice way to look at the world, you know? It's like … you see the value and beauty in the unremarkable."

I put my hands beside each other on my knees. Thumb to thumb. Neat. My fingers are very white and cold. Is it a compliment? I can't tell. It's so specific it feels genuine.

"Of course, you made a terrible snap judgement the moment you met *me*," says Baker. "But I seem to be the exception to the rule."

I roll my eyes. "Always assuming you're exceptional."

Baker laughs. He pulls his backpack over and unpacks it: a handheld shovel, a small tin.

I pick the spot, over by a tree stump with a hollowed-out centre.

Baker digs a hole and we kneel beside it.

"Doesn't this count as littering?" I say, which earns me a stern look.

"It's a time capsule and an insurance policy. Because no matter what happens you'll always know there's one shot you loved that was only for you. No one else ever saw it. One pure raw shot of Iris art. And maybe one day it will be discovered, but maybe not."

I take out my shots and shuffle them until I reach one that holds on to me. Weird that this is the one. I carefully place all my other snaps face down on my knee.

"You won't look?" I ask and Baker crosses his heart.

"You already know what I think anyway."

He's right. And a little bit wrong.

Baker has a Sharpie, writing the date and his name on the back of his print, so absorbed in what he's doing his eyebrows furrow in concentration. A laugh wants to get out, but I swallow it so as not to disturb him. I don't want Baker to think I'm laughing at him either. I'm not. Just the ludicrousness of this. Him. Me. Us being here together.

He lends me the pen to label my print. Our prints go in the box. Face down. I'm curious what Baker chose but I don't ask. We seal them and stick them in the hole. I scrape the soil back on top and pat it flat. The ground's mostly bare here. Soon the place where we planted these memories will be invisible.

We shake hands. And dust our dirty palms on our knees. Baker shifts to sit on top of the burial ground.

I shiver. Baker moves closer and lifts his arm and beckons me in. I shuffle up underneath and lean my head on his shoulder and it feels very normal even though this is the first time we've been so close. He's so warm.

A bike with no silencer goes streaking off the roundabout in the distance, shrieking into the night in a blur of light.

"Make a wish," I say against the fading hum, thinking of shooting stars again.

"I wish you'd trust me a bit more," Baker says without missing a beat and he smiles sadly.

I don't know what he wants me to tell him. *I do trust you*, I go to say, but it doesn't quite come out. It's true, though. I trust Baker to give me the right advice and to see me when I can't see myself. I trust him to bring me back.

It's me I don't trust.

When I'm with Baker, I feel different. Seen but not watched. I get lost in the rhythm of our conversation and the way he treats everything I say like it's worth paying attention to. I don't have to edit or try too hard. I don't have to rehearse the person I'll be. I exist. And I don't trust that feeling.

"Sometimes," he says, "you seem to go into yourself. Like I'm not here."

"You're used to girls falling over themselves for you?" I scoff, determined to style this out.

He looks away. For a moment, Theo flashes into my mind and I don't like it. I don't like thinking about him when I'm with Baker. And I don't like this – the fleeting feeling that Baker thinks I'm somehow wrong.

"You're annoyed?" I say.

"No. I … sometimes I find it hard to read you, that's all. And I wonder if you want me around. Especially after…"

"Oh." I've been tricked like this before. A hundred times people said they cared when they didn't. How do you tell the difference? "I don't know what happened in town the other day," I say, twisting my hands together. "I've been lied to this year … and I didn't see it for so long. I don't know…" My voice goes small. I brace myself for pushback. "Do you ever feel like everything's piling on top of you and … nothing that big or that awful has happened, but sometimes all the small things are just … heavy?"

Baker's brows dive and I wonder if he gets it. If he understands what I'm reaching for. He quietly absorbs it without fighting.

"I'm sorry I yelled," I say.

I lean into him and he says, "No, no. Sorry. I'm sorry." He murmurs it into my hair, his lips moving against my head. Baker's body is warmer than mine and I can smell his cologne. It's slightly too strong today and I wonder if that was for me. Or perhaps some other girl.

"Sometimes…" Baker says lightly, his fingertips flexing against the top of my arm. "Sometimes I think about kissing you, Iris Green."

My mouth goes dry. "Oh?"

If I was someone else, I might enquire what he means by "sometimes". I might say, "Sometimes the thought crosses my mind too". But with the warmth of his fingertips against my arm and his body pressed to mine and my heart thrumming through every inch of my skin, so hard I'm certain he can feel it, it's all too much. I'm sure he's waiting for a reaction. A movement. A giveaway. I catch my bottom lip with my teeth and fold it under.

Baker presses his head against mine. A muscle in his jaw twitches.

I focus on the cars zooming past on the horizon. Maybe he does too.

"I usually decide I shouldn't," he says.

I nod. Our skulls rub together. Head to jaw. Skin to skin. Closer than I've been to anyone since … well … in a while.

Sometimes.

Usually.

These words are liminal spaces between important possibilities.

God, I want it. I want Baker to kiss me. I want him to want everything from me so I can give it to him and he can decide who I should be. I want to be chosen for once. I want to sit here with Baker in silence for ever. I want to be friends. I want to be so much more. I have no idea what I want, so I keep my head pressed against his and hope the moment passes.

Baker claps his hands. "OK, let's do this. Get up, over there."

Baker gestures at the camera and I finally catch up. *He wants a photo? Of me?*

I say, "I have a passport photo where I look like I'm being held at gunpoint. That's all we ever need. It'll work for birthday announcements, missing person posters, obituaries..."

Baker rises and reaches back to help me up. "This isn't like that."

I put up resistance because it's what I do. And then I give up, because that's what I do too.

"You'll barely be visible," he promises. Which is an intriguing proposition.

I hold my phone so the screen points out, the glow pointed towards his lens. And I run. Sprint across the field in the view of his camera as Baker keeps the exposure long. At first, I am awkward, self-conscious, but then he shows me the test shots and the way I become a blur of shadows and light, a dark streak under the stream of headlights behind me.

In the dark I become invisible again.

So I run, spin, jump, leap, dash. I let my arms and legs be free. I let all of me be free. I move how I want to move. I laugh and scream and almost fall. I swing my body around and feel like a blur. Like light.

"I… It's beautiful," I say when he shows me afterwards.

Somewhere out of sight his hand finds mine. Squeezes.

And I take a breath. I try not to think too much about what I want. What I'm risking. What Baker means to me.

(*Sometimes… Usually.*)

I try not to hear:

(*Holy shit, O. You're making me crazy.*)

All the distracting noise in my mind.

I focus on Baker. His profile. The space he carves out against the darkness, his jaw chiselled in stars and his curls searching for the moon. I choose to believe he's real; he sees me and all the details I hide under my skin.

He smiles at me. "What?"

"Why do you decide you shouldn't kiss me?" I whisper.

His smile holds, fades. There's a pause. *Click.* A snapshot moment when something is created from nothing. And we wait to see what develops.

"Because you're a friend," he says. His features in the gloom: furrowed brow, dark eyes.

"Just a friend?"

"Not 'just' anything. I wouldn't want to ruin it. Especially… You've had a tough few months."

"Like I'm damaged?"

"No." One syllable. So fierce.

I squeeze his hand and pull him in. His other arm wraps round me, hand at my waist. His heartbeat. Mine drowning it out.

I say, "Is this OK?"

He leans his forehead against mine and turns the night warm with a low breath. "Yeah. Yeah, of course."

We hang here for a moment. Teetering on the edge.

And it's me who tips it over. Who falls first. Who reaches. Closes the distance. Me who puts my lips on his.

I put my hands in his hair. On his neck, on his shoulders. I pull him against me.

He kisses me and it's soft and warm and slow. It's different to—

He pulls back and cups my face in his palm and I twist it away so I'm leaning into his neck. He dips his head against mine and plants a kiss under my ear.

He whispers, "You're amazing, Iris. Always amazing."

And I bury my head closer so he won't see my face.

33

A night-time walk with my skin on: hand in hand with Baker Davis.

Invisible bodies and silver vision and two cameras tangling together and it's these things: Baker, my palm, his, the point where we touch. They don't feel real.

We say goodbye at my road and it's different to before. His face is closer and I can feel every second as it ticks by.

He holds our hands up, still threaded together and I can feel his breath on my knuckles as he says, "Come to a party tomorrow night? It's out the back of the Wildcroft estate. There'll be bonfires, fireworks, free booze: a whole last-days-of-freedom kind of death trap."

"I won't know anyone."

"You'll know me."

I pull my lips together and imagine it. Me and Baker.

Baker and me. Surrounded by people who will see us together. I have a flash of it: how if I went there, I would be so very visible.

Baker kisses the back of my hand. Lips to skin. A tiny patch of warmth.

"Maybe," I say.

*

In bed I hold on to the night. Snapshots I turn over again and again, because I can't believe they belong to me.

Sometimes I think about kissing you, Iris Green.

I bury my head in the pillow and take a deep breath of nothing.

And I realize how much I want to go. How much I want to be there with Baker and hold hands in the dark. How much I want to get cold and tired and tipsy and come home smelling of wood smoke and cheap booze and him. And I realize I can't.

I pull out my phone and tuck my lip under my teeth, wondering how transparent I'm going to seem. But I message her anyway:

Me: about tomorrow ... i don't suppose you'd fancy a party instead?

Bert: Whose party? On a school night? You're joking... Have you been kidnapped? ARE THESE YOUR CODE WORDS?

Bert: I thought we had plans?

Bert: Don't you want to hang just the two of us?

I do. I do want to hang with Bert.

I do.

34

Bert's room looks like a vintage toy store. Shelves lined with retro Polly Pockets, Sylvanian Families and Animal Crossing plushies. Necklaces, scarves and string lights, homemade garlands and the most stunning quote wall, the lettering constructed from brightly coloured magazine paper. It's organized chaos. It's her.

And my focus is on Bert. All my focus. None elsewhere. Definitely not on Baker or the contents of my phone like:

> **Baker:** Woke up thinking about how much I like walks in the dark. Weird, huh?

Or:

> **Baker:** You sure you're not in the mood for a party?

"OK, goodbye," Bert says to her dad after he's popped in with a tray of pink lemonade, only to be firmly sent packing. She closes the door and widens her eyes at me. "I was legitimately worried he was about to sit on the floor and start making pompoms with us. Why's that man so keen to be involved in my life?"

"Your parents are so cute."

"Aren't they? I love them, but they're too much right now. Mum has gone completely batshit since being made redundant. She's dedicating her sudden free time to helping me revise. As if I didn't do a solid enough job last year, colour-coding my revision notes and huffing so much highlighter I started to see pink elephants."

Bert flops back down on the floor and grabs her half-constructed sugar-pink pompom. I'm working on one of my own in the soft green shade of mint ice cream, helping Bert towards her dream of an entire pompom wall, despite there being no space for such an installation.

"I didn't know," I say quietly. "About your mum."

"Yeah..." Bert sighs. "I mean, honestly when would I have told you? When did you ask?"

She doesn't say it meanly, but it cuts all the same. I didn't think I had to ask. I say, "Are they OK? Are you OK?"

"Mainly. There was the awkward dinner conversation about *cutting back*, of course. I wish Saz was home. She video-calls at dinner once a week from uni, but it's not the same as having a live-in sister. And Mum's stressed. She made me a Gantt chart."

"What's a Gantt chart?"

"Oh, be happy in ignorance."

I wrap yarn. The sky outside the window is deep denim blue. Even though I shouldn't think it, it's impossible to ignore: somewhere out there Baker's getting ready. I check my phone. Six thirty.

"Are you sure you're not in the mood for a party?" It comes out involuntarily, an echo of Baker's message, straight from my subconscious to my tongue.

Bert stiffens. "Yeah, I'm perfectly sure I don't want to hang with a bunch of strangers and get wasted on a school night. Isn't your exhibition hand-in tomorrow? What if you overslept?"

"We wouldn't have to… Never mind…" *Olivia would go with me*, I think, like the world's most disloyal friend. I wind a yarn round and round the gap between my two fluffy pompom sides and pull tight, aware of Bert's gaze.

"If it's important, by all means go without me."

Bert throws a completed pompom on to the pile beside her and reaches for another colour of wool, her face rigid.

I put the wool down. This isn't how I want the night to go. "Look, I don't want to go to the party." And it's true. It's not about the party.

"Is he worth it?"

"I…"

Bert holds up a hand. "Please don't bullshit me on top of everything. You like him?"

My glasses slip to the end of my nose and Bert becomes a blur. I nod.

"Is it a thing? Does he like you?"

I push my glasses up. Isn't that the question? The one circling me since last night. There's some evidence: the kiss for one. And his messages. Even seeing him at school today – a snatched greeting between classes and frantic last-minute exhibition prep – it was friendly. Nice. Like nothing's changed. But something has changed and I need time to understand what it means. I need to know what's real. What I mean to Baker now that we're no longer alone in the dark wishing on faraway cars as though they're shooting stars.

I can't bear the idea of confiding in Bert and having it all go wrong again.

So I say, "Why would he?"

"Please don't make me throw things." Bert launches a finished pompom at me with the precision of her netball-skirted goal attack days and it bounces off my glasses.

"I guess beauty's in the eye of the beholder?"

"Oh god." Bert plucks up pair of scissors and mimes throwing them too. "Screw the beholder, why do they get all the power? You're beautiful. Luminous. Brainy and brilliant." She waves her hand to indicate all of me. "No one needs eyes to see that. Now cheese!"

The change of tack throws me and I look up into the eye of Bert's phone.

"No, no, no." I cover my face with my arms.

Bert wheedles and, in a nasty corner of my heart, I wonder what Olivia would think if I let Bert post. How Olivia might feel to be the one left aside. It's a gross impulse. I don't like it there in my brain, making me someone I'm not.

I let Bert take the photo. The filter makes my eyes huge. They pop out of my artificially smooth skin that seems to glow from within. And that's someone else I'm not.

*

Bert's dad makes macaroni cheese with cauliflower in the mix as a nod to health and breadcrumbs on top. Her mum's out with friends and I wonder when was the last time my mum went out with hers. When was the last time she took a break? What do parents even talk about? Probably us. And I feel bad for the way I left things the other night.

Under the table, I sneak my phone out of my pocket to check whether Baker's messaged me, my hands turning clumsy when I see his name come up.

Bert piles some salad on her plate and eyes me. "So I know you aren't friends any more, but I'm kind of worried about Olivia—"

"What?" That name jerks my attention more effectively than a lasso.

"I know it's probably so *not* on your radar," Bert says, and

I nod, because I can't decide what's reasonable. Whether she should be talking to me about this at all.

My phone lights up and I unlock it without trying. A photo of me on the high street. I'm silhouetted against the sun. A shadow. A mystery, but I'm tagged if anyone's curious. I remember Baker taking it with his phone but I didn't expect him to keep it. Or share. The sight of it out in public is strange. Unnerving.

I try to put my phone away and focus on what Bert's saying. Olivia.

"She's been on these apps and I think if you and her could chat…"

Another photo of me crouched and taking a shot. One of mine and Baker's shoes facing each other on the packed soil of the mound, lit up in the dark, our toes close. So close.

When I finally tear myself away, Bert's watching me pointedly.

"Sorry?"

"Forget it." Her typical Bert bluntness undercut by a weary softness. "I shouldn't have brought it up anyway."

"Help yourself, Iris," Bert's dad says, putting down a water jug and a glass of orange juice. I watch the last pulpy bits sink as he heads back out to the kitchen.

Bert glances at her own phone. Then she gasps. "Is this … you? Did you… Have you seen this?"

She saw Baker's images, I guess. "I didn't think he'd post them," I say, a little smile creeping on to my face now the initial surprise has passed. It's sweet, maybe. It's something.

Bert shakes her head. "What a creep," she says, eyes on the screen. "Such a transparent move to stay relevant to your life. So needy and embarrassing, my god."

I'm lost. "Why's Baker a creep?"

"Baker?" Bert wears my confusion. She flips her phone round and my eyes scour the screen for clues.

On Bert's screen, it's Theo, not Baker. But still me.

A photo of me there. There in Theo's room. On his bed. My hands are splayed across my giggling face, my forearms covering my body and the duvet cover up to my pits. But anyone could tell I'm naked underneath. My smudged eyes, flushed cheeks and the size of my toothy grin gives the game away.

I take Bert's phone from her hands, mine shaking lightly as I open the caption, as I turn up the sound. Theo's voice emerges from the tinny speakers of Bert's phone. A snippet of a new song. A verse, a chorus, a taster. It starts in the middle, a guitar strumming along behind the words.

But now I can see the lie
Your personality was mine
Reflecting anything I said
From your pretty, empty head
Because you?
You're blank inside

And you?
You're off my mind
Because you?
Were just a waste of time

Bert grimaces in sympathy. "What a wanker."

The loop starts from the beginning, the tune upsettingly catchy, and I hand Bert back her phone, resisting the urge to throw it at the wall.

"It's not so terrible," Bert says. I give her a hard stare. "I promise! You can hardly tell it's you. And you don't look naked. I mean … you're not naked, are you?"

"That's not the point."

Bert's dad drifts past the door doing a terrible impression of someone not listening.

But she's wrong anyway. It's a side angle, but it's definitely me. My grin's too wide, my gums on show and my cheeks are flushed and blotchy. The way my arms are clenching the sheet makes them enormous and I can't tell if it's a perspective thing or if they are indeed humongous. And I shouldn't care but I do. The point is that photo was meant to be private. It was meant to be deleted.

I remember him pretending to peek under the covers. I remember kicking him away and laughing as he snapped the shot. Him twisting the phone round to show me, bringing it close so I could see it without glasses.

"Oh no, I'm a monster," I said. "Delete! Delete!"

"OK," he laughed and prodded at his phone. "But you look fine." I squeezed my eyes shut. "Beautiful."

More lies. All of it.

"He wrote a whole song," I say. And I'm seized by the sudden hope that perhaps it's not about me. Perhaps Bert won't think it is and Bert will talk me down, but she can't even look at me and, god, that's the worst thing: knowing that she agrees with him on some level. Of course she does. It's me to a tee.

Blank. Empty. *Grey.*

"He definitely wants you to angst about it. It's all some sad-boy power play. If you ask him to take it down, he'll feed off the desperation."

"Um?"

"Oh, no. No, not desperation." Bert pulls her mouth wide. "Our boy Theo wants you under his thumb, that's all."

And she's right. Right about my desperation and right about Theo's thumb. I felt safe there once. Safe from what anyone but he thought of me. Safe from my own opinions.

She's right about him wanting a reaction too, but I've never been able to resist.

An easy target.

I unblock him and open my messages.

Me: delete that photo

Theo: now you're talking to me?

Me: delete it. take it down. i'm serious. delete the song

Theo: i would, but it goes together – the white blanket and the girl in black and white with the song

Theo: lots of empty space

Me: it's MY FACE!

Theo: look how quickly you talk to me when you want something, ris

Theo: it hurts to be ignored, doesn't it?

Theo goes quiet. He goes offline.

"Obviously this calls for elaborate schemes to take him out," Bert says with a swipe of her nail across her throat. "But at a real, practical level … is there anything you want to do? Or anything I can do? I mean, really, does he not even appreciate the irony of a song about how he's not thinking about you any more? I thought this boy was smart at least."

"There's nothing anyone can do." I reach shakily for a serving spoon, my hands pale and strange and strained, as though the skin is stretched too taut. The table slips and silvers, and the dazzle across my eyes looks like the first sparks of an idea. Because there is something I can do.

"Are you going to be OK?" Bert says.

I am. I give Theo exactly five minutes and, when he doesn't reply and doesn't take it down, I tell Bert I have a Purkoy-based emergency at home. Back in an hour tops.

"Promise me you're not going to go there? Promise you won't give him the satisfaction of seeing you upset?" Bert says, not buying my excuse for one second.

Seeing me upset? That's an easy promise. A sort of white lie of a promise.

On the street outside, I find a corner obscured by a bulky hedge and lean back until the twigs poke painfully into my spine.

I squeeze my eyes shut and summon the pins-and-needles sensation of disappearing. I imagine everyone, the whole of our year, laughing over Theo's song. All of them right now in their homes with my face in the palm of their hands, thinking about how Theo made me nothing.

A prop. A backdrop. A waste of time.

The thoughts spiral until I'm dizzy in the vicious dark I have made for myself and I wrench my eyes open.

Gone.

I've got it under control. My mind, my visibility. I'm taking it back.

35

I stare at the front door of Theo's house. It gawps back, twin slits of obscure glass above a thin letterbox mouth, but it sees straight through me.

And, OK, perhaps I didn't consider the limitations of my invisibility – like locked doors – before I arrived here, but no worries. I'll improvise.

I step up to the door and knock – hard – then step away, as if it matters. Inside there's the distant bleat of Theo's mum shouting for someone to get the door and the clatter of feet. It opens and a small face peers round. Theo's brother leans out, swinging on the doorframe to peer behind the door and standing on tiptoes to check the street. He fills all the space, leaving no room to squeeze past.

The door shuts. Inside a child's voice shouts, "There's no one there."

Luckily Theo's parents rarely have time to listen to their middle child. Luckily the word of a twelve-year-old boy doesn't count for much.

There's a scuffle within. The door's heaved open and Theo stands on the threshold, clearly pissed off. Probably pulled away from his games. His pale blue eyes search the street. For a moment, he's so close. Close enough to touch.

"No one," he shouts behind him.

As the door slams in my face a second time; it hammers home the realization that this flimsy plan of mine isn't going to work. I'm not getting in via the front door.

I knock once more for the pure satisfaction of it, but leave before anyone answers.

Theo's house is an end terrace, the only house out of four to have a side gate. I walk there now and carefully unlatch it, slipping through into the thin space between houses and closing the gate behind.

Theo's mum, Caroline, sits at a steel patio table, the open dining room doors spilling out warm light. Her head rests in one hand, a podcast emanating from her phone as she taps away at a crossword, a glass of wine beside her.

I slip past slowly, avoiding the cracked, wobbly patio slab, and carry on into the house, dodging through the kitchen-diner where Theo's filling a glass at the sink. I resist the urge to get closer, to stick my thumb under the water, or move objects around or anything as satisfyingly pointless as that. *Focus, Iris.*

As I step into the hall, Bear the Jack Russell comes careening through, yapping and tail wagging. He veers off and comes right to my feet. He sniffs, his black nose and white whiskers scuffling against my invisible toes, obsessed, as ever, with my Purkoy smell.

"No, Bear. Go, go," I whisper, balancing on my right foot.

"Sit," I hiss.

He jumps up and rebounds, then paws at my leg. A weird sight when my leg's not there. I stare in horror between Bear and the open door in front of me, where there's a small boy on the sofa watching. Hastings sibling number two.

"Bear…" he says, tiny face furrowed and I will him desperately to go back to whatever's exploding on TV.

I step on to the bottom stair and it groans. My heart ticks faster.

"Tell your bell-end mates," says Theo, walking up behind me with a drink in his hand. "If I have to answer the door to their pranks one more time—"

"Yeah?" his brother says. "It's not them, so who's the dickhead now?"

"Little shit." Theo puts his drink down on the console table, strides into the front room and tackles his brother on to the sofa.

Bear's nose pushes against my knee, wet and cold, bringing me back to the task at hand. I snatch my moment. Dash upstairs.

"Josh?" An even younger face pops out from a bedroom.

There are too many people in this house. My lungs are bursting but I clamp my hands over my mouth and try to breathe quietly as brother number three leaves his doorway to investigate. He stops close enough for me to smell his fake man-smell – cheap musky body spray and hair product. Close enough to see the freckles across the bridge of his nose, so like Theo's, each of the Hastings sibling a carbon copy of their dad, getting younger and younger, smaller and smaller, like nesting dolls. He listens for a moment, then retreats to his room.

I pause on the threshold of Theo's bedroom, held by the sight of it. Familiar and unfamiliar. His guitar, his bedsheets and the wonky stack of books beside it, the utter Theo-ness of it, but everything is out of place. There's a new poster replacing The Shins one that was always curling away from the wall. He has different shoes under his desk.

Theo's laptop's open, his headset plugged in and leaking the melancholy sound of Thom Yorke.

His phone's missing and that's a blow. But I go to his laptop and jiggle his gaming mouse.

"Get your own stuff, you freak," Theo shouts. And my heart stops for a moment before I realize it's directed at a brother. He sounds close, though – bottom of the stairs?

Between the desk, bed and shelves there's nowhere to hide in this tiny room. The bottom step creaks. *Shit, shit, shit.* Blood pounds in my ears as I cast about for a place to tuck away. I might be invisible, but if Theo walks into me, he's going to notice there's something wrong.

My imagination throws up a succession of images like a photo stack. Theo's arms holding me hostage in my invisible state. His family coming to see. Shocked faces. The police? And inevitably I have to turn back sometime. I can't stay invisible and silent in police custody.

"Theo?" I hear from far, far away beyond the noise of my own thoughts.

"What?" He's closer now. On the stairs.

"Theo?" His mum's voice.

He steps on to the landing. His profile visible at the edge of the open door. A sigh and he disappears, his footsteps heavy on the way downstairs.

I move fast now. No time to reminisce over the bad old days. I type in his password: *KarmaP0l1c3.*

His logins are all saved, so in a second I have it in front of me. And in another...

Delete post?

Click.

Just like pressing the shutter, it's that easy. And victory bubbles up in me like fury. I want more. I want to shred it all. Take scissors to the duvet, throw his books on the floor and his clothes out of the window. I want to take a permanent marker from the mug on his desk and scrawl

HOW FUCKING DARE YOU? across his wall. It's not enough. I want Theo to know how it feels to be discarded.

My chest heaves while I stand still, my mind running riot. But here's the thing: a single deleted post leads back to me.

So I delete it all. Post by post. And I should feel good. I should feel something. I should probably leave. But I stay. And I suddenly don't know how I got here. Why I thought this was justified. The adrenaline pumping through me turns to a slick, sickly feeling in the pit of my stomach. *What am I doing here?*

A message flashes up in the bottom-right corner of Theo's computer screen. My eyes track across the words on reflex.

Spade: shit, she's something else

The guilt recedes, replaced by curiosity.

I open the thread. The Theo-Ash-Spade group chat.

I scroll back for context. Above Theo's commentary there are screenshots of my messages earlier this evening, though I notice he's cropped his own final comments about me ignoring him:

Theo: look at this – over a song?

Ash: like artists haven't been writing songs about their exes since the beginning of time?

Theo: i can't believe this

Theo: this one too:

> **Olivia:** you've ruined everything between me and iris and do you even care? about me? about either of us?
>
> **Olivia:** and after all this you're just going to ignore me?
>
> **Theo:** i'm not ignoring you
>
> **Olivia:** why won't you talk to me?
>
> **Theo:** what's this if not talking?
>
> **Olivia:** you know what I mean. don't pretend.
>
> **Olivia:** it doesn't matter. other people want to talk to me

She's sent a screenshot of messages between her and some guy. He tells her she's beautiful. He's looking forward to meeting her.

Below, Olivia's sent Theo a pic. She's all dressed up and it's captioned: might wear this for my date tomorrow night, what do you think? Or don't you care?

It's none of my business. I should be over worrying what

Olivia's doing. Or Theo. Or what the two of them are doing together. The realization knocks me regardless. She told me they weren't talking any more, but of course she lied. And now an online date to make Theo jealous?

Theo: might be single for a while after this

Ash: hope you've learned a valuable lesson about juggling two friends at once

Ash: tut tut. you dog, you. I'm not angry, just disappointed etc. etc.

Spade: shit, she's something else

Impossible to know which of us Spade means. Both?

In a daze, I screenshot everything and send myself copies. And then I delete the rest of my message history with Theo. Everything. I don't want him to have any little piece of me.

It's not enough. It'll never be enough. I could walk downstairs and tell Theo's whole family what he's done. I want them to know. And, for one second, I'm determined to do it, make that scene. My fists ball and the room seems to solidify.

"What the hell?" Theo stands at the threshold and the way he's looking at me, well, the problem is, he's looking.

At me.

36

"Hey, Ris," Theo says, kind of low. Mindful, I suppose, of his family nearby. "Care to explain why you're in my house?"

"I … uh." I fold my arms. Get a grip. "I'm just leaving, actually."

But the room's too small. Theo's blocking the exit.

"How'd you even get in here?" he says.

I lift my chin.

"Whatever." He tuts. "Sneaking into other people's houses? This is unacceptable behaviour. You shouldn't be here."

"I guess neither of us have behaved perfectly then." And I realize this is why I came back. It's unavoidable and long overdue. I find my words at last. "What did you think was going to happen, Theo? You cheated on me. You wrote a song about me. You messaged me non-stop when I just wanted to forget you exist."

"Non-stop?" he scoffs. "Get over yourself. I was trying to stay friendly. Guess we're done with that?"

"Why are you posting pictures of me?"

"It fitted the song." He shrugs. "It wasn't about you, Ris. You're looking for reasons to be the victim here honestly." His eyes shift to his laptop and I block it with my body. "Did you delete it yourself? Is that it?"

"I want you to leave me alone."

"Then, just an idea, but get out of my house?" He laughs.

The injustice smarts. The way he's twisted things. I shake my head, trying to clear it of him, trying to hold on to the truth.

I step forward again, but as I twist to get past, he grabs my arm and pushes me back inside with a "Come on now."

"Theo." I hold my arm.

"Look, don't leave. I thought you wanted to chat this through," he says mildly.

I want out. My eyes skitter to the door as he kicks it closed behind him.

Every time. Every fight. Just like this. Theo calm, until he wasn't. Theo kind, until he wasn't. I am trembling now. Bravery vanished. I look at my fingers and wish myself gone. I don't care if Theo sees. I don't care if he's scared. All I care about is leaving.

But I stay. I always stayed.

"What kills me is that we were good together," Theo says. "Genuinely. No one else got it, though. Spade absolutely rinsed me for going with you. I put up with so much. For you. Do you know that?"

"You told me. Was I supposed to feel grateful?"

Theo smiles. Because he knows.

I was grateful.

"So I mess up one time. One time, when O threw herself at me at that party … what was I even meant to do?"

"It wasn't one time."

"One girl. Same thing."

"She's my friend."

"Well … not any more, is she?" His eyebrows rise. "And you still won't let it go."

My focus sinks to the floor. To the toe of Theo's white socks.

"No one else will ever like you like I did, you know?" His brow crinkles in an expression of extreme concern – almost pity – his conversational tone worse somehow than shouting or swearing or threats.

I squeeze my eyes closed.

"I mean, you think that Baker guy likes you?" I don't move. Don't react. Don't give him anything. Theo tuts. "He feels sorry for you, Ris. You're just… You need other people to hold you together constantly. You're exhausting. How's anyone meant to put up with that?"

And he's right. He's completely right.

A strange peace settles over me.

Theo steps further into his room and sits on his bed. He takes out his phone and says without looking at me, "I'm sorry, Ris. I tried. But you? You're impossible to love."

There's space, at last, to go.

I leave the house, not stopping at the sound of Caroline's surprise from the kitchen.

I slam the door and stumble into the street. Gasping.

The raw rush of shame sends me dizzy. The garden wall grates the tender surface of my palm as I fall, as I try to save myself and fail, slamming to my knees on the tarmac as the world shatters into shimmering fragments of silver.

37

I get home late. I don't bring my body. Thank god for Mum's run of nights.

I take out my phone and there are messages and missed calls waiting for me:

Bert: So I guess you're not coming back?

Bert: Are you serious?

Shit. I stare at the messages for a wretched minute before swiping Bert away.

The missed calls are all him.

Theo: pick up your phone

I leave that unread too, slipping under my duvet where I try not to think about Theo. His words. And how I'm—

Instead, I reach for Baker under the shadowy clouds. Baker against a backdrop of mundane lights made beautiful by the distance. Baker who makes me forget who I am for a while.

> **Baker:** You're probably doing way more interesting stuff involving art and creativity and the deep contemplation of life and all its possibilities
>
> **Baker:** Whereas I am drinking beer surrounded by people who are also drinking beer
>
> **Baker:** So who's missing out really?

He's sent photos. A video. I press play and get an off-balance sweep of the scene.

The field's chaos. Too many faces, too dark. There's too much noise in the background: voices clambering over music blasted from portable speakers, laughter from wide drunk mouths drowning Baker's narration. There's a constellation of flickering lights inside low metal buckets. I can almost feel it. I hate parties. The strangers. The inability to have a meaningful conversation. Too many people in one place.

But still, I want to go. I'm desperate to go, to be someone who could. Pinned down instead by the weight of the night and the weight of being me.

I flick through, searching for glimpses of Baker. More photos. Some tags. Pictures he didn't send me. Baker laughing at the girl beside him, her hair shimmering in the firelight. Baker doubled over in hilarity, his hand on her arm, her eyes alight at the sight of him. Beautiful him. The two of them standing so close.

It's captioned: Goofy lil drunk @beedumdumdavis

And I know it's nothing. It's probably nothing. It's almost certainly nothing. But I still can't stop the whisper.

He feels sorry for you.

The little voice I want to shut up.

Exhausting.

The fear that history's repeating itself.

*

I can't sleep. Everything's black. The inside of my mind is alive. Crawling. My heart's thumping.

The thought of going back tomorrow.

The thought of seeing them all and them seeing me.

The pressure.

The noise.

The judgement.

All the faces.

I raise my hands to put them against my head and they're gone and back, again and again. My silvery skin flickering like a dying light bulb.

It's disturbing.

I watch the ceiling swirl. My thoughts go with it.

I don't want to go back.
I don't want to go back.
I don't want to go.

38

I wake up this way.

The first clue is that everything's grey. Ceiling. Walls. The weak early light. And my hand on its way to rub sleep from my eye simply doesn't exist. There's a strange flattened dip in the covers where my other arm should be.

Where the duvet humps over my body there's a hollow place where I can see the pattern on the underside of the sheet as it disappears into darkness and fuzz at the edge of my vision. I'm a cave. A nothing. But it means I don't have to make a choice and that's good. My sleepless night has knocked the feeling out of me.

I flop out of bed, reach for my glasses and instinctively look to the mirror as the world comes into focus.

Nothing.

And with this sharpness comes the first flutter of panic.

I can't deliver my exhibition pieces without a body.

*

Head down, keep going, I navigate a maze of bodies and backpacks. My eyes skitter, taking everything in, making sense of nothing. I try to make a plan, but my thoughts tangle together. I just know this: find Bert, assess the damage. Later there will be Baker. The exhibition deadline. There's time.

"Did she say why?" Olivia's saying when I find my friends in the common room first thing, Olivia's face furrowed in concern and Bert's mouth stretched open in a yawn as she sits up to watch a new arrival before flopping back into the sofa.

And it's a relief, in a way, to hear them talking about me and know I exist in their minds, if not on the ground. Because I tried to come back this morning, I did, but I couldn't find myself.

"Nope. Just left and never came back." Bert sighs. "No explanation, no apology."

"That's not very Iris."

"I appreciate you haven't seen a lot of each other lately, but I can confirm it's very much her new thing. And you know what else is pretty on-brand these days?" Bert hands Olivia her phone. "Ditching your friend to party with the rebound."

I lean in closer to watch as Olivia's finger sweeps the

screen. A blur of dark pictures. Fires on fields, a crush of people. Baker by the fire.

"She's not in any of the pictures," Olivia says. "Did you see her? Are you sure?"

"She kept going on about it, O." Bert leans her head back against the wall and addresses the ceiling. "I shouldn't even be talking about this with you. She probably doesn't want you to know where she's going and what she's doing and I am, once again, being the shittiest of friends."

Olivia returns the phone. "Hardly. That's a competitive category."

Bert doesn't crack a smile as she tilts her head to look at Olivia. "You two are exactly the same, you know. Both of you thinking you're only alive when some boy's looking at you."

"We're not the same."

"She's late today too. Or still avoiding me."

"OK, so if she did go to the party, maybe she got squiffy and overslept? Everyone knows Iris Green handles wine like a toddler on a unicycle." Bert sniffs, and Olivia adds, "But I don't think she'd ditch you deliberately. She was probably more upset by the Theo thing than she let on." Olivia crosses her legs and twists towards Theo's usual corner, currently conspicuously empty. "Maybe she went to talk to him?"

"OK, but after that? Why wouldn't she come back?"

Olivia shrugs and turns her phone over beside her on the

sofa, her home screen also empty. No messages from Theo. Or the other one, the older one. That date she's meant to go on later. Does Bert know? Bert must know. Bert knows everything. I stretch my mind back to what she was saying about Olivia last night but it's one big missing piece, as if everything that happened at Theo's obliterated my earlier memories and now all I have is the feeling of standing in that room. The awful empty acceptance that I will never be enough. Not for Theo. Not for anyone.

"Either way, she's going to miss her deadline if she doesn't show. And I for one don't care." Bert cranes her head round, searching for someone in the crowd.

"Call her?" Olivia says.

"She's ignoring my messages. And she hates calls."

A pause.

"Oh."

"This is, actually, my fault," Bert says. "I should have made you tell her."

"You can't say that—"

"I knew this would happen! She had to find out eventually and if you'd just been honest with her the first time he made a move, you two would still be friends, she would still be here and everything wouldn't be so screwed." Bert lets out a huge breath and puts her head in her hands. "I should have made you tell her. I … I handled this so damn badly."

My heart goes cold.

"I'm sorry," Olivia says, putting her hand on Bert's back.

"I don't care," Bert says. "I don't! I'm done. I don't give a damn where she is; I don't give a damn if she never comes in; frankly I don't give a damn if I never see her again since she can't even tolerate me for one goddamn night."

Olivia grabs Bert and pulls her in for a hug. Against the backdrop of common-room noise, I can't hear the muffled postscript to Bert's rant or Olivia's assurances.

But I guess I have what I wanted.

I hate that I've hurt Bert, but at least now I know. Perhaps I always have. The shifting suspicion that's been inside me since this all started coalesces into something solid.

Bert knew right from the start. Of course she did. Bert knows everything.

39

Invisible – grey – I head to the toilets. I shut myself in the cubicle. I take a deep breath. I try. Try to come back. But there's nothing good in my head. I message him and he starts typing immediately. It's not enough. I call him. Fingers fumbling my phone.

Come back, Iris. Don't be so useless, Iris.

Baker picks up and says my name like it's an urgent question and it's this: the comfort of his voice, the warmth, that will bring me back. That's the only thing I need right now. Come back, hand in my work and then? Then work out what the hell to do about Bert.

But my hands around my phone are still gone.

"Something happened," I say. "Where are you? Can we meet? Now?"

"Sure. Of course, I'm on my way in. What happened?"

I shake my head.

"Never mind. I'll come," he says. "The darkroom?"

"Ye— No." I think about all my prints laid out ready to submit. Not there. The space is too cramped and I can't mess around with doors and darkness and hope I reappear. I need an open space with places to tuck myself away, to see Baker without him seeing me at first. "Oat Lane?" I say. "By the bike racks?" He'll know it. Everyone does, whether they vape or smoke or skive or not.

"Ten minutes. I'll be there."

"Baker?"

"Yeah?"

"When you spoke to me … the first time. When you asked me to the bridge … why did you ask me?"

He pauses. I unravel. Down to the floor so my thighs hit my calves. I want him to tell me something to bring me back, to put me in my skin. I want it to be that I am possible to love or at least like. I am not exhausting; I'm interesting or smart or funny or anything, anything, anything. I—

"I guess you seemed like you needed someone."

I put my hand over my mouth.

"I'm on my way, OK? I'll be there soon."

Bye, I try to say, but the word doesn't come out.

Someone's graffitied on the wall:

GOOD LUCK OUT THERE. IT SUCKS.

*

My brain needs to shush. I walk. I let my feet carry me and feel the back and forth and the solid ground under my soles. Thump, thump, thump, the ground and I colliding, solid and simple. People keep walking at me, forcing me to step aside, give way, like I'm the least important person in this whole school.

I'm at our meeting place before him. I pace the lane. My mind loops and loops over one memory and it isn't starlight and dancing and an endless, edgeless walk with his hand in mine – no – it's another time. And I see it so starkly: the shouting, angry state of me, the way I turned on him over nothing.

You needed someone.

And here I am ruining his week, again. Just like I warned him I would. I'm broken. Too much for anyone to deal with and it was unfair to ask Baker to come here, to ask him to be the one to hold me together. Constantly.

You needed someone.

But it's too late. A figure emerges from the space between school buildings. Tie askew, blazer slung over his leather camera bag. In spite of every intention to save Baker from all this, from me, I sigh and shakily stand.

I raise a hand and my relief turns to dust.

Baker's the boy who brings me back.

But I'm not back.

Why am I not back?

"Baker," I croak as panic winds round my throat and

Baker looks straight through me, not even flinching at the disembodied sound of my voice, because there is no sound. No voice.

I try to whisper. To shout.

Nothing.

And I realize I had still been holding on to that strange hope from the train: that I could never be invisible to Baker. Not even like this.

He comes to lean against the bike shelter, pushing up his sleeves as his gaze rakes the lane, the buildings, me – his expression never changing.

The school bell sounds in the distance. I imagine my feet appearing. My legs, knees.

Come on, Iris.

I press myself tight against the metal frame and try to think of something – anything – worth coming back for – how it was on the mound, the things Baker said – but all the good memories are out of focus.

Baker waits. Half an hour? More? Walking to the middle of the lane and looping.

"Iris, where are you?" he says, checking his phone on repeat. And I whisper it with him in a voice that won't make a sound.

I wait with him – almost in reach – wondering if a message scrawled in the dirt under his feet would mean anything. But what could he do, even if I tried? How could he help, even if he understood?

He waits. And I get cold waiting with him.

He sighs and I move closer. I reach for his hand, for the warmth of skin against skin and the promise that I'm real. I falter. Pull back. It would be nothing to him.

He waits. He waits. And then? He walks away.

40

No hyperbole: I think this might be the end of Iris Green.

After Baker left, after waiting, after trying and trying to bring myself back, after pacing the lane, frantic and freaked out, I come to the darkroom. And it's gone. Gone.

The frames. My prints. Everything I laid out here.

It must have been Theo. A retaliation. A deletion for a deletion.

So this is it. No work to submit, no shot at the prize.

Almost no evidence I was ever here at all, just one photo left on the work surface. It's me. Of course.

I'm grey.

I snatch it up. Into my hands. Fists. Buckled, glossy print. My face folding. My shadow disappearing into a crevasse. Imploding into a thick wad of paper. I hold it so tight it bites my palms and makes my fingers ache.

It's not enough.

I unbunch the paper, smooth it out. My grey self breathes as the print flexes against the wood. But she's not off the hook. I rip her in half. Right down the middle so her face is broken. It feels too good. Too right. I rip and tear until it's fragments.

That version of me. Gone.

And when I stop – when I *can* stop – I hitch in a breath I can no longer hear.

I look around the room and there's nothing left. And that's perfect, really. An empty room. A wasted space. So much wasted time. Because it's too late now. Too late to come back. Too late to submit anything. I pull out my phone and see the messages Baker sent me in the lane:

Baker: Have you handed in your work for the exhibition?

Baker: Are you on your way?

Baker: Are you OK? Where are you?

Baker: I don't understand why you're not talking to me

I stare at the empty space of my splayed hand.

Come back.

I try to say it with my mouth.

Come back.

And I almost see it. A flicker. A spark. Like last night. There and then gone.

My skin hurts. Prickles. The jitter of electricity everywhere. All my outsides sharp and cold and too much. My vision blurring and slipping. And that phrase comes back to me. The one from my childhood. The one Mum would use when this happened with scary frequency and I lost myself over and over. Only the phrase isn't a comfort; it's an affirmation. Because this time it is. It is. It is the end of the world.

41

This is the place I go. Closing my eyes and drifting through a tumble of green and yellow. I pick my way across the dry ground and up to the mound to sit against the bare compacted soil and look over to where cars are rushing by.

I wanted to find that moment here: the memory with Baker from only a couple of short days ago. But that place is gone. In daylight it's no longer special. It's nothing. Ugly.

I can't feel the ground underneath me. It's dizzying and disconcerting. I am untethered. Grateful simply to not be sinking into the earth. Grateful not to be drowning in soil and stones.

I curl my knees to my chest and I can't feel them either. No more skin, no more me, only everything inside, too huge to hold on to.

It's all gone. There will be no prints on the wall in their

smooth black frames. No exhibition. There will be no Bert and no Baker by my side. And that's a worse kind of failure than I imagined. This is what it means to really disappear.

I can't come back, so I fall apart. Let go.

*

It gets dark. It gets colder.

The mound turns beautiful. An early evening full of shooting stars – tiny and far away and unreal, but sometimes the light doesn't have to be all that big or bright.

Feeling returns to my fingers. Slowly, slowly. My skin against all the rough, gritty earth.

I shrug my bag off and it appears by my side. My phone spills out. No new messages from Baker. Nothing from Bert, but there's this:

> **Olivia:** i hope you're ok
>
> **Olivia:** you missed your deadline and we're all pretty worried

I sniff. "Worried" is not exactly how I'd describe Bert.

> **Olivia:** i've wanted to message you for ages and i haven't because i know you probably don't ever want to speak to me again, but i've been thinking so much about you and what i've done. i wanted to say

i understand and i will leave you alone, but i also need to say you counted, iris. we counted.

Olivia: i'm so sorry i forgot. i'd give anything not to be the me who did this

I cradle my phone.

I am suddenly back on that cramped dancefloor seeing Olivia change. I'm watching her kiss Theo. I'm in the girls' bathroom with her words on the wall. I am here, tired of apologies and blame and wanting to disappear.

So I dig.

The soil's still loose, the burial shallow. Baker and I didn't expect anyone to come treasure hunting in this corner of nowhere.

I use my phone case, then my chilly, invisible fingers, wiping the dirt away to open the box. Baker's print is on top and I move it aside carefully, face down, because it's his time capsule and his secret. But I turn mine over. An imperfect capture of an imperfect face. My selfie in the gallery.

And I think of her twin: another version of that girl in the double exposure Baker picked out in the darkroom all those weeks ago. And another in family photos. An entirely different girl in all the photos of my friends. All these girls with grey serious eyes and I see them like they're not me at all: girls who wanted to be liked, loved, wanted. Who became exhausted hiding different parts of themselves, because they didn't believe they could be loved whole. Hoping someone else might believe it for them.

Disappointed over and over again, shrinking smaller and smaller. And maybe that was necessary then. Sometimes we hide to survive.

But this is now.

I scrabble for a pen among the contents of my bag, discovering two biros and a thick black Sharpie. I uncap it and write over the surface of the print:

You see people

My eye peers out from beneath an **E**. Now it's a memory. And it means something, even though Baker was right and he was wrong. I'm not sure I do see people – I miss hidden agendas, I misjudge people sometimes, but I pay attention to other details. I do try. And what Baker said about acceptance and seeing the value in the unremarkable? That's something that feels true. A small fragile thought to hang on to.

I hold on to my portrait, let tears slip silently down my skin and fall on to my clenched hands, and the last few weeks catch up on me all at once, as if the memories are puzzle pieces slotting into positions that finally make sense.

I think I always knew. Baker's not gravity after all. He can't stop me from shrinking away, he can't stop me hiding and he can't bring me back.

No one else can do that. Only me.

And, right now, I really need to come back.

I gather my things and make a plan and when I'm done I hold up my hand – solid, real, there – to block out the lights on the horizon. I walk. I see everything spiral out ahead of me. I imagine all the ways I could fail and I know I'm going to go through with it anyway.

But first there's someone else I need to see.

42

"I came to apologize," I say. "Sorry I left last night and sorry I didn't come back and sorry I haven't been around much."

Bert sits cross-legged in the middle of her bed, her tasselled sunset-coloured duvet round her shoulders, her patchwork cushion in her arms and turquoise headphones round her neck.

One of her eyebrows twitches almost imperceptibly and I take it as encouragement. I move inside her room and shut the door, standing against it, all awkward. Not knowing whether to stand or sit or get out.

"I know I haven't been a great friend lately," I say. Because although I have my reasons and I know I haven't been trying to shut Bert out, I guess that's not her experience. I sit down, gather a cushion from Bert's floor and hug it to my chest behind my knees so the two of us are mirrors. "But I think it's because I knew no one was being honest with me. Not even you."

Bert's mouth clenches.

"You always knew? About Theo and Olivia. You knew before I did?"

She closes her eyes. "I told her to stop as soon as it started."

"But you didn't tell me," I say. "You had a choice and you chose Olivia."

This unblocks Bert. "I didn't *choose* her. I thought there was a way to fix it before you found out, that's all. I wanted the problem to go away, or for me to manage it away somehow. And I told you Theo was the worst, even before the cheating."

I give Bert a look.

"It doesn't excuse it. But it wasn't a decision one way or another. It was … Olivia confided in me and that was her decision, but if I told you? Then I'd be the one breaking us up."

"So … it was a non-choice?" I say flatly.

"People make mistakes, Iris. Huge ones. And if I don't stand by my friends when they do, what kind of friend would I be? Was I meant to chuck her away and tell her she was beyond redemption?" Bert shifts on the bed, looking like she wants an answer.

I shrug and stroke the tassel from the cushion between my fingers. The fairy lights framing the window blink on and off.

"And I make mistakes too," Bert says. She takes a deep breath. "And I'm sorry."

"It was a choice." My voice fades out.

"A bad one. I just … wanted to hold us together. I thought I could."

"You can't do everything, Bert."

Her mouth compresses in a weary smile. "OK, that's my problem. But do you want to know yours?" Bert says gently. And I don't, really, because I can hear the whisper of Theo start up in my head. But she tells me anyway. "You're so worried all the time about everyone's opinions. But your harshest judge? It's you. And I really am your friend and I didn't choose O. I chose you both, if anything. I've been right here. Even when you disappeared on me."

Right. *That.* "I… I have been avoiding you." I hug the cushion tighter, dipping my chin to it, unable to look at Bert. "Not on purpose. There's just this tipping point where I know I'm not going to be great company and it's too hard to ask you to deal with my bad company, because you never want to hear that I'm not OK."

"I always care."

"But you don't always listen. And sometimes I don't need to be told how ridiculous I am and I don't want solutions. Sometimes I don't even want to talk."

I take a breath and force myself to meet Bert's eye. "I'm worried you won't put up with me any more," I say. "If I'm too much hard work for too long, you'll just give up."

"Iris." Her face is serious. "I don't need you to be good company. I need you to be you."

"OK."

"You're never too much work."

I nod. "But I am, actually, a mess sometimes. And my mind does, actually, turn on me sometimes. And I need to tell someone who's going to believe that."

"OK." Bert smiles. "I believe that you're an utter shambles, Iris Green." She spreads her arms, her hands bookending the wide space between them. "Giant. In the sincerest and most supportive way imaginable."

I laugh, an involuntary hiccough of surprise that makes Bert's grin widen.

"It just doesn't change how brilliant you are or the way I see you," she says. "Which I wish you could see too, because that view? Magnificent."

I shake my head. That's too much. A little too much of the same old Bert always insisting I should feel OK, that I am OK, that it's all in my head and everything will pass. But I smile all the same and silently pledge to start smaller.

"You too," I say. "Obviously."

"Obviously." Bert holds out her arms. "Do I need to hug you now?"

"No, no." I drop the cushion and put my hands up. "We don't have time for that."

*

We head into town to find her. It's half seven and all old grudges are temporarily suspended in pursuit of Olivia Edis: former bestie, backstabber and maker of the very worst decisions.

OK, maybe joint worst.

I'm armed with the screenshot of her message to Theo yesterday. The selfie. The threat of a date.

Don't you care? Theo didn't, but it turns out I still do and Bert does too. I don't have a plan for this bit, but I'll improvise. A milkshake to the crotch proved effective at stopping an inappropriate date once, so I'll work with the available opportunities. Just as soon as we track her down.

Bert's on her phone, checking her chat threads for clues, and calling Olivia in between. And despite our differences, our silences, our difficulties in navigating the last few weeks, I'm so grateful Bert and I are back on the same team.

"She's still not answering?" I say redundantly as Bert lets her phone fall from her ear for the fifth time.

"There's only so many places she could be," Bert says, holding her fingers out and reeling off a list of the hottest places in town: Prego, the one decent Italian restaurant; Envy, our classiest dive bar; the Wetherspoons on Castle Street; the White Lion, which smells of feet, deep-fried food and overzealous sports fans.

It'll take a good hour of traipsing round town to cover every possibility and that's assuming her mysterious date didn't take her out of town or on a romantic walk. It depends on Olivia being sat at a table, not between venues or nipped to the bathroom. It feels impossible before we've even started.

"Try her again," I say.

"She's not answering and my phone's kind of dead." Bert looks wretched. "Why are all my friends ghosting me lately?"

"OK. We just need to start somewhere."

"You know she's going to murder us, don't you?" Bert says. "She'll never forgive the interference."

"She'll get over it."

"He's probably a standard-issue creep, not a dangerous one."

"Bert! That's—"

"Shit. I know."

We stop at a crossing. My eyes settle across the road on a wrought-iron bench in front of the low stone wall of the church graveyard.

The crossing alarm sounds and as Bert and I begin to walk, I pull my phone out.

Olivia's most recent post is a twin of the selfie she sent Theo yesterday. All dressed up. Hair sleek, eyes glittering. Pictures tell the truth, don't they? She's fine, isn't she? Flawless, confident Olivia who can hold a theatre full of people in the palm of her hand. Olivia who took Theo simply because she could, then moved on the moment it didn't work out. She'll be fine when we find her. Pissed off, probably, that we intruded on her date.

She picks up on the first ring.

"Iris? God, I'm so sorry."

Bert leans in to listen and I see my concern mirrored in her eyes.

"Where are you?" I say.

"The park. The place where—"

"Stay. We're coming for you."

*

We find her on the far side of the park, where the grass gives way to the road. She's waiting on a familiar bench. A spot that was the end of, and catalyst for, everything.

She's alone. In pale grey joggers, an oversized denim jacket, hair pulled back and skin devoid of make-up, she couldn't look more different to the girl in the photo she posted an hour ago.

A rectangle of light appears beside her, a good-looking stranger fills Olivia's phone screen as it shivers lightly against the slats of the bench.

"He's been trying all night on and off," she says in a flat voice. "My date? I'm assuming that's the reason for this little reunion?"

"You didn't go?"

"Didn't see the point in the end. I don't need that guy to feel better about myself." Olivia wipes her eye with the palm of her hand and adds with a damp laugh, "Not that I feel stellar without him. But he wasn't the answer."

"Are you OK?"

"Not really. The messages have taken a bit of a turn. Annoyed that I led him on, I guess?"

"Entitled wanker," Bert seethes.

"We're just glad you're safe," I say.

"So you haven't blocked that guy yet." Bert sits on the bench beside Olivia. "But you screened my calls?"

"Another 'I told you so' wasn't exactly what I needed."

Bert looks affronted.

"Do you know how exhausting it is to be friends with someone as perfect as you sometimes?" Olivia says. "I'm so tired of being of the useless blonde fuck-up of this friendship circle."

"Oh my god!" Bert says. "The two of you. Seriously? Look at yourself! Amazing actress, astute and articulate public speaker, wanted by the entire population of King's—"

"That's not true." Olivia darts a glance my way. "And I don't want it to be. Not any more."

Bert pauses, momentarily abashed. "You can be the tactful one then." She holds out her arms and Olivia tumbles in. It's a replay of our scene in Bert's house an hour before, Olivia in the role of Iris Green, as Bert apologizes again and Olivia apologizes right back.

I've never been the best judge of how to pick a moment, but when my two best friends – current and former – finally let go, and Olivia gets one last miserable sniff out of her system, I say, "So who wants to roast Theo Hastings?"

43

This town's mine at night. Even with my skin on, even fully visible, I feel safe with Bert and Olivia beside me. I know every nook and cranny of this place. More importantly I know where Theo stuck the ads for his next gig. They're all over town, regular reminders of him I've been unable to ignore. But over by the old Argos where the boarded-up windows serve as a town noticeboard? That's where Theo went for it. That's where we find the mother lode.

It's a shame because Spade's artwork's great. Bold portraits of the three of them, hand lettering and a swirling background in vivid yellows and reds. They're striking. From a distance they look like targets.

Bert shrugs off her bag of craft supplies and we get to work with thick markers and spray paint, scribbling out

Spade and Ash and the venue details, adding our own vital information once Theo's last man standing.

He cheated on me.

He cheated with me.

He lied.

He wrote a shit song about me.

He has no talent

He has no soul.

"How is it that you feel more strongly about this than either of us?" I ask Bert as she puts the finishing touches to that last.

"Because I love you both? And watching you break up over this thoroughly inadequate human…?" Bert gives his face an enthusiastic scribble. "He owes me for emotional damages."

Olivia pauses mid-spray. "The soul thing? Fact."

The three of us stand back to survey our efforts.

"Outstanding," Bert says.

"What if no one goes to his gig?" Olivia says, eyes widening. "Or any of his gigs? Ever. Empty room. A whole-school Hastings boycott."

Imagine. This small act of vandalism just the start. People turning on Theo, hecklers turning up to his gigs, every girl in school knowing exactly what he did, and taking our side. Looking at the cathartic words scrawled over his face, I can imagine it so clearly.

But I can also imagine Theo finding out. I trace it out over the thick black and purple lines of paint and marker and know: no one will judge Theo for this. No one will blame Theo, least of all him.

He'll be embarrassed, maybe. Angry, definitely. He'll laugh us off or he'll retaliate.

We will never get what we want from Theo Hastings.

"We have to take them down," I say with a sigh before turning back to face Olivia and Bert and their disappointment. "He'll know it was us – me at least – and he'll know it's because he hurt us."

"So? He *should* know and he should feel every word," Bert says. "You know it's not on you to shield him from the consequences of his own shitty behaviour?"

"That," Olivia says, pointing at Bert.

"He knows," I tell Olivia, gently, wishing there was another way to say, "He doesn't care. There's no way to … give this back, if that makes sense?"

Olivia nods, eyes shiny.

"It doesn't mean we're fading away, just … letting go."

I look at my friends, the three of us here together with our laughter, rage and paint-smudged skin. And it feels right.

"God, this was such a waste of art supplies," Bert says.

"It was for us."

Olivia claps her hands and steps forward. She inflates her cheeks and blows out a long breath as her gaze flicks over our night's work.

She says, "This is for us too."

Then grabs a corner and rips.

*

When there's a heap of Theo's shredded faces at our feet, Bert closes her arms round me and holds tight. She reels in Olivia with a spare arm and the three of us lock together. Coconut shampoo and Gucci perfume and the firm warmth of friendship.

When we break apart there's a moment when Bert is still touching me and Olivia and the three of us are connected. But then I take a step back and Bert lets go. "I'm heading off," I say. "Tomorrow's kind of a huge one."

Bert nods. "Everyone check-in when we get home safe?"

"Will you come to the exhibition tomorrow?" I try not to look at Olivia and the way her hands creep round her arms as I direct my invitation solely to Bert. "I missed the submission deadline and Theo took all my work, but I have a plan to fix it. And I could do with my best friend to support me."

Bert's pupils flick back and forth over my face. Of course it was too much to ask, too presumptuous after all our recent heartache. Her mouth pulls into a grimace and I say, "I'm sorry, forget—"

"No, no!" Bert puts a hand out, all smiles. All traces of hesitation gone. "I wouldn't be anywhere else."

I take her hand. Squeeze it. "Can I have a moment with O?"

"No biting, no hair-pulling, no bloodshed," Bert says over her shoulder.

And then it's just us. Me and Olivia.

"I don't know about you, but I'm swearing off romance for a while," Olivia says with a wobbly laugh. She gestures behind us, to the park, to the past, and adds, "Benches too."

I give a small smile. We start walking slowly. I scuff my feet and say, "It's OK to want someone, you know? They just have to be someone who actually sees you and gets you … or at least wants to try." My mind goes to Baker, to the lane and the silence since. And I hope I haven't messed that up. I hope he still wants to try. "I guess you have to let people in too."

Olivia nods. "Do you feel better? After…"

"A bit. Not really… Petty crime rarely solves heartbreak."

Olivia's mouth turns down. "Iris, I'm sorry."

"I know."

"You're my best friend."

"I… OK."

"I messaged him. I've been messaging him," Olivia tells the pavement. "I've stopped now."

"Why did you? For so long, I mean."

"I think … I needed to feel it was worth it somehow."

"You and him?"

"Just some love story that you were caught in the middle of – as if that would make it better. But it wasn't a love story. I'm not sure he even liked me – maybe the idea…? But the more he saw, the less he liked." She shrugs. "That would make sense. Relatable, right?"

I shake my head. "You should forgive yourself. I … I forgive you, O. I do. And your message earlier? It helped me more than you could know."

And I think perhaps I understand Olivia better than I'd like. Because I ran after Theo too and I believed without question that how he treated me was all I was worth. Olivia opened my eyes, but it's hard to be grateful. She hurt me and herself and I so wish I could put us back together, but still. "We're never going to be friends in the way we were," I say. "I don't know if we can even… We can't go back. It just can't be the same."

I watch the light in Olivia's eyes dim as my words sink in. "OK," she says.

"But I've been going to these sessions – counselling – that Mrs Coombes set up and they're helping me process everything. I think if you asked, maybe they'd set them up for you too. They helped me realize I deserve people in my life who aren't going to hurt me." It sounds too much like a reproach – and maybe it is – but I don't want Olivia to apologize any more. I open my arms and fold her inside and we hold tight.

We fall apart. We take a step back.
And then we go our separate ways.

44

I go home, but don't sleep, even though I'm bone tired. I go to the bottom of my wardrobe and pull a lifetime of discarded prints from inside and fan them over the floor. And I look. And see. And I find myself again and again. Accidentally and on purpose. There and not quite there. In some my camera hangs alone in the middle of the shot, in others I'm visible but still hidden – my face tucked away in a wing mirror while the real subject walks past, my shop window reflection swallowed by a dummy behind the glass. Obscured by ripples over the surface of a puddle here, there a shadow.

Again and again and again it's me. Silver and white and black. Shades of grey. Reflections in glass and mirrors, there and not. The confusion of all of them together, the tension. It's something.

My hand slips across a stack and reveals a glossy sheet

of white. A misprint? But when I pull it out, it's a shot of a bathroom wall: *Iris Green is grey.*

Grey?

Maybe I am. Maybe I'm silver and pearl and gunmetal. Moonlight and stone. All the in-between shades, shadows and unknowns. Maybe that's its own kind of interesting.

45

The reception desk is empty under the school crest, the corridors quiet. Unnecessary lights have been shut off and the darkness shrinks the proportions of the space, creating an intimate atmosphere.

The large wooden doors to the canteen are wedged open, the inside divided by temporary white partitions. I'm very early and it's very empty. I've swapped my clunky boots for more delicate versions and the block heels clip noisily across the tile.

On every wall other people's artwork stares down. Large-scale paintings of swimmers, delicate diamonds creating the illusion of shimmering water; plaster casts of body parts; a moody collage of newspaper articles slashed all over with black and red paint. There's a tremor in my fingers and a familiar surge of anxiety. It's all amazing. This work, these artists, this space. So what am I doing here?

And then – really – what *am* I doing here? Because there I am. My work at least.

Nine prints. A three-by-three grid. Black frames, white mounts, silvery prints. Baker on the bridge, the busker, a girl running into a crowd of pigeons, the woman in her fur coat, man versus ice cream. They're all *mine.* It was never destroyed. Never stolen.

A lump the size of a fist lodges in my throat. It can only have been Baker.

As touched as I am, it doesn't change what I need to do. It makes it a whole lot easier. I dump my academy case on the ground in front of my exhibition space. I take one last look at these prints – the work I intended to show – and it's not bad. Not bad at all. Still.

I put a screwdriver to the fixing and begin to loosen it.

*

"When I said no last-minute changes, even I didn't expect this." Ms Amin says. "It's forty-five minutes until the doors open. What exactly do you think you're doing?"

"Um … a quick switch?" I cringe, bracing for whatever's next as I sit cross-legged on the floor surrounded by my dismantled artwork.

Ms Amin hits the ground, curling her legs beneath her. As I recover from the shock of my stern art teacher on the floor, she tucks her dark hair behind one ear and swivels a frame to get a better look. A shoe shop window one half-term morning. It was early, the shop was shut. Not a single passer-by noticed my camera hanging there in mid-air as I snapped a picture of my non-reflection.

"Well then." Ms Amin reaches for an unframed print. I am skewed and strange-looking, gazing off to the side of the frame. "These are very interesting and very … unexpected … from you, if you don't mind me saying?"

"Thank you." My voice disappears with the strain of taking the compliment.

"But you can't exhibit them tonight."

"You said—"

"Everyone else met the deadline. Everyone else was ready. All your classmates have seen your previous materials. I can't allow you an extra day's work and expect no one to mind when it comes to the judging. I'm sorry, I truly am. You can keep the existing display, of course."

My hands freeze over the back of the frame I'm reassembling on the floor. It's not like I hadn't considered this possibility, but it hits me all the same. Half an hour until guests arrive is a hell of a time to fail.

The prize. The validation. Proof – unequivocal proof – that other people believe in my work. How am I meant to let that go?

I could give up on my plan. I could take out these self-portraits and put back the old ones. But those belong to a different Iris.

"What if..." I start. Ms Amin's head tilts, her delicate gold earring catching the light, even as her eyes linger on the surface of my print. "What if I withdrew from the competition? Would you let me show these then?"

Her expression's unreadable. I have the horrible feeling she'll say no. Still no. My chance has been lost and I'll have to put my original prints back in their frames and stomach the disappointment. It wouldn't be nothing. It would be my work.

"Why?" she says.

I touch my fingers to the frame by my knee. Another portrait, not a reflected fragment of my face, an accidental capture or an invisible girl, but a proper portrait. All me. There. Visible.

"I'd like to show these if I can? Please? Even if it means not being eligible any more. They're important."

Ms Amin gets up. She puts a hand on my shoulder. "Good."

And then it's just me and the work. Just me and myself.

That's not right, though. There's something missing. I dive into my bag and pull out a Sharpie. I pull a frame towards me. The first disappearance. There I am not, my camera hovering in the air in my messy bedroom. I write carefully in block capitals right across the glass:

IRIS GREEN IS GREY

The truth is, even when I'm alone, I'm not alone. I've been crowded by voices from my past. Performing for an invisible audience full of harsh words and the worst possible interpretations, scared for the longest time of getting it wrong, of falling down, failing, of all those real and imagined voices in my head.

I scrub the words through with a single dark line.

~~IRIS GREEN IS GREY~~

Perfect.

46

People arrive. One or two and then all at once. Even my classmates look unfamiliar out of their uniforms, with their hair and make-up and fancy clothes. And suddenly the room's full. A whole crowd. Adult strangers gripping their wine glass of lemonade, their eyes slipping blandly over the place where my heart is nailed to the wall, as I watch from metres away, smiling and sweating. One nods at me on her way past.

I don't know what I expected. Applause?

Applause would be nice.

I step away from my own space and wait in front of his stretch of wall where a screen plays looped footage of pedestrians walking down the high street. A pair of headphones hang beside it, inviting you into Baker's world. Not enough people stop to listen.

He walks into the canteen without looking at the walls. He stretches up and searches the crowd. His gaze lands on me. Here I am, inside all my imperfect skin and my black velvet dress and black tights. My hair brushed; my eyes lined. It was the best I could do and Baker's smile makes it enough.

"You came then?" he says. "I worried you might bail on me again."

I rehearsed this moment. I thought I was prepared, but all the words desert me.

He buries his hands in his pockets. Navy trousers with contrast orange stitching, a white shirt with the sleeves pushed up. He shouldn't look so breathtaking, but here we are.

He says, "Look at you all dressed up," at the same time as I start with, "About yesterday—"

"It's fine."

"You handed in my work?"

"Well. I went there to hand in your work. But someone got there ahead of me."

"Who? Wait … Bert?"

"She's … kind of intimidating." Baker nods and I'm sure it's a compliment.

"She's a tornado." And a sneaky little secret-keeper.

"It would have been such a waste if you couldn't see your work on the wall."

I look at Baker. Not quite believing, not quite there, but nearly – very nearly – at least starting to consider believing.

"Thank you," I say sheepishly. "I kind of … have to show you something."

*

Baker reaches up and touches a frame. Panic winds its way round my chest as he examines the work and I bite back the urge to stop him looking, to tell him to step away from those scribbled-upon images, that this was a mistake. All of it. And I don't want anyone – not strangers and definitely not people I care about – looking at the sad inside of my mind. My private library of taunts and put-downs. My carefully curated collection of all the invisible graffiti people have scribbled across my walls.

I want to shout that it's not me. I'm not her. I am perfect – the best possible version of myself all the time, the girl from the mound who shimmered under the stars. But maybe I'm her too, as well as flawed and human and never sure of anything, especially not myself.

He peers at them one by one. He lingers at the bottom-right corner frame. Inside is the sparsest print: the white interior of the girls' toilets, the worn tiles and chipped floor-length mirror where a camera hangs in the reflection, held by nothing at all.

~~BEING AROUND YOU IS SUCH HARD WORK~~

Interspersed with the pictures of me completely invisible are the ones where I'm visible. Tucked away in the corners, peeking out of mirrors, staring down the lens. On top of the glass I have filled up the dark spaces and shadows with endless scrawl telling people that I am: **CREATIVE**, **SMART**, **CURIOUS**, **FOCUSED** and all the good things I could scrounge from my memory. I've added **FORGETFUL** and **FEARFUL**. **CAUTIOUS**, **SHORT-SIGHTED** and **UNREMARKABLE** too, because they're true and they're OK.

As Baker peers closer, I wonder if he'll recognize any of the good ones. The ones he gave me.

I wait.

And I hold my breath.

"Wow," he breathes. His forehead crinkles as he turns back to me and I can't say a word. It's all I can do to stop myself from running away. "This is" – he shakes his head – "so good. You're so damn good, Green. And all these things? They're true. And so's everything you can't see about yourself yet."

I step closer so he can't see all of me. His arm encircles my shoulders. The gallery lights explode into shards as my eyes fill up and I close them to keep the tears in. I bury my head against his shoulder and feel so entirely in myself. My skin, my bones, the beds of my nails and my heart beating so hard it thrums in every part of my body. I am solid and real. I am not pretending. I know it won't last, can't last, because tonight's a dream. But for now I'm happy.

*

Much later when I've rotated with blinis and Mum and Bert have arrived and cooed over my work, Mum with tears in her eyes that I feel directly responsible for, I'm standing sandwiched between them all. We're listening to Ms Amin warble on about how proud she is of each and every one of us, with an unusual softness and a twinkle in her eye. We clap for the exhibition judge, Fiona Grieg, in her electric blue suit with her sleek hair and when we're done clapping and Fiona starts to talk about the very, very high standard and the absolutely impossible job of judging, Baker's fingers find mine and twist together in a pinkie promise.

"You got this," he whispers.

Mum nods and Bert nudges me with her hip.

And I swallow the desire to explain. To rush to tell them all that I can't win, so they won't think I lost. Calm settles over me because I absolutely do not have this.

And it doesn't matter. Because I have something else. My friends with me, my mum, all seeing me clearly, while an unfamiliar feeling fights the anxiety in my belly.

That feeling? I think it's pride.

47

Someone's turned the lights on, killing the atmosphere. The gallery space is a school canteen again. Ms Amin's in a huddle with a parent, the judge, some photographer. Mum's left with the assurance that Baker will escort me home at the end of the night and a promise that I'm "OK! Mostly. Sometimes", which I will try to expand on soon.

Almost everyone's gone now, but it's hard to tear myself away. I lean against Baker, who's just said goodbye to his sister Tash. I thought I might feel awkward around her, but she was so friendly, so like Baker, and let off such a rattle of excited chatter that it didn't matter when I didn't know what to say or stumbled over my words. She's staying local next year, she said, and we should get a coffee sometime.

"She means that," Baker clarified after she left.

I watch the screen on the wall where three lanes of traffic

flow from one side to the other, exiting to a soundtrack made up of the beeps of a train door opening. Out of its usual rhythm it's unsettling. Familiar but not.

Baker's parents didn't come tonight, but he doesn't mention their absence. I flex the headphones, let them slip round my neck and say, "Hey, you OK?"

"Great," he says. "It's been a good night." So I tuck the fact of his missing parents away for another time. Another day. Because I'm quietly confident there will be other days.

I smile into my chest. Baker clears his throat. "There's something on my mind, though. I have to correct a previous statement."

"Oh yes?" I say, as neutrally as possible, trying to supress a spike of panic.

"When I said I befriended you because I thought you needed someone? I guess what I meant was *I* needed someone." I lean away to look at him and Baker bobs his head self-deprecatingly. "This is hard to believe, but many people don't enjoy my special blend of existential dread and art chat."

"They're missing out."

"Yeah?"

I give an emphatic nod.

"And the other thing…" Baker says. "There are reasons I want to get away, you know? Just because they're not obvious, it doesn't mean they don't exist." He watches his own artwork and I resist the urge to reach for him. "Uni feels like a trap. Another three years working towards being someone I already know I'm not. For what? The world's in flux, literally on fire, and everything feels pointless."

"Everything?" I say.

"Well … no," he says softly, eyes briefly on me. "But school, work, this." He gestures at the wall. "It all feels like a distraction. A waste of time." He stares at it – his amazing heartfelt art that he pours energy and thought into – and I can't bear him putting it down.

"It's not a waste of time." I reach for him.

He leans in. We stay like this a moment and I add, "Or maybe it is. Maybe you're right and everything is. But we have time and that's something. It's brilliant. All this time to waste."

"Brilliant wasted time?" He smiles and rests his head against mine. "How poetic."

I gently nudge his head in rebuke, unsure how much he's teasing me, and say, "It's like street photography. Just ordinary moments that not everyone sees the interest in, but some of them are kind of great and … worth hanging on to. I think."

"Is this what we do?" Baker says. "Take it in turns to be the uplifting one?"

"Excuse me?" I grumble. "I'm a beam of sunshine every day."

Baker laughs a little too hard and I put my hand over his mouth and feel teeth. He grins down at me.

"I guess if you waste enough time eventually someone excellent and unnecessarily rude will turn up."

"I'm not—"

"Selfish, you called me. But I'll allow it. Only because you're kind of my favourite person, Iris Green."

I roll my eyes, unable to take a compliment. Still. Always. I hold my head down and shake it into his shoulder and I can feel Baker still looking and I can see the edge of his smile and it's too much, it's everything. I lift my chin and he dips his and our lips touch. A brief warm school-appropriate glance of a kiss.

"Sometimes," he says when we break apart and he rests his forehead against mine, "sometimes I think if I wasn't going away…"

And he never finishes that thought, because someone steps into line beside us, looking at his work. I self-consciously disentangle myself from Baker.

Blue suit. Stern brows. Fiona Grieg, the gallery owner. The exhibition judge. I'm too surprised, too starstruck to speak, so I glance at Baker and keep my mouth shut.

"What a night," Fiona says. "I didn't expect it to be such a hard decision."

I turn to Baker, waiting for him to rescue me with an appropriate response. He walks away, but I swear I see a smirk as he goes, abandoning me to the adult.

"Um, yeah," I say. "Elina's paintings were great. She deserved the win."

"There's a lot of talent here. Yours were the self-portraits? The Missing Spaces series?"

I nod, speechless to be recognized.

"Wonderful. I hope you're not too disappointed not to win?"

"No," I say, but a small pang of disappointment hits as I realize she didn't know my work was excluded. I didn't win. I genuinely didn't win.

"Keep going," Fiona says with a smile. "You have a great eye. A very bold style. In fact…"

She reaches into her handbag and pulls out a wallet, then hands me a small white card printed with her name.

"We're looking for a gallery assistant to help with weekends and holidays. It's not all chatting to customers or curatorial. It's more physical: packing, unpacking, cleaning and liaising with couriers, but if that sounds interesting and you're after a job, you can drop me an email with your CV and I'll get you in for an interview." She adds, "You'd be paid, of course."

I stare at the card and a smile tickles the side of my mouth.

She who dares.

48

"How did it feel to see your own face up on the wall?" Nicole asks, sitting back in her armchair and lacing her fingers in her lap. "That must have been a big step for you?"

"Um..." I look at the ceiling for answers. Naming my feelings has never been my strong suit. It's worse when Nicole watches, but I'm not sure I can ask her not to. "Better. Seen. On my own terms."

"And the words you put up there?" She leans forward. I've shown Nicole some phone pics of my gallery set-up. She didn't offer an opinion. I wonder if she thought it was any good: whether it was basic or profound or a waste of time.

She probably found it a bit obvious. But that's OK.

"They're all still in here." I touch the side of my head.

"But it felt good to put them there and try not to let them make me feel ashamed any more. I'm trying to choose which words I listen to, and whose, more carefully."

Nicole nods. "It's not a choice a lot of the time."

I take a sip of my water. Next session, I'm going to ask Nicole for an empty glass to add my own cordial to. Baby steps towards comfort.

"I keep thinking how anyone could visit the exhibition any time and see my stuff there. And I'll never know if they did and what they thought about it."

"Theo? Olivia?"

"All the above. And more. Anyone. My dad kind of … offered to come up … next weekend … to see me and to see the exhibition. I told my parents I want to do the whole art school thing. I mean, I worked out that the whole art school thing is what I want to do at the end of next year. And now they're taking it all quite seriously. I didn't expect that from Dad, but I think Mum had a word with him. He's throwing research behind photography careers and offered accommodation in London so I can intern."

"Some of the words on the wall are his," Nicole says, "aren't they?"

"And I do worry what he'll think. Like … it's still in me to worry about people thinking it's uninteresting and attention-seeking or antagonizing … or that they'll see it as me failing in some way. I'm worried it'll hurt him. Or Mum. But that work feels special to me and I'm going for an interview with a gallery soon… There's a lot of good that feels might come out of it."

"It's nice to see your bravery rewarded?"

Bravery? With Nicole, the desire to repel that good thought, to fling it back at her like a missile, isn't so powerful. I let her word hit me. Sit with it. I'm trying to collect the positive ones now.

Brave.

"And how are you feeling about your visibility?"

"Huh?"

"Do you still feel invisible?"

"Oh. Not in the same way."

The truth is, the invisibility has stopped. Gone. I no longer get pins and needles in my hands and sliding silver visions. I no longer go on my night-time walks. When I'm in school, I sit in the discomfort of full visibility. The impulse is still there from time to time, but so far I have stuck around.

"I'm working on showing myself more," I say. "Trying to be more myself with everyone and trying not to keep so much inside."

"Through your art?"

I shrug. "No. That was probably too much. The whole world doesn't need to know… I'm working it out."

Nicole nods. "We're all works in progress, always growing in understanding of who we are and what's right for us. It doesn't mean there's anything wrong with who we were before or who we are now."

"I guess so."

That's all I can give her right now. But it's acceptance, not rejection. It's a promise to try to see the truth in her words. Because I can't simply leave behind the old Iris, the one who was hurt. The one who wasn't good enough. She's here too.

Nicole unclasps her hands and puts them on the arms of her chair – it must be nearly the end of the session. I blurt, "I've been thinking..." I press my lips together and wait for Nicole to interrupt me and move on.

She doesn't. That doesn't happen here.

"I've been thinking a lot about what first brought me here and how to explain it. It's like ... everyone else manages to keep themselves together and I feel like I'm the only person who's failing at being" – Nicole tilts her head – "myself. Sometimes I feel like I'm a collection of spare parts constantly jamming. And I've spent my whole life trying to put myself together the right way and it's never worked."

"Trying how?" Nicole asks.

I shake my head. "Even though right now I'm OK – I'm coping – I've been so exhausted and so anxious and it keeps coming back and I don't ... I don't think it's going away. I'd like more sessions if I can? There's a lot still to say."

Nicole nods and her brow crinkles and I think maybe it's a step too far. Maybe I'm wrong. Maybe you have to wait for permission from someone else to ask for what you need.

For too long I believed people when they told me there was something wrong – that I was wrong.

And now I'm trying to tell myself with kindness: I'm fine the way I am, but I need help too. The world exhausts me. I don't understand it and it often doesn't understand me. But some people do: Baker, and Bert now, more every day. And my brain's so full, so busy, working overtime all the time and seeing all the detail and every angle of everything and often that's tiring and anxiety-inducing but sometimes it's kind of brilliant.

Maybe you just have to see the world differently when you're working in black and white – contrast, form, geometry – there's still space for monochrome alongside the colour. Maybe Nicole can help me make sense of it all.

I brace myself for her to tell me no, no, no, don't be silly, Iris. You're being overdramatic. You're wrong and everyone struggles – look at Bert, Olivia, Baker, look at your mum – it's the same.

Worse, she'll misunderstand. She'll demand I say more now. She'll ask for a label or a solution or she'll—

She moves her arms from her knees to the armrests.

"OK, if you'd like to tell me a little more about that, I'd like to hear about your experience," she says.

Nicole smiles. And I take a breath.

49

The high street is scorching. Dry and dusty. Some shoppers move slowly, sheened with sweat and hidden behind glasses or squinting angrily as though taking the sun personally. Others stride, maxi-dresses billowing and hair flowing, skin already bronze. You can tell who's ready for summer.

My camera's in my hand, of course. I stroll past a woman eating sushi on a bench. Her bamboo chopsticks are halfway to her open mouth, prawn nigiri dangling precariously, her red glasses slipping down her nose. My shutter clicks.

At the press of a button the photo appears on screen. I'm still not used to it. It still feels like cheating, but I mix it in with my old-school film work now, and I'm getting used to it – the idea that I don't need to rely on ink on paper to make my work stand out. I'm getting used to having two cameras too, but I refuse to become a gear head like Baker. This will do me.

"Nice." Baker stretches the word out as he peers over my shoulder. "I thought that'd be super unflattering."

"I mean, it captures the essence of the day. Picnic sushi, sweat and everything teetering on the edge of disaster." I push hair out of my face, grab a handful of the ends and lift it clear of my neck to enjoy the non-breeze. If I start to sweat, I'll have to go home. There's nothing worse.

"How's the camera working out for you?" Baker reaches over to lift it out of my hands.

I tell him it's fine. Sure, it's not my two-thousand-pound dream camera, but after the disappointment of not winning the art grant, I had to temper my expectations. It's a nice camera and it's mine. At least twenty-five per cent mine and that'll increase every month as I slowly pay Baker back thanks to my new job at the gallery. I tried to make him charge me interest, but he renamed me Stubborn Darkroom Girl and refused to do it, so instead I buy him coffees.

And when that's paid off, with my new digital gear and the money I'm saving on supplies, everything else will go straight into next year's exhibition fund. I'm working on something already.

"Her?" Baker says, pointing up the high street, but I don't even see who he's talking about because I'm distracted by someone else I've spotted.

An old man with blue glasses and a white ring of tufty

hair above his ears. He looks familiar and it makes me hesitate. "He's right up your street," Baker says, following my gaze.

Baker's right. I swallow the nerves threatening to flutter up my windpipe and put on a burst of speed to catch him up.

"Excuse me," I say. "I'm a photographer and I'd love to take your portrait if you don't mind?"

The man's expression is warm but he cups a hand to his ear and frowns, and I realize I've cocked this up. Too quiet, always.

"Sorry, we already give a lot to charity," a younger woman says, sweeping past me. "Come on, Dad." She shoots me a frosty glance from under a heavy fringe.

"Oh! No! I'm a photographer and I'd love to take your dad's portrait, that's all." I speak up, I put on a smile, I take a small step forward and brandish my camera, working to my little script. "Yours too if that's OK?" I add to the woman.

"Why?"

This is the moment for giving up. I want to do it. Apologize and scurry away and pledge to never, ever speak to another living soul about my photography. Never, ever speak to another living soul, full stop. And this moment would appear again in my dreams as I wonder what these two people thought of me, that strange girl who approached them out of nowhere. But I want this. I want to be able to do this.

"You just … both caught my eye on a crowded street."

The woman looks ready to go, but the man puts both

hands on top of his walking stick and throws his head back. "Like this?"

His daughter cracks a smile.

I snap the portraits and they look good, even on the back of my screen. With a little work in post-processing they'll sparkle. I give the woman a card with the details of the basic gallery website I built so they can find the portraits later.

Baker comes swishing up, hands in his pockets, long self-conscious strides, face full of smug.

"Will you ever stop?" I say.

"I'm not sure it'll ever get old seeing you do that. Iris Green voluntarily talking to strangers?" He shakes his head. "Can't get over it."

"Imagine taking so much credit for other people's personal growth."

Baker's mouth twitches, definitely laughing at me.

We meander up the high street, but it's too hot to be serious, even about photography, even after I've bought us both iced smoothies and Baker's given himself brain freeze with his lack of self-restraint.

We leave the high street behind and head for the bridge. We slurp frozen juice and watch the traffic stream past while we stand perfectly still above. The silence is companionable in a way I never thought silence could be.

"I paid for my ticket last night," Baker says.

"Oh?" Something big starts struggling in my chest. It strangles my voice. "When do you leave?"

"I'll get a summer job, save a bit more. The Eurostar's booked for September."

I sneak a look sideways at Baker. Our elbows almost touch where we're leaning on the metal barrier. Baker watches the road.

"I start at the gallery next weekend," I say.

So this is it. We'll have snatches of summer together and then who knows? Baker goes travelling. I'm left behind. There's email and messages and old-school postcards. There's following and liking and comments back and forth. There's photos of Baker at the Colosseum and trekking the Alps, sweating on the beach and learning to surf while I revise the same old subjects for one last year.

And then I'll leave too. Everything around us will change. New friends, new homes, new lives. We'll stay in touch – at least for a while – I know we will. Because I know how Baker feels about me and I know it's real. Before he goes, I'll tell him how I feel and I think he'll say it back. We've stepped along that cliff face so many times and neither of us has had the courage to look over. It's only right that I jump first.

"I think it'll be good," Baker says. And he could mean Europe, the summer, the job, the two of us or the whole future stretching out ahead and all this time waiting to be wasted so brilliantly.

"I think so too," I say.

"There's something else. I booked a return."

"Oh?" I know my expression isn't right. I can feel the edges of my mouth tugging down. "You're … returning?"

"At Christmas. Just for a bit. Don't look at me like that." He leans his head to the side and closes one eye against the sun. "Of course I'm coming back for you."

Baker's arm shifts infinitesimally closer and as his hand closes the gap, his fingers find mine. He leans his head on me. Our bones press together. On the railings our two littlest digits wrap and hold tight like a promise.

No matter what, it'll be fine. It'll all be fine. If this isn't for ever – and I guess nothing's for ever – I'll survive. Not by myself but with myself. With the things and people I love, knowing that I can be loved.

My phone vibrates and I fish it from my bag.

> **Bert:** I made an M&M's cake and I'm not saying it's my finest work to date, but I am saying you'd better declare it a masterpiece and eat at least two slices or you'll be dead to me

It's six twenty; Bert's dad gets tea on the table for half seven. I unwind my pinkie from Baker's with only the slightest twinge of regret.

"I have to go," I say.

"Bert?"

"Uh-huh. Can't be late – it's First Exam Eve for Bert and I think she needs talking down. I'm going to meet her at school tomorrow for a coffee and debrief when she's done too. There'll be… I think she'll be there." I swallow, my stomach fluttering. "Olivia."

Baker raises an eyebrow. "OK?"

"Yeah. Yeah, I think so." I nod.

Baker takes my hand and presses his lips to it in a kiss that shoots through my bones.

"I'll let you know when today's haul is online," I say, letting go of his hand.

"You better."

"I promise."

Baker grins and his eyebrow twitches. He knows the tussle that's going on inside me. The desire to put myself down. To diminish my efforts before I've even seen the result. He knows it's all on the tip of my tongue.

"I will," I say. "I … I think I got some good ones."

And Baker breaks out in silent applause as I turn away, shaking my head at the ridiculousness of him and me, at this. At the sheer discomfort of saying it aloud:

I did this.

I tried.

I think it was good. At least OK.

And me? I'm OK too.

Author's note

When I started writing *Iris Green, Unseen*, I was thinking a lot about all the small (and sometimes not-so-small) ways the world chips away at us and about how we pick ourselves up and carry on despite that, how we find the positives in all that noise and find ourselves too.

Although *Iris Green, Unseen* sees Iris making progress towards support and self-knowledge, this isn't a book about finding answers, or feeling miraculously transformed by the final page, because real life is rarely so neat and tidy.

For me, one of the brilliant, comforting things about books has always been the way characters and their struggles can help us feel less alone with our own. So, while some uncertainty remains at the end for Iris, I wanted to write about how, if you can find the courage to speak up, often the right people will be there for you. Most of all, I wanted to write about how love and acceptance can find you, regardless of whether you feel worthy, because no one is an incomplete or broken person. No matter how you feel right now, you are already good enough.

Although Iris is fictional, she was inspired by a time in my life when I felt particularly adrift. She means so much to me and my hope is that this book will resonate and, perhaps, make someone, somewhere feel seen.

Lou x

Acknowledgements

First thanks to Becky Bagnell, my wonderful agent, for all your guidance and encouragement over the last three years, and for being such a calm, reassuring voice of reason in the face of my authorly anxiety.

I'm endlessly grateful to all my brilliant editors: Linas Alsenas for seeing the potential in Iris's story and starting her on the way, and to Genevieve Herr for your insights. Many thanks to Tierney Holm for bringing a fresh eye, and seeing this book over the finish line with such kindness, wisdom and enthusiasm.

Enormous thanks to Jennie Roman, Wendy Shakespeare, Isabella Haigh, Christine Modafferi and everyone else in the wonderful team at Scholastic who helped in bringing Iris's story to life. Thanks to Sarah Baldwin for the stunning cover. I feel very fortunate to work alongside such a skilled, passionate team of people and am very grateful this book has been in such good hands.

Thank you, Nicky Watkinson, for your insightful sensitivity read. Any oversights or missteps are entirely my own.

I might have never managed a second book if it wasn't for all the support for my first. Many thanks to Matthew Parkinson-Bennett, Siobhán Parkinson, Kate McNamara and Elizabeth Goldrick for making so much possible.

There are many amazing people going above and beyond to champion writers and new writing, making it just that bit easier for us all to keep going on this journey. To everyone who ever said a kind word about *The Eternal Return of Clara Hart*, gave it a push forward or recommended it to another reader, thank you. I could fill another book with people I'll always be grateful to and they include the Bounce team, the crew at WriteMentor, PaperBound Magazine, Paper Lanterns, Big Kids Book Club, Charley Robinson, Shelly Mack and so many others. Thanks to the judges and organizers of the Yoto Carnegies, the Branford Boase Award, the YA Book Prize, the Great Reads Awards, and everyone at the Kirkus Prize.

Putting words down on the page is a solo pursuit, but writing is never lonely thanks to brilliant writer pals. I'm particularly grateful to all the 2022 debuts, the WriteMentor Class of 2020 and my SCBWI gang. Thank you, Aislinn, Jess, Jinny, Alison, Jan, Sue, Kari, Hannah, Kelly, Zoe and many more who have listened, read and provided invaluable advice, suggestions and support. I'm so privileged to be among you and to get to read your stories. I can't wait to see where you all go from here.

To Eve Ainsworth, thank you for your kind and encouraging support in the early stages of *Iris*, and Emma Finlayson-Palmer for your valued input so near the end.

Thanks to Rebecca Anderson for being both wise and hilarious, and for looking over the counselling scenes. If I mucked them up in subsequent edits that is, of course, on me.

Thank you, Daisy Jervis and Becci Fearnley, for being there from the very start with *Iris*, especially knowing what a long and fraught journey it was likely to be! I'm grateful every day to have such understanding and talented humans in my life.

Thank you, Melanie Garrett, for coffees, excellent brownies, even more excellent stories and endless patience. Would I have survived these last three years without you? I doubt it. Thanks above all for making me want to be a better writer.

Writing and publishing a novel or two would be impossible without the most understanding friends. Thanks, Bex, Ella, Lauren, Davina, Rebecca and Anne, who have all taken turns being shoulders to despair on. Thank you, Faith, for being both family and friend – I'm so lucky to have you in my life.

Thanks to my lovely family, on both sides, for being so supportive and encouraging.

Mum, thank you for everything, from filling my childhood with stories, to being behind me every step of the way as I navigated this new chapter of mine.

Dan, you're my favourite person. Thank you for inspiring Iris's passion for street photography, for dog walks and brainstorms, pain au chocolat and unfailing support.

Finally, thanks to all the booksellers, librarians, teachers, bloggers, reviewers and readers. If you've bought, borrowed or mentioned one of my books, if you're reading this … thank you so, so much!

Daniel Cook

LOUISE FINCH

Louise lives in the southeast of England with her photographer husband, their two small dogs and too many house plants, surrounded by books, craft supplies and vintage furniture.

She is the author of one other book for young adults, *The Eternal Return of Clara Hart*, which was shortlisted for the 2023 Yoto Carnegie Medal for Writing.